D1311594

HOW TO MAKE
FRIENDS AND
MONSTERS

ZONDERKIDZ

How to Make Friends and Monsters
Copyright © 2013 by Ron Bates

This title is also available as a Zondervan ebook.
Visit www.zondervan.com/ebooks.

Requests for information should be addressed to:

Zonderkidz, 5300 Patterson Ave., SE, Grand Rapids, Michigan 49530

978-0-310-73607-3

Editor: Kim Childress
Art direction: Deborah Washburn
Cover design: Deborah Washburn
Illustrator: André Jolicoeur
Interior design: Ben Fetterley and Greg Johnson/Textbook Perfect

Printed in the United States of America

13 14 15 16 17 18 /DCI/ 20 19 18 17 16 15 14 13 12 11 10 9 8 7 6 5 4 3 2

HOW TO MAKE
FRIENDS
AND
MONSTERS

BY
HOWARD
BOWARD
WITH A
LITTLE HELP FROM
RON BATES

CHAPTER 1

How-I-Am

You know how there's always that one kid who can't find a place to sit in the cafeteria because people "save" empty seats for imaginary friends whenever he heads their way? So he has to carry his Salisbury steak, potatoes, and hot roll all the way to the table in the very back of the room? Only he trips and falls before he gets there and, when he stands up, he's got cream gravy in his shirt pocket and green beans where his eyebrows should be?

I'm that kid.

My name is Howard Boward (yeah, thanks Mom and Dad), but most people just call me "How." Well, not just How, they call me "How Weird," or "How Lame," or "How Did You Get That Chair? It's Saved!" Things like that. Until a few weeks ago, I was more of a "Who" ("Who's the dork by the water fountain?"), a "What" ("What is wrong with that kid?") or a "Why" ("Why is he wearing a unitard?"). So, when you think about it, the fact that I am now a "How" is kind of a step up.

Not a *giant* step or anything. You can only go so far up the popularity ladder when half the seventh grade has seen you running down the hall in a unitard—which, for the record, was part of an experiment I was doing on invisibility. My hypothesis was correct: unitards cure invisibility.

I've actually created a chart of the popularity ladder and I fall somewhere between gym-class asthmatic and that dog that bit Vice Principal Hertz. It's not as bad as it sounds. A lot of people love that dog.

The point is, it's become increasingly apparent I need to improve my social status. And I need to do it fast because, in middle school, being unpopular is like having a disease. *Symptoms include fear, loneliness, wedgies, and a sudden, unexplained loss of your lunch money. If you think you may be experiencing unpopularity, ask your bully if daily beatings are right for you.*

I'm kidding! You can't ask a bully to cure a disease. Bullies are the disease! And Dolley Madison Middle School (Go Manatees!) is the center of the epidemic. I should know, I'm like candy to those people. It's weird—there's just something about me that attracts the big, brainless, and angry. I'd like to say it's my sparkling personality, but since the only thing about me that sparkles are my braces, it's probably one of these things:

Reasons I Am Bully Candy

1. I'm built for it. If they ever make a movie about those rubber stick figures that have bodies like pencils and flexible, spindly arms, Hollywood will knock at my door.

2. Somewhere behind the massive construction project in my mouth are the remains of my original teeth. I'm told I'll probably have a magnificent smile someday. I just can't imagine why I'd ever use it.

3. I have G.A.S. (Goosebumps Addictive Syndrome). I am totally addicted to the **Goosebumps** novels by R.L. Stine. I read them in the bathroom at school because, when I get to the scary parts, I tend to scream. This is a completely involuntary response. Coincidentally, pretty much the whole school thinks I have some painful digestive-disorder, though I've told them repeatedly, "No, I have G.A.S." This doesn't help.

4. I use big words like "digitibulist" when I could just say "thimble collector."

5. I am a digitibulist.

6. My hair is cotton white and stands bolt-upright on the top of my head so that I constantly look like

I've been frightened by a creature in an Abbott and Costello movie.

7. I watch Abbott and Costello movies.

8. I have "nerdism," a condition that requires me to love science and wear bulky, un-cool eyeglasses.

9. The other kids are all jealous of me. (This one is kind of a long shot but it makes the list come out with ten items. I like to list things in groups of exactly ten.)

10. I am smart.

Number 10 is the worst offense, and the one most responsible for my problem. See, your average bully can smell a big, juicy brain from up to three blocks away. That's bad news for me. Imagine roaming through a pack of wild dogs with bacon in your head.

(FYI, I don't actually know what a brain smells like. But intelligence smells like bacon.)

Now, about the "incident" … I guess it would be easy to blame what happened in the fall of seventh grade on the bullies, but I won't. No one made me do what I did. Everything that went wrong, and all the madness that came from it, is my responsibility. Judge me as you will.

All I ask is that you keep in mind I am only twelve years old, I had a ton of homework, and these were my first monsters.

CHAPTER 2

The Mother Load

It all started the day Mom walked into my room, and, out of the deep blue nowhere, said, "Howard, why don't you bring a friend home to play after school?"

My gut instinct was to say, "Great idea, Mom! Whose friend should I bring?" But I didn't because she might actually have picked one. Anyway, I knew what was happening. I could tell by her too-eager smile and the way she kept rolling the tips of her hair around her fingers. This wasn't a real question—this was Mom-language! You know, that secret language of double-speak moms use when they're trying to say something without saying it.

Something like, "You don't have any friends, do you, Howard?"

I gulped.

See, this opens up a whole gray area because it really depends on how you define "friends." I mean, I interact with a lot of people. Wedgies, for example, can be a

9

bonding experience, and I get no less than one a week. That has to count for something.

I stepped away from my desk and looked up at her. My mom's got this thick mop of dark-brown hair and these puffy bangs that flop down just across her eyebrows. Except this time she had the front pulled back, and I could see these little wrinkles on her forehead. Not old-lady wrinkles. Worry wrinkles.

I'm pretty sure I gave them to her.

Don't ask me how she does it, but Mom has a way of getting to me. All of a sudden, those wedgie-relationships felt as flimsy and unsupportive as my overstretched underpants. Funny, being friendless had never bothered me before. But now, having to say it out loud and having to say it to someone who actually worried about these things, it felt, I don't know ... wrong.

So I did what any son would do in my position. I told her a fictionalized version of the truth.

"Kids don't go to each other's houses anymore," I said. "We all hang out online. You'd be surprised how much the Internet has streamlined the friendship process. I'm close personal friends with a lot of people I don't even know."

Her worry lines deepened.

"What do you talk about?" she asked.

"Oh, sports. Politics. How to build better parent-teen relationships. That kind of thing."

OK, I was grasping at straws. I had to. It would be humiliating to tell my own mother the last thing I got on my FaceSpace page was a survey titled "Who Looks More

10

Like a Mole Rat?" It came with two photos: me and a mole rat.

My advanced algebra book was sitting on the edge of my desk so I picked it up and started to leaf through the pages. This seemed like a painless way to wrap up the conversation. After several seconds of intense fake-reading, I glanced up. She was still standing in the doorway, half-swallowed inside one of Dad's old, gray sweatshirts. What was she waiting for? My mom is a smart woman, she knew how we played this game—I pretended to answer her questions, and she pretended to believe me.

But this time was different. It was like she kind of wanted to believe me.

"All right, then," she said at last.

I didn't know what it was, but something about her tone bothered me. Because she didn't say it like, "All right, then. I guess I'll leave." She said it like, "All right, then. That goldfish isn't going to flush itself."

It was a tone of action—the kind of tone people use when they're trying to talk themselves into doing something unpleasant. I'm wrong about a lot of stuff. But I know my tones.

☆ ☆ ☆

The unpleasantness was Reynolds Pipkin—and it was in my room.

"Howard," Mom said cheerily, as if the universe was not imploding. "Look who stopped by to see you!"

As I mentioned earlier, there is a lunch table in the back of the cafeteria that is the final destination for kids who have been rejected at every other place they tried to sit down. It is the saddest table in the world. If I had known how this situation was going to escalate, I'm sure I could have dragged home someone from the sad table. Not to play with, you understand, but just for show.

I pulled my covers up over my head.

"Howard?" my mother poked. "Aren't you going to say hello?"

"Hello, Mom," I said from the safety of the bed tent.

Reynolds was a year younger than me, which meant he was in elementary school, which meant he was a different species.

"Hello, Howard," I heard him blink behind his oversized owl-style glasses. "Your mother asked my mother if I could come over for a play date."

Oh, the agony! No one in seventh grade has play dates! If I was too big for footie-pajamas, the most comfortable PJ ever, I was too big for this. I pulled down my covers and shot powerful, imaginary laser beams at his pumpkin-shaped head.

"Not now, Reynolds," I said through gritted teeth. "I'm doing middle-school stuff."

"What kind of middle-school stuff?"

"I'm growing a mustache."

"Neat," Reynolds said. "Where are you growing it?"

"Why don't you show Reynolds your chemistry set?" Mom said.

At this suggestion, I filled both my cheeks with air and then blew it out hard so that my lips made a flapping noise. This is what you do when you don't like something, but you're not allowed to say bad words.

I got off my bed, walked to my closet, and pulled a large, rectangular, plastic box off the top shelf. The cartoon-covered front said "Li'l Genius Chemistry Set!"

None of this, I remind you, was my idea. You may hear some talk about an explosion. Don't believe it. It was more of a pop, the kind you get when a balloon breaks. I knew this would happen if I mixed certain chemicals together. What I did not know is whether it would happen if I had Reynolds mix them together.

Reynolds's skin was back to its normal, non-greenish color in less than a week. His parents insisted he still had a weird smell, but I think that's because they forgot how Reynolds usually smells.

Mom made me write an apology letter and not one that said, "Dear Reynolds, I'm sorry you stink," but it was worth it. Her Pipkin-plot had gone up in smoke—just like Reynolds's black, flame-kissed eyebrows.

☆ ☆ ☆

A few days later, I walked into my room and saw a rectangular package wrapped in plain brown paper on my pillow. Written on the wrapping were these words: "You are special, Howard. Love, Mom."

It was a book: *How to Make Friends*.

CHAPTER
3

Guru of the Den

Ordinarily I would've gone to my mom and thanked her for my present. That's because, ordinarily, my presents are good.

I just didn't see how a book could teach you how to make friends. Were there rules I was supposed to follow? Did the other kids know these rules? What about the UPs? UPs have more friends than anybody, and I don't think they've ever read a book in their lives.

"UPs" is what I call the "uber-populars," the superstars of Dolley Madison Middle School (DMMS). A single word from an UP can send you plunging to the bottom of the popularity ladder or raise you to that glorious place where even the eagles get nosebleeds.

I picked up the book. *How to Make Friends* had a hard-cover and felt lightweight but stiff as a two-by-four. It was the kind of book a bully might check out of the library if he needed something educational to beat you with.

"I'll pass," I said aloud. Then I chucked it onto Mount

Wash-Me, the pile of clothes that is always sticking out the top of my laundry hamper.

Now, I don't want you to think I have anything against books in general. In fact, in my bookcase right now are a dictionary, a Bible with my name on it, my dad's old copy of *Where the Sidewalk Ends,* a few *Goosebumps* paperbacks, and pretty much everything that's ever been written about hobbits. I know that doesn't sound like a whole lot, but I only have eleven other shelves and those are reserved for science. Chemistry, physics, biology, astronomy, botany, mineralogy, zoology, ichthyology—you name it. If it's the kind of reading any other seventh grader would consider torture, it's in my collection.

☆ ☆ ☆

I couldn't sleep. I kept wondering why Mom had given me that book in the first place. What was she not telling me? Was something terrible going to happen if I didn't start making friends? I remembered the time in third grade when my class went on a field trip to the museum, and you couldn't go inside without a buddy. Everyone paired up, and I was left standing there outside the door. I eventually got in. Still, it's kind of hard to enjoy dinosaur bones when you're holding hands with Mrs. Feeney.

You don't think you have to pick a buddy to get into college, do you? I hope not. I don't think I could stand spending four years with Mrs. Feeney.

It turns out not sleeping is surprisingly thirsty work. I

headed to the kitchen for a bottle of water, and on my way back, I noticed a flickering light coming from inside the den. It lured me. When I looked through the doorway, I saw a wad of messy hair peeking over the top of the recliner. I didn't need to see the other side. I knew he'd be there stretched out in his favorite, old T-shirt and goofy pajama bottoms, the light from the TV making his face kind of an eerie blue.

"Dad?"

"Hey, champ," he answered.

When my dad is watching TV, he calls everyone "champ." That way, he doesn't have to turn his head to see who he's talking to.

"What are you watching?" I asked.

"Monster movie."

"Why do you like monster movies so much?"

"They have monsters."

"Oh," I said. "Which one is this?"

"*Frankenstein.* You want to watch it with me?"

"No thanks," I said.

Don't even get me started on *Frankenstein.* I can't stand that movie. First of all, I don't like the monster. He's big, he's strong, he's scary, and he can barely put two syllables together. If I wanted to see a creature like that, I'd go to school and wait for one to stuff me in my locker.

The other thing I don't like is how everybody calls the monster "Frankenstein." Frankenstein is the scientist! You know, the guy who created a person out of spare parts in the coolest laboratory ever? He should be the star of the movie!

But he isn't. Nobody watches the scientist when there's a big, ugly monster to look at.

"Dad, can I ask you something?"

"What is it?" he said, and I heard fear in his voice. I'm pretty sure he thought I was going to ask if I could have some of his popcorn.

"Is being popular important?"

"Oh, that," he said, reaching back into the bowl and pulling out a fistful of buttery kernels. "Ask your mother."

It would save my family a lot of time if Dad just had "Ask your mother" tattooed on his forehead.

"Well, she's kind of the reason I brought it up. She gave me a book about making friends."

"A book, huh?" Dad said, and he licked his fingers like five salty popsicles. "Well, if it's all right with her, it's all right with me. You tell your mother you have my permission to be popular. OK, champ?"

In fairness to my dad, there was an eight-foot monster on the TV screen terrorizing villagers, so the fact that he was paying any attention to me at all was kind of a miracle.

"Sure, Dad. Thanks."

I went back to my room and pulled the book off the mountain. I figured it couldn't hurt to read just the first couple of pages—it might even put me to sleep.

Only it didn't put me to sleep. It did the opposite. The truth is, I had a whole new respect for *How to Make Friends* the minute I saw what was on the first page.

CHAPTER 4

The New Place

The first page said, "Chapter 1: Try Going Someplace New."

Right away, I could tell this book was going to help me a lot. See, I'm the kind of guy who likes to hang around the house, which is a terrible place for making friends. Everyone knows me there.

That's why I decided to follow the book's advice and go someplace new—the garage.

By "garage" I mean that thing that looks like a garage, but isn't. To be considered an actual garage, a structure, in theory, would have to be able to hold a car. This particular space had no hope of holding a vehicle of any kind, including a theoretical one.

That's because it was literally packed with junk—old appliances, discarded wires, patio furniture, Christmas decorations, outdated clothing, the possible remains of a UFO, and boxes and boxes of things we had forgotten we ever owned.

But to me, the best thing about the garage was what it

didn't have—my family. This was a place where I could be alone. A kid my age needs some alone time for pondering and stuff. You can't ponder when family's around. It makes them think you're up to something.

I have a large family composed primarily of people I'm related to. Maybe you'd like to meet them. The Bowards, in no particular order, are:

1. Mom and Dad, who I've already told you about.
2. Our dogs—Frisco Boward and F.P. "Pants" Boward.
3. Orson.
4. Three guinea pigs—Moe, Larry, and Shirley.
5. Uncle Ben.
6. The TV (who is not really family but she talks to me when no one else will).
7. Birdzilla—the world's most insulting cockatoo.
8. Katie Beth.
9. An ant farm with over 400 ants all named Antoine because I cannot tell them apart.
10. The Stick.

Now, there are a few things about my family this list doesn't tell you. For example, Uncle Ben doesn't actually live with us, but he's over so often it feels like he does.

That's fine because I like Uncle Ben a lot. He owns a used electronics store, and if I ever need a particular piece of equipment for one of my experiments, he can usually come up with it.

"Hey, that's what uncles are for," he tells me, and he's probably right. I can't think of anything else uncles are for.

As for Orson, he's my five-year-old brother, and he almost never speaks. Trust me, I'm not complaining. He's a neat little kid, it's just he isn't real interested in communicating with other people. This makes him the exact opposite of my 17-year-old sister, Katie Beth. In theory, Katie Beth has the ability to detach herself from her smart phone, but as far as anyone knows, she has never done so. Once, when she was watching a movie and nodded off on the couch, I saw her sleep-texting.

I didn't read the message, but I'm guessing it said, **"Zzzzzzzzzzz."**

Last of all, there's the Stick. I was going to leave the Stick off the list completely, but it's been in our house since before I was born and some of the other family members are attached to it. Also, it is my older brother.

His real name is Nathaniel. Nathaniel is 15 and has always been under the mistaken impression that he is the boss of me. I try to avoid speaking to him but, when I do, I call him the Stick. I used to call him "Ugly on a Stick" or "Lame on a Stick" or "Stink on a Stick," you know, things like that. If something was so horrible you could put it on a stick, to me, that was Nathaniel. Then one day, I couldn't think of anything disgusting enough, so I just called him "Stick."

It stuck.

To be honest, getting away from Stick was the main reason I wanted to spend time in the garage. I couldn't read a book called *How to Make Friends* in front of my arch nemesis. He'd destroy me!

So after breakfast, when no one was watching, I slipped outside and lifted one of the white, roll-back doors on the garage. There it was—my oasis of uselessness. Stacks and stacks of glorious clutter filled every spider-webby corner. No one would look for me here! I pushed my way through old, brown boxes and swallowed older, browner dirt until I found a nice, undetectable spot between a beat up sofa-bed and a leaky canoe.

This was paradise.

Is it just me or is there something magical about having a secret place all to yourself? Mom sure knew what she was doing when she gave me that book! Oh, I realize most people would tell you a junky, old garage isn't the best place for making friends, and they could be right.

Then again, it really depends on how you make them.

CHAPTER 5

"Be Yourself"

Now that I had a new place to hang out, I moved on to chapter two: "Be Yourself."

Be myself? Were they insane?

They'd have to be. Being myself was the reason I didn't have any friends! Before some guide-to-life has the gall to tell anyone to be me, it should really consider who I am.

I am the anti-UP.

I am the eclipse to their sunlight, the crater to their mountaintop, the sweaty armpit to their cologne-scented cool. In fact, if there is one thing all uber-populars have in common, it is that they are not me!

"Be yourself" didn't sound like good advice at all, it sounded like one of those crazy, random things my dad is always saying. You know, things like "It'll all work out," and "Have a nice day." Things we both know are impossible.

Then he gives me a cookie.

To be fair, Dad spends most of his time talking to animals and Stick—creatures that may not understand the words but are still happy to get a treat. See, my dad is what they used to call a dogcatcher, but now they call an animal-control specialist. I used to think that meant he could control animals with his mind the way Aquaman does fish. When I told Dad this, he said, "What makes you think I can't?"

I like that he answered that way. It makes it not really a lie when I tell people that he can.

Oh, about Aquaman. In case you haven't heard, he's a comic-book character who lives underwater and telepathically commands sea creatures. He was invented by Paul Norris and Mort Weisinger in 1941, and the only reason I know this is that a very large portion of my brain does nothing but store information about who invented what and when.

In my own way, I'm a lot like Aquaman. He has all these crime-fighting abilities, but he only gets to show them off when the bad guys go into the water. With me, it's science skills. I can do some pretty amazing things with a chemistry set, but no one would know that unless they came into my world.

At the moment, that world was a two-by-two-foot clearing in the middle of a dark, clammy garage. I felt comfortable there. I couldn't put my finger on it, but there was something very familiar about the place—the dim light, the mechanical parts, the general feeling of creepiness.

Then it hit me—Dad's movie.

That was it! The garage looked sort of like Dr. Frankenstein's laboratory! OK, his lab was more of an underground lair, and the garage was more of an aboveground dump, but they both had that same shadowy, enter-at-your-own-risk quality.

Almost subconsciously, my eyes fell back to the book and those two stupid words:

BE YOURSELF.

Only this time, they didn't sound so stupid.

This time, I understood what the book was telling me to do. It wasn't telling me to be myself—the spazoid who wore a unitard to school. It was telling me to be who I was on the inside. It was telling me to be a scientist!

A scientist who had just found his laboratory.

CHAPTER
6

The Secret Lab

I couldn't believe I hadn't thought of this sooner. The garage would make an awesome lab. Now all I had to do is keep my family from finding out about it.

Over the years, my family has become less than enthusiastic about my scientific activities. The final straw happened about a year ago when I was closing in on a breakthrough that has eluded inventors since the beginning of time: glow-in-the-dark footprints. Brilliant, right? I mean, how else are you supposed to find your way back to your seat when you have to go to the bathroom at the movies? Anyway, I guess I messed up something with the chemicals because, after a while, a mysterious, green cloud formed above our house. Also, my shoes melted.

This is what we scientists call "a setback." My parents just called it being grounded for a month.

So, for obvious reasons, the new lab was going to have to be my little secret—my last *little* secret. After that, they got a whole lot bigger.

When I flipped on the light switch in my bedroom, the ceiling fan started moving.

Strange. I hadn't had that fan on all day. That meant that somebody had come into my room and pulled the short, silver chain attached to the light fixture. In a normal house, this isn't a particularly suspicious event. But I don't live in a normal house.

I live in a house with Stick.

For as long as I can remember, Stick and I have been engaged in a war of annoyances. Anything one of us can do to pester the other in even the smallest way is a victory. But this? This didn't make any sense. Why would he just turn on my ceiling fan? All I had to do is pull the chain and turn it off.

I decided I was being paranoid

A second later, my head exploded.

"AHHHHHHHH-CHOOOOOO!"

It was the single, largest sneeze ever to erupt from human nostrils. The next one—a full-fledged sneeze-quake—nearly popped my eyes out of their sockets. There was a third and a fourth and a fifth, each one louder and more sinus-scorching than the one before it.

I ran out of my room in a desperate flight for tissue and grabbed the Kleenex box that we keep on the end table at the bottom of the stairs. It was empty—but not completely empty. Inside was a small, square note.

"Don't ever touch my phone again!" it said.

"Howard, what are you doing?" my mom asked. I whirled around and saw her standing there in the baggy, red sweatpants she only wears on housecleaning days. Apparently, my nasal blasts were even louder than the horrible shriek of the vacuum cleaner.

"Snee-snee-snee-sneezing!" I said, and then demonstrated.

"Well for heaven's sake, use a tissue! You're spreading germs."

Poor, naïve Mom. She didn't get it. Something was being spread all right, but it wasn't germs. It was evil.

The sneezing fit had opened not just my sinuses, but also my mind. Now I saw everything clearly. Stick had pulled the chain on my ceiling fan, but not before sprinkling the blades with ample piles of black pepper. When the fan started moving, the pepper filled the air, and eventually, my nostrils. He'd turned my entire room into a self-service sneeze factory!

I picked up the note and read it again. Then I blew my nose in it.

Here's the thing—if Stick didn't want me touching his cell phone, he shouldn't have left it in a place where I could so easily get my hands on it. I mean, it was right there on his nightstand! Did he expect me to just leave it alone? Now, I'm not saying he *wanted* me to secretly record him singing in the shower, and to make that recording the ringtone on his phone, and to call him nine times in a row when he was hanging out with his friends.

I'm just saying we both knew that was what was going to happen.

The pepper still stung whenever I sniffed. But what hurt more was the agony of defeat. Stick would pay for this ... eventually. First, I had a lab to build.

☆ ☆ ☆

I spent the next few days in my soon-to-be laboratory, quietly throwing stuff away, hauling boxes to the attic, and—most important—arranging the remaining clutter so that it formed a solid wall across the front of our garage. Anyone opening the door would see nothing but a great barrier of household junk, the perfect camouflage for a super-secret lab.

The only problem would be getting inside. I'd need an easily accessible yet cleverly disguised door to evade the science groupies. OK, I didn't think science groupies actually existed, but what good was a secret hideout without a secret entrance? Besides, it was the best excuse I could come up with for building myself a tunnel.

Here's how it worked: I took an old, blue, vinyl cooler—the kind with the hinged lid—and cut a large hole in the bottom. That was my gateway. To get into the lab, all I had to do is open the lid, crawl into the cooler, make a left turn, slither through an empty file cabinet, and pop out through the swinging door of an old clothes-dryer. Piece of cake.

Now that I had a secret lab entrance, I could move on to something even more vital—secret lab stuff. I needed equipment. For starters, I made a work-table out of an old bathroom door and outfitted it with an electric burner from a broken stovetop. Since chemistry is a big hobby of mine, I already had plenty of test tubes and beakers and cylinders lying around. I brought them over along with the microscope from my room. Then I dug through the garage's various junk piles for wires, gizmos, and other kinds of "tech-orations" that make any lab feel like home. Finally, I found a set of those old, "rabbit ear" TV antennas that look like a giant letter "V" and ran them up to the rafters. With a little tinkering, I was able to make an electrical arc leap ominously from one of the metal rods to the other. I don't know if you've noticed, but in the old movies all the secret labs have leaping electrical arcs. This particular one didn't serve any actual purpose, but it sure looked scientific. Cool too.

CHAPTER 7

Impossible Dreams

Why didn't someone tell me physical labor was such hard work? I'd been moving large, heavy objects for days, and I ached in places where other people have muscles, but it was worth it. My laboratory was ready!

I crawled through the secret door and entered a world of invention.

Inventing, if you haven't guessed, is kind of my thing. I can't remember a time when I wasn't trying to come up with amazing, new technologies. Some of them, like the automatic flyswatter, fizzled out on the drawing board. But I also have my triumphs, like the never-ending candy jar, which does great as long as you keep refilling it. Katie Beth says this makes it exactly the same as a regular candy jar, but that's because she doesn't understand science.

Science isn't about making something that works, science is all the stuff you learn when you make something that doesn't work. I didn't realize what huge successes my failures were until Mr. Z explained it to me.

Mr. Z is Mr. Zaborsky, my favorite teacher, and the only person I know who likes inventing as much as I do. Mr. Z doesn't laugh when I tell him about my ideas, even the really, really weird ones that involve wizards.

"Keep dreaming, Howard," he says. "Dreams are what inventions are made of."

As I looked around at my brand-spankin' new lab, I wondered, *What if I couldn't dream big enough?*

I didn't want to waste premium space like this doing the same old science I used to do in my room. I wanted to make something fantastic—a spaceship or a time machine or a cure for wimpiness. I wanted to create something impossible!

Of course, the problem with creating something impossible is that no one can tell you how to do it. I sat on the edge of my work table and thought about how nice it would be if there were books out there with titles like **How to Make an Interdimensional Bicycle** or **How to Make Anti-Gravity Gum**—and that's when I saw it.

It had been right in front of me the whole time—*How to Make Friends*.

"No ... no," I told myself as I stared at the book that had led me to this lab. "You're reading it the wrong way, Howard. It's **'HOW to Make Friends'** not **'How to MAKE Friends!'**"

Just so you know, from time to time my brain will generate random weirdness. I acknowledge that. But this was a ridiculous idea even for me. Kids make friends at school and church and summer camp—they didn't make them in a laboratory! Then again, technically speaking, most kids didn't have a laboratory. And if there was one thing I'd proven beyond all doubt, it was that I was no good at making friends the regular way.

"Forget it!" I yelled at the book. "It's impossible!"

And I was right. It was absolutely impossible. I was ready to drop the subject then and there, but the book wouldn't let it go.

"You disappoint me, Howard," it seemed to be saying. "Isn't the impossible exactly the kind of thing you were looking to invent?"

This is why you should never argue with a book. They're surprisingly good debaters. I felt a big, marble-sized opportunity rolling around the little crevasses of my mind.

Could I really do this?

And before you say anything, yes, I knew how insane the whole idea was. But I'll bet unicycles and stuffed-crust pizza sounded pretty crazy until someone made them real. Besides, what was the worst that could happen? I'd fail? Failing was one of the few things I was good at.

I looked down at my arms. They had goose pimples—possibly even goose acne. I felt tingly all over, the way you do when you lick a 9-volt battery. Here was my chance to accomplish something I never dreamed I'd do in my entire life. It was settled.

I, Howard Boward, was going to make a friend!

CHAPTER 8

What You Want In a Friend

The hardest part about any project is getting started. I picked up the book. The title of the next chapter looked promising: "Think About What You Want in a Friend."

That sounded easy enough. I grabbed a pencil and started a list.

Big smile. Big heart. Regular-sized liver, lungs, spleen, kidneys...

I'd read enough biology to know that these were all good things to have in a friend. Trouble was, I didn't know where to get them. I mean, where is a 12-year-old inventor supposed to find a decent supply of fresh, raw organs?

I decided to check the refrigerator.

Over the years, I've discovered the kitchen is a valuable source of scientific ingredients. Particularly the back of the fridge. There's some stuff in there you'd swear must have escaped from a laboratory. So I swung open the big, stainless-steel door and stuck my head inside.

Pickles, mustard, something that might once have been cheese—nothing especially interesting. I was checking the lettuce crisper—the "mystery drawer," as I like to call it—when Stick walked into the room.

"Do we have any liver?" I asked him.

He pushed me out of the way and grabbed a Gatorade bottle from the top shelf.

"What do you want with liver?"

"It's for an experiment," I said. "I'm trying to determine if there's anything in the house that smells as bad as you."

He walked away from me and over to the kitchen table. A second later, a pair of his sweaty socks landed on my head.

"How about those?" he asked.

I was about to retaliate but a foil-covered dish caught my attention. I peeled back the aluminum.

"What's meatloaf made out of?" I said. "Intestines?"

"You are such a spaz. What are you up to anyway?"

I didn't answer. The last thing I needed was for Stick to get suspicious. It was time to go see Uncle Ben.

☆ ☆ ☆

Ben's Electro-A-Go-Go—Uncle Ben's electronics store—was in an older part of the city between a used record place and a Vietnamese donut shop. All day long the store sounded like the rockin' hits of 1973 and smelled like cinnamon buns.

It was the most fantastic place on earth.

When I walked in, my uncle was up to his elbows in computer guts.

"Uncle Ben," I said. "How do you make a friend?"

"With a logic board, a microprocessor, and about eighty pounds of raw hamburger," he said.

That's what I like about Uncle Ben. We speak the same language.

"What if I wanted to make a real-live-thinking-acting-doing kind of friend?"

"Oh, that kind!" he said, pushing back his messy, black hair and wiping his hands on his jeans. "I'm sorry to tell you this, squirt, but you can't make one of those from electronic parts and premium, grade-A beef."

"I guess not," I said, disappointed.

"Of course not! You'll also need DNA."

We'd learned all about DNA—deoxyribonucleic acid—in school. Basically, it's the building block of friends, enemies, athletes, dogs, cats, bugs, flowers, and lots of other things. I, myself, am absolutely loaded with it. Unfortunately, my DNA comes with one big drawback—it turns into me.

Forget that. I didn't want to have to hang out with myself twice as much as I did already.

No, there was some prime friendship-DNA out there. And I knew just where to get it.

CHAPTER 9

Middle School Gets Hairy

Josh Gutierrez plays middle linebacker on our school's football team. He smiles a lot, especially in the mirror, so I guess he's happy. He's got brown eyes and black hair, and for a seventh-grader, he's enormous. And talk about strong! Of all the people who have ever held me upside down by my ankles from the athletic-field bleachers, Josh made it look the easiest.

"Josh," I said, catching him at his locker between classes. "Can I ask you a question?"

"If you're asking if you look like a geek, the answer is yes," Josh said.

"I was wondering if I could have some of your hair?"

"How much?"

"Two or three strands."

He poked me in the chest. Even his poking finger was strong. "I mean, how much are you willing to pay for it?"

Pay for it? It never occurred to me I might have to buy someone's DNA. Since they got it for free, I naturally assumed they'd give it away.

"Well," I told him, "when we were in third grade, I gave you my lunch money every single day for a year. How about we call it even."

"That was you?"

"Yes."

Josh smiled as if reliving pleasant memories.

"I'll tell you what. For old time's sake," he said, "give me your lunch money."

I did.

Josh walked off down the hall and every hair on his head went with him.

Things didn't go any better with Missi Kilpatrick or Dino Lincoln. It wasn't until I was about to approach Kyle Stanford, who I'm pretty sure would rather part with his brain stem than his hair, that it hit me.

This was a very bad plan.

What was I thinking? These were UPs! Uber Populars! If I were to make a friend using Uber-Popular DNA, I would almost certainly be creating a friend who hates me.

The science nerd is the natural enemy of the UPs.

My feet swiveled 180 degrees, and I walked quickly in the other direction—right into Winnie McKinney.

"I'm sorry! I didn't see you!" I said.

"Slow it down, slick. One fender-bender and the whole hallway backs up."

Winnie McKinney has always puzzled me. She's average height with average-length hair and green eyes that sit about an inch apart from each other, which seems about average. Yet if I had to describe her total effect, I'd call her above average. Mathematically speaking, this makes no sense at all, but that's probably because she's a girl.

Girls never make any sense to me.

The thing about Winnie is she doesn't fit on my popularity chart. She is not an UP, but she knows all the UPs. And all the UPs know Winnie. But Winnie also knows the jocks, the brains, the rebels, the band buddies, the posers, the leeches—pretty much everybody.

In fact, about the only person Winnie McKinney doesn't know is me.

"I should have been watching where I was going," I said. "I was just trying to get away."

"Get away from what?"

"Nothing," I mumbled. "A bad idea."

"My name's Winnie," she said and she held out her hand.

I tightened my neck muscles. It's a reflex. Normally when someone holds their hand out to me, it's to wrap it around my throat. But as Winnie's hand made no sudden, aggressive move, I gave it the benefit of the doubt.

"I'm Howard," I said.

"Howard Boward? No way! Have you been asking people for their hair?"

In my school, weird news travels fast ... unfortunately.

"It was just a stupid experiment," I blushed.

"About DNA, right?" Winnie said, reaching up and plucking a strand of her own shoulder-length blonde-ness. "Here you go. I pulled it from the scalp because I figured you'd need the root. You're not going to clone me or anything?"

"No. It's just sort of ... a project."

"Cool. You must be some kind of pre-teen Einstein," she said.

"Hardly," I told her. "Maybe a young Lloyd Groff Copeman."

Winnie scrunched up her face.

"I don't really see what DNA has to do with flexible ice-cube trays, but whatever."

Then she smiled and walked off down the hall.

Unbelievable. Winnie McKinney knew that Lloyd Groff Copeman invented the first rubber ice-cube tray! Nobody knew that! Was it possible that someone in the world besides me spent their spare time memorizing inventor trivia?

I looked at the silky, golden strand clutched tightly in my grip. It was now the most valuable thing I owned.

I told Winnie I wasn't going to clone her, and I wasn't. Cloning means making an exact copy of someone. Winnie McKinney was one of a kind, and I intended to keep it that way.

The truth was, I didn't want my friend to be an exact copy of anybody. I wanted it to be unique. While I hadn't worked out all the details, my plan was to take only the coolest characteristics from a lot of different people and combine them into one super-friend who would be completely new and totally awesome.

So, ideally, my friend would have some Winnie-like qualities but also the best features of other people. All I had to do is figure out a way to get my contributors' good parts without having to take the rest of them. For instance, I wanted my friend to be as strong as Josh Gutierrez but without Josh's tendency to shake me until I spewed pocket change. That meant I'd need to get DNA from somebody big, but who?

Stick was pretty big. I imagined what it would be like having even the tiniest part of a second Stick in my life.

My body shuddered.

Oh well. These were the kinds of questions that had baffled scientists since the beginning of time. I supposed it wouldn't hurt to give myself one more night to sleep on it.

CHAPTER 10

Riding with Aquaman

Early the next morning, Dad crept into my room as quietly as a rodeo bull and flipped on the light. My dad is a master of rude awakenings. Didn't he know Saturdays didn't start until noon?

"Howard, I need you to come down to the office with me," he said.

Dad's office was at the animal shelter. If he was taking me, it meant he was having trouble with his computer. I dragged myself out of bed and got dressed.

We were about halfway there when the radio in his truck squawked.

"Johnny, what's your twenty?" an electronic voice asked.

"What's your twenty?" is code for "What's your location?" All the guys in animal control talk in code. I think it's to keep the dogs from figuring out what they're up to.

"Headed in now, Slate," Dad radioed back.

The voice on the radio belonged to Slater. I don't know if that's his first name or last name, it's just what everybody calls him—either that or "Slate."

"You know that guy west of town that keeps animals on his place?" Slater asked. "Well, one of them got loose and is roaming the neighborhood. Can you head out that way?"

I saw Dad's jaw clench. He didn't turn and stare at me or anything, but his eyeballs were definitely pushed in my direction.

"I've, uh ... I've got my son with me right now," he said.

"Take him along. He might be a lot of help," Slater said. "I've told you a hundred times, Nate's a great kid."

"It's Howard," Dad said.

"Howard!" the radio voice screamed, and then it got quiet for what seemed like forever. "Maybe you could drop him off somewhere."

"I'm not dropping my kid off ..."

"Well I don't mean on the side of the road!" Slater said. "I mean someplace like a mall or a basketball court. A place where he could hang out with other kids for a while."

"It's Howard," Dad repeated.

"Oh ... right."

Apparently, my reputation had reached the animal shelter. This explained the looks I got from the animals.

43

"I want to go," I said. "I won't cause any trouble, Dad. Honest."

Dad wasn't buying a word of it. I couldn't really blame him. Me promising not to cause trouble was like a porcupine promising to be careful with a balloon. But we were the closest truck, and we were already most of the way there. So after hesitating a minute, Dad picked up the handset.

"It'll be fine, Slate. We're on our way."

"You know best," Slater answered. "Oh, and Johnny— it's a bear." A bear? Had he just said a bear? I sure hoped so—this was probably as close as I was ever going to get to a big-game hunt. Plus it sounded like a lot more fun than spending my Saturday debugging the world's oldest computer.

"Me and you tracking wild bear, Dad!" I said. "Maybe we should go pick up the dogs?"

I had trained our two dogs, Frisco and Pants, to hunt by having them track down my guinea pigs. They were great at it, mainly because I had never trained the guinea pigs to hide.

"No dogs," Dad said. "The bear will be in a garbage can."

"How do you know?"

"He's a bear. He'll be after food."

I felt like a doofus. Of course the bear was after food! Wasn't that the point of every single Yogi Bear episode ever? Obviously the bear would be in a trash can. Trash cans are like restaurants to bears! How could I have not known that? I tried to redeem myself by explaining how we could set a trap using a picnic basket and an anvil, but Dad cut me off.

"You'll be in the truck."

"As your back-up?" I asked.

He didn't answer but his look said "I'm already sorry I brought you." I stopped talking.

We pulled into a rural neighborhood with big yards and long, country roads. Sure enough, at the end of the main road, a black bear was making a face-first plunge into a garbage can.

"Keep the windows rolled up. Stay in the truck," Dad said.

He got out and walked toward the bear.

My dad is not a small man, but he looks even bigger in his uniform. I don't know why, it's just a khaki-colored shirt with a flag on the sleeve, but it makes him seem six inches taller. He had on his sunglasses, and his black cap was pulled down tight so you couldn't see those little streaks of gray in his hair.

I mean, I knew it was still the same guy who watched monster movies in ridiculous pajamas, but when he was walking up on that bear he looked, well, like a hero.

"Get out of that can!" he yelled.

The startled bear jumped backwards streaming

garbage in his retreat. For just a second, I thought he was going to run away, but at the last minute he stood on his hind legs and started moving forward. I watched as my dad disappeared behind a large, furry eating-machine!

"Rollo!" Dad yelled. "Get down!"

He pushed his hand against the slobbering bear and the animal fell back to all fours.

"Get over there!" Dad yelled, pointing toward the truck.

To my enormous surprise, the bear walked to the back of the vehicle and crawled through the open gate. Dad slammed the cage door behind it and got back in the cab. I stared at him and tried to push my speechless mouth closed but it wouldn't stay shut. Had I really seen what I thought I just saw? I couldn't believe it.

My dad was Aquaman!

CHAPTER 11

The Bear Necessities

"Dad!" I gasped, still dizzy from the excitement. "That bear tried to maul you!"

Dad turned the key and the engine roared—roared like the truck of a beast-master!

"Who, Rollo? Rollo just wants to play. He thinks he's people, that's his trouble."

I didn't know which surprised me more—that the bear thought he was people, or that he'd apparently been confiding in my dad.

"You know this bear?" I asked.

"Oh yeah, me and Rollo go way back. He gets out now and again and we have to come round him up. It's kind of a sad situation."

There's something you should know about my dad. He loves animals. That's why he's great at his job. I remember this one time there was a bobcat caught in a drainpipe, and my dad had to go get it out. When he came home that night, he had twelve stitches in his arm.

Mom asked him why a grown man would reach into a pipe knowing he was going to get clawed by a scared cat. Dad just shrugged.

"You didn't marry me for my brains," he said.

That's true. I've heard Mom say the same thing on several occasions.

We drove on down the road. Since this was my first carpool with a bear, I wanted to know all about Rollo.

"Why did you say this was a sad situation?" I asked.

"Oh, it's just one of those things," Dad said. "Rollo's been in a cage since he was a cub, and humans are all he's ever known. That's not much of a life for a bear. I wish there was something we could do about it, but there's no way he could make it in the wild now."

"Did you know it was going to be Rollo when we headed out here?" I asked.

"No, but I sure hoped so. The guy's got a couple of other bears on his property that aren't nearly so friendly. They're really too big to be in those cages. That's why I'm trying to find zoos for them."

I turned around and looked through the thick, rectangular window into the back of the truck. It's weird how people can seem one way when you first meet them then very different once you get to know them. In case you're wondering, that also applies to bears. Just a few minutes earlier, Rollo had looked like a fierce creature that was going to mutilate my dad. Now he looked like a big teddy bear who, at worst, might hug you to death.

"Are we taking Rollo back to his owner?" I asked.

"Nope," Dad said. "He's got a pretty nasty cut on his front leg. We'll run him over to the vet at the zoo."

☆ ☆ ☆

The zoo hospital had yellow walls and three huge examination-tables and some of those blinking machines that made it look like a spaceship—or maybe a space ark since it was filled with animals.

The veterinarian, a woman with short, black hair and big, black glasses, had given Rollo something to knock him out and, lying there, he didn't look scary at all. He looked sweet and harmless. I've noticed the same thing with Stick—he's only terrifying when he's awake.

"I need to talk to the doctor about what we can do with the bear," Dad said. "Wait for me out in the hall."

I walked past some holding cages and through a pair of large, swinging doors. The hallway was lined with pictures of animals doing interesting things you never see them doing at the zoo. Things like catching fish and stalking zebras. I sat down in a chair against the wall and waited.

"Excuse me, coming through," a thin man in dark-blue coveralls said.

He shoved a wide broom across the floor as he came through the double doors that led into the treatment area. When he reached me, I lifted my feet the way I do when Mom vacuums because, as I've told her many times, that counts as "helping." The big broom was pushing all kinds of useless material in front of it—bits of string, a few

wrappers, and a couple of thumb-
tacks. But mostly, there was hair. Lots
and lots of hair.

"Mister," I asked, "is that animal
hair?"

"Probably," the man said.

"What kind of animal hair?"

"I expect it's a little of everything,"
he said. "They got animals coming in
and out of this place all day long. And
they shed like you wouldn't believe!"

He bent over and picked up a
handful of the sweepings.

"Could be hyena, zebra, tiger, ape. Might even be a little
of mine in there!" he laughed, rubbing the top of his nearly
bald head.

"Are you just going to throw it away?" I asked.

He looked at me like I belonged in one of the cages.

"Do you think the animals want it back?" he said.

Then he swept the pile into a dustpan and dumped it
into a green garbage can on wheels before walking back
through the double doors.

Now, I don't know why—maybe it was because Rollo
looked so peaceful and kind—but for some reason, I found
myself thinking about animals the way my dad does. To
my dad, animals aren't wild, ignorant beasts. They're furry
people who spend a lot of time outdoors. I'd studied enough
biology to know there were other differences, but all of a
sudden those didn't matter so much. They didn't matter

because animals had at least one quality that was sorely lacking in the human population—generosity. While most of the kids at school had refused to part with even a single strand of their hair, these animals had donated loads of it without my even asking!

Was it exactly the kind of hair I was looking for? No. But sometimes inventors have to work with what's handy.

So, like a thief left alone in a bank vault, I approached the fuzzy treasure in the green, rubber can. Here was a genetic mother lode, all the DNA I could hope for, literally dumped right in front of me. I figured some of the hair had to come from an animal as strong as Josh Gutierrez—and probably smarter than Kyle Stanford. All I had to do is scatter a few of these strands in with Winnie's and I'd have the perfect spices for my friendship stew!

Moving quickly, I stuffed my pockets with enough DNA to upholster a yak. Then I sat back down and waited for Dad and tried very hard to pretend my pants didn't smell like nature's barbershop.

CHAPTER
12

Oh, Brother

Someday I'm going to invent a calendar with no Mondays. They're a bad influence on the rest of the week. I only mention it because this particular Monday was oral report day in Mr. Z's class—it did not go well.

In my defense, my underwear hasn't fit properly since National Wedgie Week. I'm not trying to make excuses, but it's pretty hard to concentrate on paleontology when parts of your elastic waistband are rubbing against your kneecaps.

All I'm saying is if I hadn't been distracted, I would have noticed something unusual was going on with my visual aids. My report was on life in the Jurassic period, so I jazzed it up by downloading pictures of the great dinosaurs to project on the roll-down screen behind me. Mr. Z doesn't require us to use visuals, but if there's one thing I pride myself on, it's showmanship.

But something was wrong. The creatures being shown

on the screen were not the creatures I had in my report. Ask anybody—never once did I say a word about a dork-a-saurus, a butt-a-saurus, or a Mr. Potato-saurus. Yet there they were behind me big as life! I heard people laughing but assumed that was because my underwear was tucked into my belt.

I might never have figured out what was going on if Mr. Z hadn't stopped me.

"Howard," he said, "why is Luke Skywalker riding a triceratops?"

I turned around and stared at the strange image.

"I don't know," I said. "They didn't even exist in the same era."

Mr. Z looked confused, which was understandable. But I knew exactly what had happened.

Stick was going to wish he was never born.

☆ ☆ ☆

I knew Stick hadn't done this alone. It was beyond the limits of his chimp-like brain. He'd obviously had help from a master, someone who could create a dozen images like these before naptime.

Orson.

It was too perfect to have come from anyone else. My little brother is only five and he never opens his mouth, but he is to computers what Mozart is to music. So if Stick told him to sit down at the keyboard and create some funny pictures of dinosaurs, Orson could make it look easy.

Naturally, Stick wouldn't tell him they were playing a

trick on me. That would be mean—Orson has no meanness in him. But he must have realized something was up because the morning before my report, he was as mad at Stick as I'd ever seen him.

Pity it didn't last. It never does. If Orson has one weakness, it's that he really loves Stick. I'm hoping he outgrows it before there's permanent damage.

Even though I had no idea what Stick had done, I knew Orson had forgiven him when I saw the Slinky. Stick found it in the pocket of his jacket later that same day. That's how Orson lets you know he's not mad anymore—he hides a present somewhere you're sure to find it. It's always one of his toys so you'll know he's the one who put it there. I guess that seems kind of weird to people whose brothers actually talk to them, but what can I tell you? It's Orson's way.

Mom says not to worry, he'll talk when he's ready. In the meantime, it's free toys for the rest of us.

My point is I knew Orson hadn't sabotaged me on purpose. This was strictly between me and the Stick.

☆ ☆ ☆

"I heard about the dork-a-saurus. Tough break," Winnie McKinney told me when she showed up at my locker.

"Oh that. No big whoop," I said.

"It must have been humiliating."

"I have had my head flushed in the girl's bathroom—by girls," I told her. "This is nothing."

"If you say so," she said.

Winnie was half-a-head shorter than me. Her blonde hair was all one-length, and she combed it over to the left side of her head so that it made an even part. It was an organized look, which I appreciate.

"So how's the experiment coming, the one with the DNA?" she asked, her green eyes showing this wasn't just pity—she really wanted to know.

"I've kind of hit a snag," I said, which was true.

That was the other reason this was a lousy Monday. It turned out finding the DNA was the easy part. I'd spent the rest of the weekend trying to make it do something amazing, but it just sat there on the table like a big pile of hair.

"You'll figure it out. Everybody says you're the smartest kid in school."

With that, Winnie smiled, turned, and moved on down the hall.

Only her words didn't go with her—they hung around and repeated themselves in my ears. Had I heard her right? Did she really think I was the smartest kid in school? I mean, lots of kids said I was smart, but they meant it in an unappealing, nerdy kind of way. Winnie McKinney actually made intelligence sound like a good thing.

CHAPTER 13

Operation Get Really Even

When I got home, I headed straight to the garage. The DNA would have to wait while I launched a more urgent project: **"Operation Get Really Even"** (or **O.G.R.E.** for short). I was going to just call it "Operation Get Even" but the "Really" made it sound extra-fiendish. This one needed to be special.

The idea was simple. I'd secretly coat Stick with a stink-spray that would be activated by his own perspiration. I didn't actually have a stink-spray, but I figured I could come up with some kind of reverse-deodorant pretty quickly. I mean, how hard could it be to make Stick smell bad? He was most of the way there already! I considered several fragrance options—bouquet of broccoli, sour milk, Grampa's bathroom—but in the end decided to go with plain ol' skunk.

I've always been partial to the classics.

The hard part would be making sure Stick started perspiring at just the right time. Fortunately, I had that covered. All I had to do is rig his bike to play the same music they blast from the neighborhood ice-cream truck. See, every morning on his way to school, Stick had to ride his bike past a group of kindergarteners waiting for the bus. It's a well-known fact that kindergarteners will chase any vehicle playing ice-cream truck music—they're drawn to it like mice to mozzarella. Naturally, Stick would panic. The faster he pedaled away from the sugar-crazed five-year-olds, the more he'd sweat. By the time he walked into homeroom, he'd be sopping wet—activating my skunk-funk formula!

It was a perfect plan.

Well, it was perfect as long as nothing went wrong. Mr. Z says every experiment has something that can go wrong—it's called a "scientific variable."

"Just because you *can* do something doesn't mean you *should* do it," he told our class. "Part of science is being aware of the possible consequences."

That was good advice. After careful consideration, I decided the possible consequences of **O.G.R.E.** were:

a. Stick would be humiliated in front of all his friends, and;

b. He'd come home, pin me down, and stick my face into his unbelievably stinky armpit.

It was risky—but totally worth it.

By the next morning, I'd created the formula and applied it to Stick's clothes. After school, I rushed home and hid out in the lab, confident I had achieved the final victory in the Boward Wars. If all had gone well, Stick had just endured the worst eight hours of his life!

Yet even in my moment of triumph, something told me my plan didn't work.

That something was Reynolds Pipkin.

"Your plan didn't work," he said.

"Reynolds!" I screamed. "How did you get in here?"

"I crawled through the cooler, turned left at the cabinet, took the tunnel to the dryer, and came out the door. Why, is there an easier way?"

I was speechless. Reynolds Pipkin was inside my secret lab! It was like some terrible dream.

"Nobody knows about this place!" I yelled.

"I'm not going to tell anybody. I have a secret place of my own under our kitchen sink. No one can find me."

"No one wants to find you!"

"This place is neat," Reynolds said.

I held my arms out in exasperation.

"How did you know the way in here?"

"It seemed like the logical path," he said. "I saw you standing by your garage yesterday and, a second later, you were gone. The only thing that had a door on it was the cooler so that had to be the way in. The rest I just figured out as I went along."

"You realize I'll have to erase your memory," I told him.

"That's what I'd do," Reynolds said.

As upset as I was by this invasion, I was more bothered by what he'd said about Stick.

"What do you mean by 'my plan didn't work'?" I asked.

"That spray you made for Nathaniel—it made him smell like cotton candy," Reynolds said. "Is that what you were going for? I assumed it was something smellier."

I shook my head in defeat. Then something occurred to me.

"Wait a minute, how do you even know about my plan?"

"It was in your notes," he said. "I came across them on a sheet of paper while I was going through your garbage."

"You go through my garbage?"

"Not yours. Everybody's. You'd be surprised what you can find."

I know I should have rained blows down on the little weasel, but I was too disappointed. The only part of my plan that had actually worked like I wanted was the ice-cream truck music. Even that didn't go as expected.

"After school, Nathaniel bought a bunch of popsicles and sold them from his bike," Reynolds said. "He's made like twenty bucks already."

So **Operation Get Really Even** was a bust. Stick smelled like a candy store, and Reynolds Pipkin knew the location of my secret lab. This was not a good day.

But you know what they say—when life gives you lemons, have your lab assistant make lemonade. Since I didn't have a lab assistant, I gave Reynolds the job.

CHAPTER 14

Wonder Putty

"You're trying to combine DNA, aren't you?" Reynolds said.

I gave him the look, the one that let him know he could be replaced by a trained monkey.

"Reynolds," I said. "What are the duties of a lab assistant?"

"To wash things, fetch things, assist the scientist, and keep my mouth shut."

"Oh, that's right," I said. "All the things that you're terrible at!"

I turned away, leaving him to stew in his own shame.

Here's what bothered me about Reynolds Pipkin—he gave intelligence a bad name. I'll admit he's smart, and he was right about what I was trying to do with the DNA. But did he have to be so annoying? Did he have to button his shirt all the way up to his chin? Did he have to blink like an owl every five seconds?

The worst part was realizing that the way I felt about Reynolds was the exact same way the seventh grade felt about me. Mom's suggestion to "treat others the way you want to be treated," well, it was clearer than ever my only real chance at friendship was the pile of hair sitting on my lab table.

But after spending days staring at a giant fur-ball, I was no closer to a friend than when I started.

"That's a very impressive hair collection," Reynolds said. "What does it do?"

Even his questions irritated me.

"Reynolds," I said, rolling my eyes. "Don't ask about things you can't possibly understand. You don't know the first thing about how to change one substance into another substance."

"Yes I do," he said.

"Liar!" I shrieked. It's my standard response when someone says they know something I don't.

"Really, I do," Reynolds said. "Look."

He reached into his pocket and pulled out a small, plastic container.

"What is that, and why is it in my lab?" I asked sternly.

"It's Wonder Putty," Reynolds said. "It's the neatest toy ever because it changes from one substance into another substance."

"It does not."

"Sure it does. See? Right now it sticks to things, like gum does."

Reynolds stuck the wad to the leg of the lab table.

"Get that off of there!" I ordered.

"But if I flatten it, like this," he said, mashing the wad in his hand, "it absorbs ink like paper."

Grabbing a comic book I had on the counter, Reynolds pushed the gummy wad against one of the pages. When he peeled it back, a drawing showed on the flattened putty.

"That's not what I'm talking about at all," I grumped.

Reynolds ignored my disinterest and continued his blabbering.

"And if I roll it like this," he said, working the goo between his palms, "it turns into a ball."

Reynolds threw the putty ball hard against the concrete floor and it bounced skyward. In fact, it bounced so high that it passed through the leaping electrical-arc at the top of my lab.

When the ball hit the electricity, it shot out like a missile and ricocheted around the room before finally landing in the middle of my hair collection which, an instant later, fizzed, bubbled, and caught fire.

"Reynolds, get some water!" I yelled.

He handed me a beaker, and I instinctively flung the contents onto the burning putty. What I didn't realize was that this particular container wasn't filled with water—it was filled with the **Operation Get Really Even** formula that I'd used on Stick.

It did the trick. The fire was out and the only thing left on my lab table was a scorched, smoldering putty-blob with an awful lot of hair in it.

"That was close," Reynolds panted.

I glared at him, wondering how difficult it would be to put his brain into a lab monkey.

Now, what happened next might be hard for you to believe. It's hard for me to believe, and I was there. But strange as it sounds, the hairy, wet blob began to bubble. A moment later, it spewed liquid like a boiling volcano! A dense, black smoke blew from its center and the gross, slimy substance pulsated. With each throbbing pulse, it grew bigger and bigger and bigger!

I was certain we were dead, or grounded, or both. There was only one thing to do.

"Reynolds," I said calmly. "You're fired."

The next thing I saw were the bottoms of his shoes disappearing through the dryer door.

It was just me and the blob. I couldn't take my eyes off it. The hideous thing kept expanding like a giant bag of microwave popcorn. Its outer skin was nearly transparent, and I could see small electrical-charges erupting inside. Before long, the terrifying bubble had engulfed half the lab! Its crown extended almost to the roof, and even though I was as scared as I have ever been, I knew I wouldn't leave this place for anything. This was what it meant to be an inventor! The blob's interior glowed as flashes of actual lightning cut through the smoke inside it. The surface throbbed—it throbbed like a beating heart!

The explosion was breathtaking. I defied gravity for several feet before slamming against the back wall of the garage. When I regained my senses, I noticed the room was eerily still. It was also filthy. Green globs of slime covered the walls and ceiling. Without Reynolds, or at least his monkey equivalent, clean-up was going to be a nightmare.

There was no use putting it off. I picked up the mop in the corner of the lab—then instantly dropped it. I dropped it because clean-up wasn't going to be a problem after all.

That's because the ooze—every disgusting spot of it—was moving! I couldn't believe my eyes. The pasty bits slithered back to the table where they recombined into the big, unexploded squish-ball. All of my lab materials—the animal hair, Winnie's golden strand, a yogurt I had been saving for a snack—were visible beneath the mysterious, transparent skin.

What happened next should make anyone think twice about trying to make DNA pudding. The bubbling blob began to stretch and form shapes. At one end, I saw the jellylike tail of a tiger. At the other, pushing out like spikes, were the legs of a rubbery zebra. A lion's head emerged and then faded. For an instant, I saw the mustached face of the janitor from the veterinary hospital, then Winnie's face, then Rollo's face, all of which vanished in a drain-like swirl. A second later, tiny monkey-heads cropped up like goose-pimples across the pulsating flesh.

The pattern continued with faces and body parts emerging blobbishly for an instant before disappearing. Looking back, the process actually made a lot of sense— this thing was loaded with DNA and didn't know what to do with all those molecules. I took a deep breath (which

smelled surprisingly like cotton candy) and assessed the situation.

The blob was a quivering mass of jelly with no sustain- able form. Somehow I had to help it decide what it was going to be.

But how?

I looked down. There on the floor was my copy of

How to Make Friends. It had fallen open to a chapter called, "Making Connections."

Connections?

Well, the book had gotten me this far. It was worth a shot.

As quickly as I could, I rushed around the lab grabbing electronics from my various stashes. I picked up a logic board, microprocessors, wiring, and a lantern battery, then dropped them into the ooze.

This next part is not for the squeamish. I forced myself to reach inside the festering blob. "Icky" does not begin to describe the sensation. It was like being in the belly of a whale that just ate a Radio Shack. When I finally got the battery in my hand, I ran a wire from the spring terminals to the circuit board.

Instantly, the blob stopped throbbing.

Instead, it vibrated all over.

The book was right—I'd made a "connection"!

I'm not saying it was huge progress, but it was definitely different. To keep from having to re-enter the grossness, I installed a small serial-port on the surface of the skin.

The port allowed me to connect my computer directly

to the blob. It was a long-shot, but what choice did I have? I attached the cable and pressed "Enter." To my enormous surprise, the blob twitched.

As impossible as it seemed, I was data-streaming to Wonder Putty!

CHAPTER
15

Going Online

I had no idea what I was supposed to do next. All I knew was that when the computer connected to the blob, a message appeared: "New hardware detected. Installing driver device." A second later, there was another message: "You are now connected."

Well, at least I knew what was happening. My computer was reading the blob as a port "I," like an external hard drive. But so what? It was a twitching blob instead of a throbbing one. That was still a long, long way from being a friend.

In desperation, I went back to the book.

"A good way to make friends," it said, "is to spend time online."

Online, huh?

I went to my laptop and googled "human." That seemed basic enough. It took me to a website showing the anatomy of a cartoon-style male, which I downloaded to the blob.

This got a response. The stretchy goo shook and

expanded then pulled itself together in an incredible feat of blobular gymnastics. When it was through, the gelatinous thing in front of me had a recognizable shape. It was oozy, drippy, and disgusting—but it was human!

OK, maybe that's an exaggeration. It had the basic shape of a human, kind of like a department-store mannequin made out of jelly, but that was about it. Still, it was a huge improvement. I tried to imagine what the thing would look like as a real, live person but the creepy, bubbling flesh distracted me. It was like looking at some kind of mutant, plucked chicken. So I dressed it.

Astonishing what a makeover can do. All of a sudden it didn't look like a big, naked blob anymore. It looked like a blob in a baseball hat, sunglasses, and striped necktie.

Just my luck—my goo sack was a total fashion-feeb.

I wasn't criticizing. I myself have been known to wear black socks with a glittery-gold unitard. That was all right for me, but it would never do for my new pal. He deserved better. So as much as I hated the idea, I was going to have to teach us both the art of looking spiffy. I went back to the computer

and googled the phrase "middle school style." It pulled up a website called "Teen Trendz" filled with advice on color coordination, hair care, and shopping like a celebrity. I felt my brain gag.

"The things I do for you," I told the blob.

While I was waiting for the page to load—there were a lot of pictures—I picked up a broom and started sweeping up the wreckage on the floor. Stick says I'm a neat freak, but I don't think so. It's just that disorder gives me a rash.

Suddenly, out of the corner of my eye, I saw something move. I looked up from my broom. Let me tell you, what I saw next caused my eyes to bug out like two super-sized cereal bowls. The shape on the table—the one I'd just been talking to—was sitting straight up! Actually sitting! Then, as casually as you please, the thing raised an arm and loosened the tie around its neck.

I don't think it loosened it because it was choking or anything. I think it just wanted to look ... cool.

"No ... way!" I gasped.

What had just happened? How had it happened? Then I saw the answer—the cable was still hooked up to the serial port! Whatever was on the computer was being fed directly to the blob *and was teaching it to dress better!*

This changed everything! I dropped the broom and rushed to the keyboard.

There was a whole world out there that the putty-man knew nothing about—and the world-wide-web was the fastest way to explore it.

I quickly typed in the name of a website that taught the

English language. I mean, what good was finally having someone to talk to if he couldn't understand anything I was saying? But the important thing was that I now had a way to reach this incredible creation—my creation. I looked at the thing sitting there in sunglasses and a ridiculous tie, and I just couldn't hold back any longer.

"It's alive!" I screamed. "It's alive!"

CHAPTER 16

Things Change

"Hey, whiz-kid, how's it going in Scienceville?" Winnie McKinney asked when she saw me in the hall the next day.

Part of me wanted to say, "Not too bad, I have a mass of Jell-O in my garage that can dress itself," but some things should stay between a boy and his blob.

"Things are fine," I told her.

"Whatever you're working on, I hope you wrap it up in two weeks," she said. "I'll bet you can win first prize."

"First prize? I thought the science fair wasn't for three more months."

"It's not, goofus. I'm talking about the talent show!"

"Oh that!" I laughed. "Last I checked, being the biggest geek in school wasn't a talent."

Winnie frowned.

"Don't do that," she said. "Don't call yourself names. You're not a geek, you're a scientist. Science takes talent. I'll bet if you put your mind to it, you could make a lot of people see that. Anyway, whatever you do has to be better than watching Kyle Stanford smash another watermelon."

Kyle Stanford was the winner of last year's show. His talent consisted of taking an ordinary watermelon and smashing it with his forehead. It was pretty gross—I could see why it took first prize.

Few things are more entertaining to middle schoolers than watching squishy objects splatter. Kyle would be hard to beat. Then again, I was pretty sure what was sitting in my lab was a lot better than a watermelon. Grosser too. "Maybe you're right," I told Winnie. "Maybe I can show them science is a talent. I'll have to let you know."

☆ ☆ ☆

The lab was exactly as I had left it except for one thing—there was no blob on the table.

Oh, there was a blob. It just wasn't on the table. It was sitting at my computer!

That was disturbing enough, but what really gave me the chills was when he turned around and looked at me.

The last time I saw Blobby, he didn't have any eyes! He had them now. I looked into those two dark-brown beauties bulging out of that big, hairy head.

Hairy? When did he grow hair? This experiment was changing faster than I could process the information. I thought about running for the safety of the clothes dryer, but the blob didn't seem to be dangerous. I'm not saying he liked me or anything, but at least he was wagging his tail.

Wait a minute—he had a tail?

This day was full of surprises.

I took a few careful steps toward the rapidly evolving creature. He ignored me. I didn't know whether to be relieved or insulted. I took another step, but he just kept clicking the mouse and staring at the images that flew across the monitor.

I inched forward.

"Hey, you," I said nervously. "I'm talking to you. Do you understand me?"

I couldn't be sure, but I thought he looked surprised. Of course, when you don't have any eyelids, it's pretty hard to look any other way. I picked up the sunglasses from yester-day's fashion experiment and stuck them over his freaky, bulging eyeballs.

"THIS IS A COM-PU-TER," I yelled, emphasizing every syllable and pointing at the laptop.

He stared at me for a minute. Then ... he nodded.

My heart raced. We were communicating!

"I AM HOW-ARD. I AM YOUR FRIEND," I said even louder and slower.

He stared at me just like before. But he did not nod.

I gulped. This was what I was afraid of. The blob was

becoming more human by the minute—and humans didn't like me. What if he didn't *want* to be my friend?

"Think, Howard, think!" I told myself. "How do other kids make friends? How do normal kids who don't have laboratories and thimble collections make friends?"

Like emailed lightning, the answer hit me.

FaceSpace!

Normal kids made friends on FaceSpace! Of course! I connected the cable to the port in the creature's back and sat down beside him at the computer. Then I pulled up my personal FaceSpace page. As it loaded, I found myself holding my breath. Was this a good idea? What if he didn't like my online profile? It was full of information about me—everything from my birthday to my hobbies to my favorite food. The monitor flashed and, a second later, there I was sporting my happiest, braces-baring grin. I'd always liked that picture. It was taken the day Stick left for summer camp.

I only hoped the creature would like it too.

At first, he just looked sort of confused. I'm not sure, but I think he was trying to figure out how I could be in the chair next to him and on the computer at the same time. But after a while, it was like everything clicked. His face turned toward mine and, in that instant, I could tell he knew me. I don't mean he recognized me—*he knew me*.

In that moment, a strange, new feeling came over me. It wasn't that we were friends—I didn't know how it felt to have a friend. But I knew how it felt not to have one.

And it didn't feel like that.

A Side Order
of Bully

"Good news, nerd. I've decided to give you my hair."

The voice was cold and threatening, like day-old cafe-teria meatloaf. An UP had come to the back of the lunch-room—and was talking to me!

"Listen, uh ... what's your name again?" Josh Gutierrez asked me.

"Howard," I smiled uncomfortably. I hoped I didn't have food in my braces.

"Oh yeah, How-weird. Classic! Anyway, I've been thinking it over and decided I was wrong to come between a dweeb and his dream. So I'm going to give you that hair you wanted. And then you're going to write my term paper."

He put his giant hand on my shoulder and squeezed. It wasn't one of those

75

friendly, little squeezes, it was the kind you give an orange to make it give up its precious juices. I flinched and closed my eyes for a second, and when I opened them again, the room seemed a whole lot smaller. That's because Kyle Stanford, Skyler Pritchard, and Bulldog Busby had formed an impenetrable wall around my chair.

"What are you guys doing here?" I asked.

"We got hair too," Kyle Stanford said.

"Funny thing, guys," I said nervously. "As it happens, I'm not really in the market for hair anymore."

Josh flashed his straight, white, non-metal teeth.

"Isn't that too bad?" he said. "I need that paper a week from Friday."

He shoved a notebook page at me containing his assigned topic. The others pulled out pages of their own.

"Week from Friday. Don't be late," Kyle warned. Then he thumped me on the back of the head, which is UP-speak for "thank you."

I suppose I could have said no, but these guys were football players—they spent their afternoons hitting people for fun. I folded the four sheets and put them in the Chewbacca lunchbox I use as my briefcase.

Sitting there alone, I felt a dull pain in the pit of my stomach. I was pretty sure it wasn't the meatloaf.

CHAPTER 18

Monster Meets World

Back at the lab, there were several developments. Development number one was that my friend had sprouted a mane like a lion. Development number two was that the mushy exterior of his body now looked more like hairy, human flesh. The biggest change, however, was that he'd grown a mouth.

"Woah hoord," he said when I crawled out of the tunnel.

I didn't have the slightest idea what he was saying, but they were the sweetest sounding words I ever heard.

"That's awesome!" I told him. "I mean, for your first try. And that's a very nice mouth you have there."

I really did like the mouth—particularly his fangs. They reminded me of our dogs, Frisco and Pants.

"Now," I said, "let's try that again. Say 'Howard.' Come on, give it a try. 'HOW-ard. HOW-ard is my friend.'"

"Hoord ... fween," he tried.

"Yes," I told him. "Hoord is your best fween."

I gave him a drink of JuiceAid as a reward.

The next couple of days brought incredible prog-ress. My friend got bigger, hairier, less slimy. He grew claws and eyelids. But when little surprises stopped popping out of his skin, I figured my buddy was as finished as he was going to get. In his completed form, he was tall with wide shoulders and massive arms that fed into long, hairy fingers. His mane was thick and wild and blonde like something you'd see in the jungle or at a rock concert.

As for the eyes, they were large and bright brown and reminded me a little of my sister's. He had Winnie McKinney's smile. I liked that. Overall, I'd have to say the creature looked sort of human-ish but with enough animal stuff left over to stay interesting.

A long tail and permanent fur coat are interesting, right? Maybe they were just interesting to me.

Anyway, it wasn't only the physical changes. He was learning at an amazing speed.

"How-ward," the former blob said while clicking away on my computer, "what is this?"

He was pointing to an image he'd pulled up on the web. I looked at it.

"That's a cow," I said.

"Cows are beautiful," he said, touching the screen with his hand. "They're so nice and blue."

Blue? Cows weren't blue! And since when were they beautiful? I figured out then that he wasn't pointing to the animal in the picture at all. He was pointing to the sky behind it. I'd never thought about it before, but if you've never seen a sky, how do you know what it is?

"The blue stuff is the sky," I told him. "Would you like to see the sky?"

"I'm seeing it right now," he said, and pointed again to the computer screen.

That's just sad. When your monster can't tell the difference between a real sky and one in a box, you've had him cooped up too long. It was time to push this experiment to the next frontier.

☆ ☆ ☆

That night, when the street was dark and everyone was sleeping, I went back to the lab. I'd told him we'd be taking a little trip, so he was expecting me.

When I crawled out of the dryer, the sight of him stopped me in my tracks. He was decked out in an old Hawaiian shirt he'd found in a box of Dad's clothes, and he wore long shorts and flip flops. Completing the look were the baseball cap, sunglasses, and necktie I'd given him when he was still a blob. He held a small suitcase.

"I'm taking a trip!" he said happily.

We were going outside, no farther than the driveway. But if you've never seen anything but the inner walls of a garage, I guess that's the journey of a lifetime.

I led him to the dryer. Understand that the passage from the dryer to the cooler was a pretty tight squeeze even for me. This guy was twice my size. But he was a trooper, pushing himself through the file cabinet and then making the L-turn toward the exit. As a scientist, I can tell you it defied physics. My theory is that he must have somehow maintained enough of his earlier sponginess to shoot through the tunnel like toothpaste through a tube.

His head emerged first, and the expression on his face said everything. There was a whole world out there, one without walls, and it was bigger and more amazing than anything on the Internet. He closed his eyes and took a long, cool sniff. You can't download the smell of fresh air.

"Come on," I told him. "It's one small step for monster, one giant leap for monsterkind!"

Like a baby taking his first steps, he crawled out of the tunnel. Instinctively, he headed for the grass, reaching down and touching the soft, cool blades with his hands. And there he sat listening to the crickets and smelling the flowers and looking at the ocean of stars above. Everything was new and amazing, and not just for him. I'd seen all of these things thousands of times—but I'd never seen them with a friend.

"This is where you live?" he asked me, and he stretched out his arms to take in the great outdoors.

"This is where everybody lives," I said. "This is the world."

"I like the world," he said, and he fell back in the grass and felt its coolness on his back.

And you know something? On that particular night, I liked the world, too.

CHAPTER 19

The Gooshee Run

Mr. Z says science is a process. One discovery leads to another discovery and it goes on and on because no matter how much you think you know, there's still a lot more to learn.

The important thing, he says, is that you keep expanding the scientific frontier.

So that's what I did—at least beyond the limits of our driveway.

Over the next several nights, my friend and I extended our journeys to the far reaches of the neighborhood. One excursion took us to the all-night convenience store, a land of cars and lights and self-service gas pumps. For my new friend, this might as well have been Disneyworld.

I decided it was time for the ultimate test—human contact.

We went inside.

"Two Gooshees, please," I said.

Gooshees are a semi-frozen, sugary slush available

in various flavors. I had Rainbow Extreme, but since my friend was a novice, I started him out on basic strawberry. The clerk behind the counter took the money from my hand and, for the first time, looked up at us. Then the strangest thing happened.

Nothing.

This man put a strawberry Gooshee in the hair-covered grip of a monster and never batted an eye.

Science demanded an inquiry.

"Excuse me," I said. "Do you notice anything unusual about my friend and me?"

"You're out kind of late," he said.

"Yes, but I mean about our appearance."

"Well, I don't think I've seen a necktie with flip flops before," he said.

I asked if there was anything else. He shrugged.

"This is the night shift, kid. I've seen it all."

Imagine that. By late-night convenience-store standards, we were totally normal!

We walked outside, and I took a gulp of my extreme Gooshee. Extremely satisfying. Watching my technique, the monster drew a long sip from his straw.

"What do you think?" I asked.

He didn't answer. He didn't have to. His body began to jitter like a sugar-charged jackhammer and, in the light of the neon sign, I could see his pupils enlarge to the size of quarters.

"Woo-hoo!" he screamed, and then he was gone.

It was a dead-out, full-on sprint and I could not believe how fast he could move. He ran like he was part cheetah which, for all I know, he was. This continued for several blocks, and I had no hope of keeping up. When I finally caught up, he was flat on his back and panting hard on the lawn outside the school building.

"Are you all right?" I asked him.

At first, he didn't answer. Finally, he was able to wheeze a sentence.

"Can I try your Gooshee?" he asked breathlessly.

"You couldn't handle my Gooshee!" I told him.

We both knew it was true. He rested a while then took in the sights.

"This is your school, isn't it?" he asked, pointing to the cruelty factory that looked even more menacing in the dark.

I nodded.

"I think I would like to come to your school," he said. "I'd like to see your teachers and meet your friends."

Friends? I hadn't gotten around to telling my creation that I was about as popular as foot fungus.

"It would be great to take you to school, big guy," I said. "I'd like nothing better. But middle school is a tough place. Kids can be pretty mean to outsiders. Trust me, you're better off hanging out in the lab. You'll thank me someday."

"I thank you now," he said. "You're only trying to protect me. You're a good friend, Howard."

"You're a good friend, Howard." No matter how many times I heard that, it never got old.

What Big Eyes You Have, Mrs. Morrissey

"Bwaaaaaak! Here comes El Dweebo! Bwaaaaak!"

It was Birdzilla, Mom's enormous and irritating cockatoo.

"Shut up, Precious!" I said.

Precious is the bird's real name. I call it Birdzilla for two reasons: first, it has been overfed to the point where we're about one sunflower seed away from an ugly, feather-spewing explosion; and second, it's pure evil.

"Howard's a dork-burger. Bwaaaak!"

"SHUT UP, Precious!" I said louder this time.

"Precious, you shouldn't say such awful things," Mom said as she stroked the bird's beak with her finger. "Nathaniel, why did you teach Precious to say such mean things about Howard?"

"I didn't teach her that," Stick lied. "She must have figured it out on her own—like everyone else."

Stick was sitting directly across from me at the dinner table. I always sit someplace where I can keep both eyes on him and, if necessary, launch a counterattack. He's a pretty easy target. Like that night, he was wearing a green football jersey with a big number **12** on it.

"Nice shirt. Just trying to make sure everyone knows your I.Q.?" I said.

He shot me a look that could melt steel.

I tried to shoot him one back but couldn't keep a straight face. Stick's hair makes me laugh. It makes me laugh because it never moves. I don't know what he does to make it look like he's constantly wearing a permanent, reddish-blonde helmet, but whatever it is, it involves hogging the bathroom for like two hours a day.

"Howard's here! Doofus alert! Aaaaaaaaaaak!"

"I mean it, Precious!" I screamed, and I showed her my fist.

Mom shook her head.

"Precious, if you don't stop saying those things there will be no crackers for you. Do you hear me? No crackers for Precious!" she scolded.

"Bwaaaak! Precious loves you!" the bird squawked.

Mom squealed with glee.

"Did you hear that, Katie Beth? Give Precious a cracker!"

Katie Beth rolled her eyes. That was her standard reaction when anyone in the family told her to do something, asked her a question, or spoke to her in any way. I don't know what it was about turning 17 that made her suddenly find our family so annoying. We've always been this annoying!

To be fair, Katie Beth's eye-rolls are more noticeable than other people's because she wears very large glasses that make her eyes seem huge. Sometimes when you look at her, I swear all you see are a pair of giant, brown eyes sticking out of a bunch of long, dark hair. But that's probably because the rest of her is so small. My sister is what my mom calls **"petite."**

That's French for **"mean."**

It was Wednesday. That meant we were having chicken. I always wondered if the sight of deep-fried bird on the table made Precious nervous. I hoped so.

"Children, I want you to keep your windows closed at night—closed and locked," Mom said as the plates moved around the table. "This neighborhood isn't as safe as it used to be. Mrs. Morrissey said she got up last night to let her cat out, and she saw a boy walking the streets with some kind of bear!"

I laughed. So did Stick and Katie Beth. Orson looked a little scared.

"It wasn't a bear," I said and instantly felt the eyes on me.

"How do you know what it was?" Mom asked.

Uh oh. I should have known better than to open my mouth around my family. Orson had the right idea—never say a word.

"I mean, I'm guessing it wasn't a bear," I said, trying to undo the damage. "Who would go out walking their bear at two in the morning?"

"Two in the morning?" Mom asked.

"Or whatever time it was. That's just crazy. Crazy ol'
Mrs. Morrissey!" I said louder than usual, which is what I
always do when I don't want to sound nervous.

Mom stared my way for a long time as if the heat of
her gaze could sweat out a confession. Fortunately, after
twelve years in this family, I have developed a kind of
immunity.

"All right, it wasn't a bear," she said at last. "She didn't
actually say it was a bear, but I was giving her the benefit
of the doubt. She's older, you know, and her eyes have
started to go. But that doesn't mean she's crazy. You're
not crazy just because you think you see a boy and, well,
something else."

"What else?" Stick asked.

Mom hesitated. Her eyes jetted around the table as she
pondered whether to take the story any farther.

"Bigfoot," she said at last.

The eruption at the table even made Precious laugh.

"What exactly did Mrs. Morrissey say the abominable
snowman was doing at two in the morning?" Stick
snickered.

Mom bit her bottom lip.

"Drinking a Gooshee," she said, and then she burst out
laughing along with the rest of us.

But I was only laughing on the outside. On the inside, I
was worried. Mrs. Morrissey had seen not just me, not just
the monster, but the Gooshee! That old woman's eyesight
was better than I thought.

"Crazy ol' Mrs. Morrissey!" I said in a really, really loud voice.

"We don't call people crazy, Howard," Mom said sternly. "Remember last week's church sermon?"

"All right then, she's not crazy," I said. "Maybe she's just got an irrational fear."

"An irrational fear of what?" Mom asked me.

"I don't know. Bigfoot?"

"Bigfootaphobia?" Katie Beth said.

Mom threw up her hands.

"Everything isn't a phobia, Katie Beth. Anyone would be afraid if they saw Bigfoot because Bigfoot is scary. A phobia is when you're afraid of something you shouldn't be, something ordinary."

"When we were in kindergarten, Josh Gutierrez was afraid of the See 'n Say," I said.

This was true. If you're not up on your toy-ology, the See 'n Say is a talking device that has a spinning farmer in the middle of it. When the farmer stops on a certain barnyard animal, it utters a phrase like "The cow says 'Mooooo'." It's about as terrifying as a clock radio.

"You're kidding!" Stick said.

"No," I told him. "When it talked, he used to wet his pants."

Everyone burst out laughing again. *Maybe my family isn't so bad,* I thought. The only one at the table who didn't find this hilarious was my dad. He'd been quiet all evening.

Mom asked him what was wrong.

"It's nothing. I guess I just wasn't in the mood to talk about bears," he said.

Dad turned and looked at me. "They're sending Rollo back to his owner."

Now I knew why Dad wasn't laughing. I felt my stomach sink. That sweet, friendly bear was going back to his life in a cage. It didn't seem fair.

CHAPTER
21

Traps and Cages

At school on Friday, I delivered the completed term papers to the bullies. The work was excellent if I do say so myself.

They had each been assigned a different topic: Patrick Henry; Frederick Douglass; Amelia Earhart; and Buffalo Bill Cody. So I opened with the following sentences:

"Patrick Henry is a great American hero."

"Frederick Douglass is a great American hero."

"Amelia Earhart is a great American hero."

"Buffalo Bill Cody is a great American hero, as long as you're not a buffalo."

Then, for the second sentence, I wrote this:

"But not as great as another American hero, Benjamin Franklin."

The remaining 2,500 words were the same in each paper. They discussed, at length, Ben Franklin's unparalleled achievements as a statesman, publisher, philosopher, scientist, and, more recently, one-hundred-dollar bill.

I did this for two reasons. First, Benjamin Franklin is

the greatest inventor of all time. Period. I'm not saying Alexander Graham Bell and Thomas Edison weren't geniuses; I'm just saying that, without Franklin's electricity, they'd be two guys sitting around in the dark with nobody to call.

Second, I don't like being thumped in the back of the head.

If you recall, I had "agreed," under threat of pulverization, to write four papers ... but I didn't say they'd be four *different* papers. And never, ever did I say they wouldn't be about Benjamin Franklin. I knew what would happen next. When the teacher saw 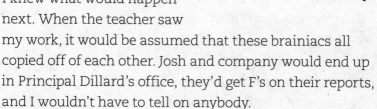 my work, it would be assumed that these brainiacs all copied off of each other. Josh and company would end up in Principal Dillard's office, they'd get F's on their reports, and I wouldn't have to tell on anybody.

Few things are harder to live down in middle school than being a tattle tale.

Was it a perfect plan? No. Was retaliation coming just as sure as Precious looks like a volleyball with wings? Absolutely. But if I was going to take a beating it was nice to know that, for once, I'd earned it.

I wasn't planning on visiting the lab until later that night, but something drew me there. I opened the cooler door and sneaked quietly through the tunnel.

When I emerged, I saw him sitting on his table. He wasn't doing anything, just sitting and staring at nothing in particular.

The expression on his face wasn't like the one I'd seen when he'd sniffed the great outdoors or sampled the heavenly delights of a Gooshee. It didn't show joy or sorrow—or anything.

He was just ... there.

I looked hard at him. This is what I'd always wanted, a friend who would be there for me day or night. I didn't have to worry about him joining in the taunts of "How-weird" or "How-lame" because he'd never hear them. You couldn't hear those things from the lab.

That's what made the lab so perfect. It was the perfect cage.

When he saw me, he smiled.

"Hello, Howard. I thought you'd be coming back later."

"What were you doing?" I asked.

"Waiting for you."

"Is that what you always do?"

He looked puzzled.

"I'm your friend," he answered.

"Yes," I told him. "You are. But what were you doing before I came in?"

He didn't know what to say.

"OK then," I said. "What would you like to do?"

The question took him by surprise. I guess that's because I'd never asked it before.

"Well, we could play a game," he said. "Or we could talk and you could tell me about your day, I don't know. Whatever you want to do, Howard."

I sort of nodded. "And what do you want to do tomorrow, and the day after that, and the day after that?"

He sat there a minute not saying anything at all. I was asking him something unimaginable—something that wasn't about me.

He shrugged, but I knew the answer.

"You'd like to go to school, wouldn't you?" I said.

He lowered his head. I recognized the look—it was the one where you're afraid to let yourself want anything because if the answer is no, well...

"I know that's impossible, Howard," he said. "I know I can't go to school."

Looking into those big saucer eyes it was hard to believe a week and a half earlier he'd been a slimy ball of putty.

"If I've learned anything from meeting you," I told him, "it's that nothing is impossible."

CHAPTER 22

Monster Makeover

"Is that what I think it is?" Uncle Ben asked.

"I am a foreign exchange student," the monster said.

His answer was perfect—just like we'd practiced it.

"Foreign exchange student? From where? Mars?" Uncle Ben said, looking at the tail sticking out of the baggy, over-sized shorts.

I quickly corralled it.

Uncle Ben's reaction was pretty much what I'd expected. My uncle had seen things a lot more weird than this, mostly on the Internet. Last year, he went to a UFO convention in Roswell, New Mexico, and brought back a picture of an actual alien brain. I thought it looked like a jellyfish with the tentacles pulled off, but I guess that's what alien brains are supposed to look like.

Uncle Ben circled us once, grabbed the creature by the jaw, and looked inside his mouth.

"Logic board and microprocessors?" he asked.

"They're in there," I said.

"Eighty pounds of hamburger?"

"Nope," I said. "Wonder Putty."

"Good call. He won't need refrigeration."

I'd put the creature in an extra-large sweatshirt and baggy sweatpants to hide the tail for the walk to the electronics store. It had a big hood, which kept people from getting nosy. You can't be too careful when you've got a monster in your garage. That's why I didn't tell Uncle Ben absolutely everything about how I'd managed to make a friend—it was for his own protection. If my uncle ever found himself on the receiving end of one of Mom's interrogations, the less he knew about what I'd done, the better.

All I really told him was that I was ready to take my new friend to school, and I'd prefer we weren't greeted with pitchforks and torches.

"You leave that to me," Uncle Ben winked, and he picked up his cell phone.

After he'd hung up, he led us past the donut shop next door and into Yolanda's Clip Joint, a girly looking place that smelled like wet hair and fingernail polish.

"Oh my goodness. That's not right," Yolanda said when she pulled back the monster's hood and a blonde, furry jack-in-the-box popped out at her.

Yolanda was the kind of woman you'd expect to find in a beauty parlor, and by that I mean she had really nice hair. It was black with little curls everywhere, and it came down just a tiny bit past her shoulders. She was tall and had long, pink fingernails and a baby blue dress that kind of looked like a uniform. Maybe it was a uniform because all the women who worked there wore the same thing.

I'd never seen Yolanda before, but I knew right away that I liked her. She was about the same age as Uncle Ben.

"I told you on the phone it was a special case," Uncle Ben said.

"I know, I know. But there's special and then—there's this!"

She grabbed a handful of the vicious mop.

"Can you do anything?" Uncle Ben asked.

Yolanda's eyes got squinty, and she crossed her arms like Vice Principal Hertz does when he's on guard duty in the cafeteria. She was biting her lip so hard I thought she'd draw blood.

"You know, we don't take men," she said. "This is a ladies' place. The ladies come in and sit under the hair dryers and they talk, you know? With him in here, well ... you can imagine what they'll be talking about!"

"So ... no go?" Uncle Ben said.

"Are you kidding? These ladies haven't had anything new to talk about in years! You just stand back and give Yolanda room."

We did.

"I appreciate this, Miss Yolanda," the monster said as she wrapped a cape around his huge neck. "I know I'm a bit of a challenge—and without even an appointment."

"Forget it, kid. Some people just have weird hair. Look at this boy," she said, pointing at my crazy mop.

She was grinning when she said it, but I still wanted to crawl down the shampoo sink.

Judging from the crowd, Saturdays were busy at Yolanda's Clip Joint. The wall on the opposite side of the room was lined with hairdryers connected to about a dozen chatty, curler-topped heads. Some of the dryers had stopped, but the ladies refused to give up their seats. They didn't want to miss the show.

Yolanda clipped her way through the wild, blonde jungle, then called for a pair of manicurists to join her. The summoned women didn't exactly rush over, but once they got hold of those sausage-sized fingers, they went after them like pros.

Two hours later, the transformation was complete.

The figure in the swivel chair looked like a monster—but a monster with a really nice haircut.

His mane was gone, replaced by a close-cropped style that fed into a pair of longish sideburns. The thick hair on top was pulled back and tied into a short ponytail behind his head. His shaggy beard was a thing of the past, and while his fingernails still looked like claws, they were polished and clean.

My friend eyed himself in the mirror, but I don't think he recognized that freshly sheared fellow staring back at him. When he finally did, he grinned from pointy-ear to pointy-ear.

Yolanda was a makeover genius.

Now, I'm a Pappy's Happy Cut customer myself and therefore clueless about any style that costs more than six bucks. I had the uneasy feeling this one could be twice that much—or even more! Nervously, I dug inside my pocket, hoping my allowance had somehow cloned itself.

"Put your money away. Yolanda charges for haircuts, not for art," Yolanda said. "Besides, any friend of Benny's is on the house. Shop policy."

I couldn't believe it. Then the same thing happened when we walked down to the other end of the mini-mall and picked out a couple of monster-sized outfits from the used clothing store. The shop-owner there wouldn't take a dime either—not from "friends of Benny's."

Uncle Ben—who I couldn't imagine being the same person as this "Benny"—shrugged it off.

"You know how it is," he explained as we walked back to his store. "In an old mini-mall like this, there are bound to be a few electrical problems. Can you believe not one of these store owners knows how to install a satellite dish? It's like being next door to cave people! Anyway, when they run into trouble, I help them out with the technical stuff.

They're just returning the favor by helping out my nephew. That's what neighbors do, right?"

How do you like that? Uncle Ben—who I didn't think had a friend in the world that wasn't attached to a power cord—was popular!

There might be hope for me after all.

CHAPTER
23

A Nerdy
Treasure Island

On the way back to the lab, we stopped at one of my
favorite places.

"Where are we, Howard?" my stylish new friend asked.

"The dump!" I proclaimed, stretching my arms out to
take in its greatness.

"What is the dump?"

"It's an island of treasures," I told him. By this time, my
excitement had climbed to amusement-park levels. "Wires
and circuits and components—you name it, they've got it.
And the best part is they don't belong to anybody!"

"Why don't they belong to anybody, Howard?"

"Because the owners didn't want them anymore! They
threw them away," I said.

He picked up an old alarm clock, the kind you had to
wind. It looked like it still worked.

"Why would someone throw this away?" he asked.

"I don't know. Maybe they got something better. Who cares? It's just more treasure for us!"

The monster nodded. But I don't think the dump's bounty brought him the same pure joy it did me.

"I guess if nobody wanted a thing, it could still have a home here," he said.

"A home? It's the dump!" I said. "This is where you find stuff you want to take home!"

We sorted through a ton of really neat junk that for inexplicable reasons someone decided was garbage. When I looked at the creature, he was holding an old, stuffed panda that was missing one of its eyes.

He wasn't hugging it or anything, which would have been creepy. He was just looking at it. I thought he looked kind of sad.

"What's wrong with you?" I asked.

"Howard, does everything end up at the dump?"

"Everything cool," I said.

"You're cool."

"And proud of it."

"Is this where you'll end up?"

"What do you mean?" I said. "Like when I die?"

"I guess."

"Of course not, goofus! When people die, they don't go to the dump."

"Where do they go?"

"Well," I said. "They go to heaven."

"Is that where I'll go, Howard? I was just wondering because I'm ... different."

He was different, all right. For that matter, so was I. We were both fairly unique individuals. In a way, being different made us the same—but not exactly the same. I was different like everyone else. He wasn't like anyone. I have to admit his question surprised me. How was I supposed to know where he'd go? I didn't even know what he was. But I knew what he wasn't. He wasn't a blob of goo.

You can't be best friends with a blob of goo.

"Don't worry about it," I told him. "You leave it to me. If I can get you into middle school, I can get you into anywhere. Plus, I'm sure God will have no problem with you."

CHAPTER 24

The New Kid from Canada

"I didn't even know we had foreign exchange students in middle school," Mrs. Ogilvie, the registrar in the front office, said.

She looked bewildered as she stood there staring at the large, eager student on the other side of the counter.

"Oh, it's a brand new program," I told her. "We're the first family in the district to get one. I'm sure you'll be getting the paperwork in the mail."

Mrs. Ogilvie was a thin-faced, gray-haired woman who had worked at Dolley Madison forever and didn't like surprises. I'd just brought her a big one. My hope was that she'd approve almost anything just to make us go away.

"And you?" she said. "You're Howard's ..."

"Uncle. I'm his uncle."

Uncle Ben was sweating, but that might just have been because he was wearing a tie. My uncle is not the kind of person who wears ties. They make him look confused and desperate, like a dog trying to get a Christmas bow off its head. I probably should have let him wear his usual outfit—a loose-hanging, button-down shirt, a pair of ratty-old jeans and white high-tops—but I wanted him to look like he was responsible.

And in a way, he did. He looked like he was responsible for a crime.

I felt a little guilty about pulling Uncle Ben into this scheme, but I needed a grownup. Most grownups would have said no, but that's what's different about Uncle Ben. When it comes to adulthood, he's kind of like a twelve-year-old in a thirty-six-year-old body.

I knew he'd help, not just because I wanted him to, but because he was as anxious to see the monster get into middle school as I was. Plus, it was a caper. I have seen at least a dozen movies about capers with my uncle and, after every one, he tells me how he could have done it better. I think Uncle Ben would have made a great jewel thief or secret agent if he hadn't found his calling in the used electronics business.

But I did wish he'd stop sweating.

Mrs. Ogilvie looked up at the enormous enrollee in front of her. She moved her glasses to the tip of her nose and leaned in close to me.

"What is he?" she asked quietly. "I mean, what nation-ality is he?"

"I am from Canada," the monster said.

I suppose I could've given him any nationality, but, I

don't know, something about him just screamed "Canadian."

"He seems kind of big for the seventh grade," Mrs. Ogilvie said suspiciously.

"Yeah, they grow 'em big up there. It's something in the water," Uncle Ben said, tugging at his sopping wet shirt-collar.

"Right," I added. "Everything is big in Canada. Just think about all those moose. They're huge!"

Then we both laughed uncomfortably while Mrs. Ogilvie stared at us with all the amusement of a face on a totem pole.

"If you say so," she said at last. "All right, what's his name?"

My plan was going flawlessly. I had made sure the creature had the right look and the right clothes. I'd devised a fantastic cover story about him being a foreign exchange student. I'd even brought him up to speed on our seventh-grade coursework.

But as hard as it may be to believe, one small detail had slipped my mind.

"His name?" I asked, panicking.

"His name?" Uncle Ben asked, double-panicking.

"I am Howard's friend," the monster said.

"Good for you," Mrs. Ogilvie told him, "but I still need a name."

"Of course! Of course you do," I agreed nervously, wondering why this was so hard—I knew hundreds of names!

Unfortunately, none of them was finding their way out of my mouth. I could tell Uncle Ben had gone into total brain-lock so this was all up to me. I did have a favorite name, a great one—Benjamin. But that was Uncle Ben's name, and this situation was confusing enough already. It was a shame, though. I really wanted the big guy to be my tribute to Benjamin Franklin.

"That's it!" I cried out. "Franklin! His name is Franklin!"

"I like that," the new Franklin said.

"Congratulations," Mrs. Ogilvie said. "Franklin what?"

I looked around for a last name—anything! Franklin Desk? Franklin Chair? Franklin Book? Oh wait, the book! I looked down at the book I was carrying. It was one of the Goosebumps series, by R.L. Stine.

"Stine," I told her.

"Franklin Stine?" she asked me.

I gulped.

"Yes," I said apologetically.

Uncle Ben looked stunned.

"It's . . . a very common name in Canada," he said at last.

Mrs. Ogilvie stared at me for a long time without

blinking. Then, to my great relief, she wrote the name on her form.

"Franklin," as I now knew him, was in.

"He's living with your family, correct?" Mrs. Ogilvie asked me.

I nodded.

"And you are part of that household?" she asked Uncle Ben.

He hesitated for a second but then nodded. He was in too deep to back out now.

We left the office, and finally I could breathe again. Uncle Ben looked almost giddy. So did Franklin Stine. Who could blame him? Only three weeks old and already starting his first day of school.

Monsters grow up so fast.

CHAPTER 25

First Impressions

Right away I could tell there was something different about the classroom: there was my desk, then Franklin's desk, and then space—lots and lots of space.

All the other kids had pushed their desks out against the walls, leaving me and Franklin sitting there like the hole in the middle of a donut. No one wanted to sit near the new kid.

"How ... how long have you been in the States?" Mr. Abdullah, my homeroom teacher, squeaked. It was kind of a loud squeak because he was sitting as far across the room as he could possibly get.

"Not very long," Franklin replied politely. Then he smiled.

Mr. Abdullah looked pale. You'd think he'd never seen fangs on a seventh-grader before. For the rest of the period, he avoided looking in our direction.

As for my classmates, their eyes never left us.

This didn't bother Franklin. "Hello," he would say whenever he'd notice someone staring. "I am a new boy from Canada."

"Ix-nay on the anada-kay," I growled in Pig Latin—just in case Franklin was part pig.

He smiled and sat quietly until the bell rang.

"Everyone seemed nice," he said as we walked out of the room.

"This is middle school—no one is nice," I corrected him. "And stop smiling so much. It's a sign of weakness."

He had a lot to learn. It was funny how I felt this need to protect him—even from things I didn't really worry about for myself. Since I'd never had a best friend before, I hadn't realized that breaking one in was such hard work. I stopped at the water fountain for a drink.

That's when I heard the voice.

"Help! Help me!"

Now, I have been in enough school hallways to know you don't go rushing to every cry for help. By taking your time, you greatly improve the chance that someone else has already handled the problem. I mean, aren't these exactly the kinds of situations we have hall monitors for?

If they didn't want to be heroes, they never should have put on the sash.

Franklin, however, did not understand this. Before I could say anything, he was a blur running willy-nilly toward the commotion. I followed him and rounded the corner just in time to see Dino Lincoln holding Corky Dorfman by his underwear. Corky's feet were a good eighteen inches off the floor.

"Does someone need help?" Franklin asked.

"He's trying to stuff me in my locker!" Corky screamed. "Help!"

"Of course," Franklin said in the friendliest possible way.

This was the day I realized Franklin was a very helpful creature. He reached out with his giant hands, grabbed Corky by the shoulders, and removed him from Dino's grip. Corky looked relieved. Then Franklin stuffed him in his locker.

"There you go," the monster said, closing the door.

Dino Lincoln was stunned. He stood there with his mouth wide open, but, after a couple of seconds, it turned into a grin.

"Thanks, Big Stuff," he said at last. "You're all right."

"I'm glad I could help," Franklin said.

As we walked away, I explained that Corky Dorfman actually wanted help staying out of the locker—not getting into it.

Franklin thought about it, then shrugged.

"The taller boy must have been confused, too," he said.

At that moment I learned something about Franklin Stine. He had absolutely no concept of cruelty. He didn't know about bullies or wedgies or the social structure of the popularity ladder. In a way, it was kind of nice.

Middle school was going to eat him alive.

CHAPTER 26

All's Fair in Love and P.E.

The bell rang for second period—the moment I'd been dreading. This was the point where my schedule took me in one direction and Franklin's took him in another. I could protect him as long as we were in adjacent desks—but from all the way across the school? A knot formed in my stomach as we came to the fork in the hall.

"You'll be fine," I told him, biting my lower lip. "I know you can do this."

"I know you can do this, too, Howard," he smiled.

I turned right toward my algebra class. He made a left toward phys ed.

About halfway down the hall, Winnie McKinney caught up with me.

"Who's your giant shadow?" she asked.

"Just some kid from Canada. He's new," I told her.

"So I heard. He's monster big."

"I wouldn't say 'monster' big," I blurted out. "He's probably just Canadian big."

"What's Canadian big?"

"You know that maple leaf on their flag?" I said. "That's actual size."

She gave me an odd stare. It made me uncomfortable.

"Anyway, he's big," Winnie said. "What's his name?"

"Franklin ... Stine."

I added a pause between the names thinking it might sound better. When Winnie's jaw dropped, I knew I was wrong.

"No way!" she screamed. "I'll bet he hates whoever stuck him with that!"

OK, I'll admit it. I am terrible at naming things. I should have figured that out when Dad let me name our dog. Not Frisco—Stick got to name him. I named our other dog, Pants. Actually, Pants is his nickname. Most people think we call him that because he pants a lot, but that's not the reason. The real reason is that he has kind of a bluish coat that reminded me of a picture at the library. The picture is of a boy wearing the nicest blue suit I have ever seen. It's all satiny and comes with knickers and a hat. I now know the name of that picture is "The Blue Boy" by Thomas Gainsborough. I wish I'd known it then. Blue Boy would have been an awesome name for a dog.

Instead, I made the mistake of pointing to the picture and asking my dad who it was. He said, and I quote:

"Who? Fancy Pants?"

So now you know how our dog got the name Fancy Pants Boward. It was because my dad knows nothing about art.

But *Franklin Stine*? That one was all on me.

"I've got to get to class," I told Winnie.

"Me too. So are you going to be science-boy in the talent show or what? Come on, say you will. I want you to."

The sound came through like music. Winnie McKinney wanted me to do something—and it wasn't her homework. I was nearly speechless.

"Oh ... all right, then," I gulped. "I'll do it."

"Awesome! I'm on the talent committee, I'll sign you up," she said.

Then she trotted down the hall.

My head felt light and fluffy. This girl actually believed I had talent! What a nice thing for her to say—was she out of her mind? My momentary lapse into happiness gave way to the certainty of public humiliation. What was I thinking? I couldn't demonstrate science in front of an audience. These kids came to assemblies to get away from science! They'd destroy me!

But that's when I got an idea—a big one. I'd show them a side of science they'd never seen before. And I wouldn't be doing a solo act.

"Put Franklin's name down too," I yelled after Winnie.

"Howard Boward and Franklin Stine are going to shock the world—with science!"

☆ ☆ ☆

After class, I waited for Franklin by my locker. It was a few minutes before I saw him walking down the hallway. A small person was tucked under his arm.

"I told you I'm all right," the armpit-hostage said. "Will you put me down?"

"Just have the nurse look at it, Wendell," Franklin said.

Wendell Mullins was tiny, even compared to me. His hair was dark and still wet from gym class, and his eyes were long, narrow slits that disappeared when he squinted.

"What happened?" I asked.

"Nothing!" Wendell screamed. "We were playing soccer in P.E. and I was the goalie. He scored nine times! So after the game, I said, 'you kicked my butt out there!'" Franklin's lip quivered.

"I didn't mean to!" he cried. "It's just so small! Do you think it's broken?"

I shook my head.

"You didn't hurt anybody, Franklin. 'Kicking butt' is just an expression. It means you won."

"I did?" Franklin said.

"Of course you did! Now, let me go, Gargantua!" Wendell exploded.

The monster gave a huge sigh of relief, and Wendell

117

dropped to the floor. When he got up, he gave Franklin a hard shove. It wasn't a shove like he was trying to knock him down—which I'm pretty sure would have been gravitationally impossible—it was just the way a kid shoves another kid.

I couldn't believe it. Franklin had gone to a physical education class and fit in!

"Hey, Wendell!" he called after his fleeing gym-mate. "I enjoyed kicking your butt today!"

"I'll get you next time, goof-bag!" Wendell called back without turning around.

I stared down the hall and saw a half-dozen kids with wet hair and the unmistakable slump of defeat—sure signs they'd just come from P.E. One had a black eye, two were limping, the others were rubbing various bruises.

Franklin looked pleased.

"I kicked their butts today too," he said proudly.

Then he turned and strolled confidently toward his next class. I was about to do the same when one of the walking wounded approached me.

"Your friend is one seriously weird dude," the boy said. "But he is the best soccer player ever to put on a pair of gym shorts!"

CHAPTER 27

An Invitation to the Palace

It was a memorable Sloppy Joe day. The cafeteria lady dropped three trays before she worked up the nerve to actually hand Franklin his food. This made it the sloppiest Joe day ever.

Also, for the first time in my life, I got to sit at the front table.

"Gee, Howard. Do you always get a whole table to yourself?" Franklin asked when we sat down.

I looked around the cafeteria. The back tables were jammed so tight that it was impossible to know whose apple-cinnamon surprise you were digging your spoon into. I guess nobody wanted to be too close to Franklin at feeding time.

"Ummm . . . ," I muttered. "All my really close friends have a different lunch period."

That seemed to satisfy his curiosity. Then we tapped our milk cartons together in a toast, and dined.

Franklin loved the Joes. He liked the milk too—not as much as a Gooshee, but then again, that's hardly a fair comparison. The one food that concerned me was the lima beans—he went ga-ga over them. This was trouble. If Franklin was going to scarf down a plate of lima beans like it was a hot-fudge sundae, we'd never convince people he was human.

I watched him happily licking his tray. Then I looked down at my own plate. The buns had been cold, the fries were frozen, and the rest of the meal had tasted like cardboard. It was the best middle-school lunch I'd ever had.

Franklin and I didn't have any classes together in the afternoon. When school was out, I waited for him by my locker.

I saw Mr. Z walking down the hall.

"Hi, Mr. Z," I said. "I'm just waiting for my friend."

I really liked being able to tell people that.

"Oh, hello, Howard. This friend you're waiting for—is it that new boy?"

"Franklin," I said.

"Right," Mr. Z said. "He's, uh … he's not from around here, is he?"

"He's from Canada," I said.

"Oh? What part?" Mr. Z asked.

"All of him," I said.

Mr. Z gave me a funny look, probably because he never met anybody who was friends with a Canadian before. Then he changed the subject.

"I hear you're going to be in the talent show."

"Yes," I said. "I'm doing an act with Franklin. I think you'll like it. It's all based on science."

"Science? Well, that should be different."

"It's going to shock the world!" I said.

"I'm sure it will, Howard," Mr. Z said. "We'll see you in class tomorrow."

"See you, Mr. Z."

I went back to waiting for Franklin. I figured I'd see him coming from a mile away. A guy as big as Franklin is pretty hard to miss. Of course, you could say the same thing about Josh Gutierrez, but I didn't see Josh coming until it was too late.

"That was real funny, dork-face," he said, grabbing my collar like some tough guy in a black and white movie. "We got our papers back today."

He held the paper an inch from my glasses. It had a large, red "F" with three exclamation points, which had to be some kind of record even for Josh.

Funny how my plans always seem like really good ideas right up to the part where I'm beaten senseless. Josh and Kyle Stanford each grabbed an arm and dragged me out of the building.

I struggled a little, mostly because it's expected. The objective wasn't so much to break loose as to delay the journey—you never know when a miracle might need an extra second or two.

We stopped at the place I had been trying not to think about—Beatdown Palace. The Palace was a schoolyard legend. To hear the kids talk, this was a torture chamber where the walls dripped blood and nerd skulls sat atop spiked fence-posts. That's why I don't want you to get the wrong idea when I tell you that, when I finally saw it, I was, well … disappointed. Relieved, sure, but it was kind of a letdown.

That's because the notorious Beatdown Palace turned out to be nothing but an old metal barn beside the athletic field. It's where they kept the various balls and nets and practice equipment used by the sports teams.

In fact, the only scary things inside the Palace were Skyler Pritchard and Bulldog Busby—the other two F recipients from my plot. They were waiting for us.

"All right, now it's a party," Skyler said. "Let's do this!"

They surrounded me. It was no use fighting—every single one of them was at least as big as Stick. But as far as I could tell, size was the only thing they had in common. Josh was dark with dimples the girls called "dreamy." Kyle was blonde and dressed like a surfer even though we live nowhere near the ocean. Skyler had long, stringy hair and a facial fungus, which might have been a mustache. And Bulldog looked like his name.

Josh and Kyle lifted me into the air until the back of my jacket caught on a large utility-hook. I was dangling like a strip of bacon above four hungry dogs.

"You're a real funny dude, you know that?" Josh said. "We all failed history but at least you got a good laugh out of it. Tell me, was it worth it?"

He poked me hard in the chest and I started to sway.

"I should explain," I said nervously. "Term papers aren't really my thing. Now if any of you guys need help getting something ready for the science fair, well …"

Kyle Stanford squeezed the sides of my face.

"I am going to mess you up!" he said, his words arriving with quite a bit of saliva.

Personally, I don't care for a lot of chat before a beating, especially when it's moist. Kyle must have sensed my impatience because he pulled his fist back into launch position. I closed my eyes and prepared for the familiar smack of knuckles on flesh, but it didn't arrive. Instead, I heard something else—a soft tapping on the metal door.

"Tap. Tap. Tap."

I heard it again. Everyone froze.

"Howard?" a quiet voice said. "Howard, are you in there?"

"Franklin?" I called.

The door creaked open.

"Hello, fellas," Franklin said, that pleasant smile glued to his face. "I am looking for Howard."

As he stood there in the doorway, the sun setting behind his giant head looked almost like a halo. But probably just to me.

"Who is that?" Skyler gulped.

"What is that?" said Kyle.

"Whatever it is, it wasn't invited," Josh said coldly.

Franklin took a step toward the group. The group took a step backward.

"What's everyone doing in here?" Franklin asked cheerfully.

"Nothin'," Bulldog barked. "We're just hanging out with our little buddy How-Weird!"

"It's 'Howard'," Franklin corrected him. "HOW-ward. I had trouble with it at first too. You have to practice."

"Franklin!" I said as my feet swung back and forth like a pendulum. "You don't understand what's ..."

"Shut up!" Josh screamed at me, pushing a finger in my face.

I stopped talking. It seemed like the best course of action. I didn't want to make Josh any madder; Franklin was doing enough of that on his own.

Josh let out a disgusted groan and squared his shoulders.

"Hey, meathead!" he yelled at the creature. "You need to get lost!"

"I already did," Franklin told him. "It was between fourth and fifth periods. But a nice teacher found me and told me where to go."

I had the feeling this was not how things usually went in Bully-land. Franklin's answers seemed to confuse my abductors, especially Kyle. But if you knew Kyle, that wouldn't be exactly surprising.

"Look, dude," Kyle said. "I don't know who you are, but this is none of your business!"

"I am Franklin Stine," Franklin said politely. "And Howard is always my business. Howard is my friend."

The four nerd-nappers lined up in a row that stretched across the width of the Palace. Josh took a step forward.

"As you can see," he said, extending his arms. "I've got friends too."

"I'm glad," Franklin said. His grin was as warm as a new puppy.

All this non-violence seemed to be taking a toll on Kyle's tiny bully-brain. He stormed over to the spot where I was dangling and gave me a hard, angry push.

Then he aimed a finger at Franklin.

"Look! If you don't get out of here right now, we're going to start kicking some serious butt!"

Franklin's face lit up like the candles on a birthday cake.

"Really?" he squealed, unable to contain his happiness. "That would be awesome! Everyone says I'm very good at it. Watch this, Howard!"

Franklin rushed to one of the metal racks at the front of the barn and came back with a ball. It wasn't a soccer ball like before. It was a basketball, but that didn't matter. All Franklin cared about was that it was round, it was filled with air, and it could hit things.

He dropped the orange dribbler, and in one effortless motion, kicked it with the force of ten ninja-mules.

It took a fraction of a second for the cannonball to collide with Kyle's face. There was a loud thud—and then a louder one when Kyle collided with the ground.

"Hey!" Bulldog yelled.

He didn't have time to say anything else. A football hit him in the stomach and knocked him against the back wall.

"Did you see me, Howard?" Franklin asked gleefully. "I'm kicking their butts!"

I was about to congratulate him when Josh yelled, "That's enough!"

The building went silent—well, except for Kyle's moaning and Bulldog's wheezing. I'm pretty sure those were involuntary.

"We're done here," Josh said. "Let's go, guys."

He shot me a menacing look before making his way toward the door.

"Oh, is the game over?" Franklin asked as the group took a wide path around him. "Thanks for playing then. I had fun."

In case you're wondering, there were no taunts or threats or salty names thrown back at us, which I found refreshing. The tough guys seemed to want to put the Palace—and everything in it— behind them.

"Hey! You want to go get Gooshees?" Franklin called after them. "They're super good!"

When he got no reply, he shrugged, turned around, and lowered me from my hook.

"Boy, am I glad you showed up when you did!" I told him.

"You weren't at your locker. Were those the really close friends you told me about at lunch?"

"More like acquaintances," I said. "How did you know where to find me?"

"I smelled you," Franklin said.

Now that's something you don't hear every day. I sniffed my armpits to see if I'd left behind some kind of stink trail, but it was no more than usual. That's when it dawned on me—an awful lot of Franklin came from the zoo. That included his nose.

Bears, my dad had told me, could pick up a scent from several miles away.

I looked up at the creature who had found me just when I needed him most. He was one amazing package, all right—best friend, bodyguard, and my own personal bloodhound.

CHAPTER
28

Extracurricular Activities

That night, Franklin and I prepared for the talent show in the lab.

"Do I have to wear this, Howard?" he asked, holding up the costume I'd given him for our performance.

"Yes," I told him. "Presentation is everything. We're going to make you look spectacular. But more important, they'll never look at science in the same way again."

"If you say so, Howard."

"Oh, I do. Now, let's practice. We've got a million things to do and the talent show is on Friday."

☆ ☆ ☆

Franklin's second day of homeroom was a lot like the first. Mr. Abdullah still wouldn't look at him, and there was a national park between us and the nearest desk. But at least that eerie silence was gone. The gossip machine was rolling again, and I could hear the day's headlines as they moved from person to person:

"Have you ever seen a weirder-looking kid in your life? The big one's weird-looking too."

"I heard they kicked him out of Canada—for punching a Zamboni!"

"Did you see Kyle Stanford's new forehead tattoo? It says 'Spalding'!"

But mostly what I heard was, *"Wow! We gotta have that kid on the team!"*

I was pretty sure they didn't mean me. The bell rang. We were barely in the hallway before something stopped our progress like a concrete wall. It was Coach Fritz.

"I was talking to your P.E. teacher about what you did in class yesterday," Coach said to Franklin.

"Was it about the whirlpool?" Franklin asked. "Because nobody told me not to drink out of it."

Coach Fritz was a large man with a crew cut, a bulbous nose, and a whistle permanently attached to his chest. I'm willing to bet this was the first time he'd come across a seventh-grader who could look him straight in the eye.

"It was about your kicking," he said. "I hear you have a leg like a mule."

"A zebra," Franklin corrected.

"Whatever. The thing is, I'm the football coach here. Do you play?"

"I play with Howard."

"What's a Howard?"

It occurred to me the coach didn't realize I was there. Anyone under 120 pounds was invisible to Coach Fritz.

"Me, Coach," I said. "I'm a Howard."

"I see," he said, then looked back at Franklin. "How would you like to play with us?"

"I'd like that."

"Fantastic!"

"Can Howard play too?"

The coach looked down—way down—until his eyes landed on me. He had this look on his face like a guy who buys a shiny new car then finds out it comes with a Howard in the passenger seat.

"Well ... I don't know," he said. "He's kind of scrawny."

"Wait a minute!" I yelled. "I never even said I wanted ..."

"That's OK," Franklin said. "Howard and I can play something else."

This was not the answer the coach was looking for. His eyes squinted, and he stroked his chin.

"I suppose we could make him a place kicker," he mumbled. "Some of those guys have no athletic skills."

"But Coach ..." I pleaded.

"Good," Franklin said. "It wouldn't be any fun without Howard."

"Sounds like a plan," Coach said. "So what do you play?"

"Chess. Kickball. Yahtzee ..."

"I mean what position?" the coach asked.

"He's from Canada, Coach," I said quickly. "The game's a little different there. But as soon as we download—I mean read—the rulebook, he'll be ready."

"Report to the practice field after school today," Coach told us.

"Report to the practice field"—that was a sentence I never expected to hear in my whole life.

☆ ☆ ☆

I had always been under the impression that, since I did not have muscles, they could not hurt. I was wrong. After a couple of days of football practice, I ached in places I had never ached before. It hurt to think—maybe that's why some athletes chose to stop doing it.

Franklin, on the other hand, did not have any pain—but he delivered a lot of it. Once he'd absorbed the official rules from my computer, he fit the game the same way a hammer fits a nail. When

Franklin was on defense, he got a tackle on every play. Sure, the tackle-ee didn't always have the ball but that didn't matter. He just kept tackling people until someone blew a whistle. Sometimes he made four or five tackles on the same play.

And if one of the players he put his giant meat-hooks on did happen to have the ball, he didn't have it for long. Franklin would simply take it away. Heck, sometimes they gave it to him!

"If this were a real game, you'd set a league record for penalty yards!" the coach barked in his direction. "But great Caesar's ghost—can you play football!"

Yes, he could. On offense, he was the fastest guy on the field. Once he got into the open with the ball, no one could catch him. So Franklin waited on them. He'd actually stop there on the field and wait. If the defender ran away, he chased them. It all went back to the first day of practice when Coach said he wanted "to see some hittin' out there on every down!"

You kind of have to be specific when you're talking to Franklin.

As for me, I played a position known as "blocking dummy." I'd hold a cushion, stand perfectly still, and wait for someone twice my size to do their best impression of a windshield hitting a Junebug.

I couldn't imagine where my blocking-dummy skills would come in handy in a game situation. But if they ever did, I was ready.

☆ ☆ ☆

Getting between classes took a little longer in my semi-mutilated condition. I'd been practicing football for two days, and yet I had a whole season's worth of pain.

That's because I'm what they call "advanced."

The worst part was that there were three games left in the season. I didn't know how the guys who had been doing this all year could stand it. I tried to inch my way down the hall, but my feet refused to budge. Winnie McKinney stopped and looked at me. She shook her head.

"If you're looking to make it to class, you're generating the wrong kind of inertia," she said. "What, you think you can just ignore Newton's first law of motion?"

"Newton didn't play football," I groaned.

"Of course not! He was a science-boy like you!" she laughed. Then she grabbed my hand and dragged me down the hall.

"Ow! Ow! Ow! Owwwww!" I yelped with every step.

The painful trek stopped at the door of my history class.

"So how'd a smart kid like you end up on the football team, anyway?" Winnie asked.

"It was a package deal," I said, "if they wanted Franklin, they had to take me."

"So what's in it for you?"

"A full-body cast, I expect," I said.

She laughed, and I liked it as much as her smile.

"You know the talent show is tomorrow. Are you ready?"

"We've been practicing. If I can move, I'll be there," I told her. "We're going to shock the world!"

"With science?" she asked.

"Of course. Everything is science," I said—because it's true.

"And you're sure you don't want to do this alone? Your friend doesn't seem all that sciencey to me."

"Oh, he's sciencey, all right."

Winnie's eyebrows went up, which made her nose twitch a little. I liked that too.

"You know a lot of people are scared of him," she said.

That was putting it mildly. The lunch ladies had started making Franklin two trays—one to serve and one to toss wildly into the air.

I gave her my most reassuring smile.

"That's because they don't know anything about him. Trust me. Friday is going to be a *monster* success!"

CHAPTER 29

The Amazing "Super Science Duo" Show

My body still hurt on Friday but only when I moved or thought or breathed. It was a big improvement. At least I could get through the talent show.

Franklin and I waited backstage for our turn. In the meantime, I checked out the competition.

Kyle Stanford, last year's winner, was up first. It turned out his face was too tender from having a basketball slammed into it to perform his usual act of smashing a watermelon with his forehead. So instead, he squashed a tomato with a hammer.

It was pretty gross but I thought it lacked a certain pizzazz. I'm guessing the audience agreed with me because the applause was lukewarm at best. We had a real shot here!

Next up was Latoya Gentry. She went out there with her French poodle and did something called "dog dancing."

They were good, but if you ask me, the dog was doing most of the work. And he didn't even go to our school.

I hoped the judges would take that into account.

Then came the big moment—we were next! The lights went low on the stage and we walked into the darkness. This was it! At last, I could share my gift of science with the entire school.

Winnie stood at the microphone.

"Our next act promises to shock the world," she said. "Friends and classmates—the Super Science Duo!"

The music started—a low, tension-building blast of synthesizers and horns and drums. At the same time, a rented fog-machine spewed a milky-white mist across the floor of the darkened stage. Then, when the audience was at their peak of anticipation—my voice burst from the speakers!

"Throughout history, mankind has marveled at the mysteries of the universe," I bellowed from the shadows. "But of all the wonders of science, none is more amazing than the miraculous act of creation. Prepare to be astounded! People of Dolley Madison, I give you ..."

The stage lights came up! The spotlight flashed! The fog rolled! The music boomed!

"Hawaii!" I proclaimed.

The audience was stunned.

Unfortunately, they were not stunned by science. They were stunned by Franklin.

Franklin was the centerpiece in my salute to Hawaii, which is why I'd dressed him in flowers, a Hawaiian

137

shirt, and a long skirt made of real grass. He was gently strumming a ukulele and moving his hips in an authentic hula-fashion.

"The Hawaiian islands are a string of igneous rock formations spawned by volcanic activity in a wondrous act of creation that continues even today," I began my presentation.

I was aiming a laser pointer at a large map of Hawaii being projected onto a screen at the rear of the stage.

"You stink, Boward!" someone yelled.

I sensed we were losing the audience.

"From a geological standpoint," I continued, "the composition of the islands is fascinating."

"Boo! Booooo!" rose from the darkness. The responses were getting louder.

Still, Franklin was a trooper. He kept a smile on his face and continued to strum and sway. I'm not saying he looked happy about it, but the point is he didn't give up—not even when it started raining spit-wads.

He just kept hula-ing his way across the foggy stage, a big, sweaty monster dancing on a cloud.

"Get off the stage!" someone yelled. I think it was my history teacher.

"Some of the minerals found in Hawaii are ..." I tried, but it was too late to win them back. The room had erupted into a full-fledged riot.

Larger objects reached the stage—pencils, Sharpies, snack foods. One kid threw his cell phone. I ducked. Well, I'd had enough! This was the thanks I got for trying to make science entertaining? Did they know how much work I'd put into this? Did they know how difficult it was to fit so many different sciences into a single performance?

Of course they didn't! Which is why I've made a list:

- Hawaii was made by volcanoes: volcanology
- Franklin's skirt was made of grass: botany
- I choreographed his hula-dance movements: kinesiology
- A map of the islands was projected onto a screen: geography
- I used a laser pointer: technology

And if all that weren't enough—the ukulele was being played by a blob of goo I made in my garage!

What did these people want from me?

I held my head high and walked off as a barrage of debris pelted the stage. But here was the curious thing, Franklin didn't follow me.

He didn't even stop playing. He just stood there strumming the ukulele while a year's worth of school supplies whizzed past his head. He closed his eyes like he was shutting out the world around him, and after a little while, he started to whistle.

The tune wasn't the one we'd rehearsed. It wasn't even Hawaiian. Then he started playing something different on the ukulele, and I recognized it as a song we'd heard when we'd gone to see Uncle Ben.

And then something happened that no one expected. This skirt-wearing giant opened his mouth, and out came what I can only describe as a miracle.

"I look at you all, see the love that's there sleeping
While my guitar gently weeps . . ."

His voice was like an Extreme Rainbow Gooshee poured into both ears. It was amazing. After a while, he stopped singing but kept playing the ukulele, and the song got faster and faster, and his fingers were flying across the strings in a blur, and the crowd was standing and screaming and clapping. ·

And I knew, for certain, that not one of them was cheering for some enormous, performing monster. They were cheering for Franklin Stine.

We won first prize. My major contribution, of course, was getting off the stage quickly enough so that everyone forgot I was part of the act. That was all right. The plaque would be in the trophy case for a long, long time, and somewhere on it would be three impossible words: Howard Boward—Winner.

☆ ☆ ☆

After the show, things changed for Franklin. People wanted to sit by him, have lunch with him, learn to speak Canadian.

At football practice, the guys voted him team captain, and the cheerleaders made up a routine about him.

"DEFENSE, Hold that line! Smash 'em! Crash 'em! Frank-lin Stine!"

A few days later, Winnie McKinney caught up with me on my way to algebra.

"I gotta hand it to you, slick, you shocked the world," she told me. "The Super Science Duo was a big hit."

"Yeah, I guess," I said. "But I don't think people got the science part of it."

"Are you kidding? How could they miss it? Botany, kine-siology, technology ..."

"And I was so sore I had to take an ibuprofen just to get out there."

"Pharmacology!" Winnie yelled. "It was a science show-case for the ages."

"That's what I thought!" I said. "Still, I've got to give Franklin some of the credit."

She considered it.

"Well, he did keep the crowd from throwing their chairs."

Ouch. I had been hoping Franklin's performance made people forget about the bombing of Honolulu. But Winnie smiled, and even though I didn't want to, I smiled back. I just couldn't help myself.

"People are looking at that guy a lot different today," Winnie said. "I guess you really can't judge a book by its cover."

Franklin was full of surprises all right. He wasn't the same creature I'd kept hidden away in the lab. He was out of the box now, and he was meeting new people and learning new things. In just a few days at school, he'd already learned how to make his classmates like him.

And he sure didn't learn that from me.

After school, I waited by my locker until the hallway was almost empty. There was no sign of Franklin. I looked at my watch a couple of times and tapped my foot impa-tiently, which is the international sign for "I'm waiting for someone." You do it so that anyone who sees you standing there won't think you're a mugger or some dork with no friends.

It kind of worked. I'm pretty sure no one thought I was a mugger.

A few minutes later, I saw Wendell Mullins, the dark-haired kid from Franklin's gym class.

"Hey, Wendell, have you seen Franklin?" I asked.

"Yeah. He told me to tell you he was going to PizzaDog. I guess with Dino and that gang."

"Dino Lincoln?" I asked. Dino Lincoln was the coolest kid in school.

"Yeah," Wendell said. "I saw him getting into Dino's mom's car."

Dino's mom's car? Dino's mom had a sports car! A convertible! Dino had once punched me in the kidney just for standing too close to it. And now Franklin was riding in it? That sounded like a lot more fun than rolling down our driveway in Orson's red wagon. And to top it all off, they were going to PizzaDog, probably the greatest hot dog–pizza restaurant in the history of the planet.

The more I thought about it, the more it bothered me. While I was standing there waiting at my locker like a chump, Franklin was riding in sports cars and having a delicious pepperoni-dog with cheese. He'd abandoned me! How could he do that? Before I came along, he was just a tub of Wonder Putty! Why would he leave me for Dino?

It wasn't a hard question to answer. Dino rode in a convertible. Dino had friends. Dino was an UP.

I was "How-Weird," the science geek.

I walked home alone.

I didn't go to the lab that night. Franklin was a big boy, he could find his way back on his own. Instead, I went to bed early and, for the first time in three weeks, I didn't tell my best friend I'd see him in the morning.

Because who knew if I would? Clearly, I couldn't count on him being there. And now that Franklin had met other people, I couldn't count on him being my best friend either.

CHAPTER
30

How to Lose
a Friend

My first thought was that we had a gas leak. When you're awakened from a sound sleep by this "psssssssst" noise, a gas leak is a logical conclusion. Of course, gas pipes don't also whisper "It's me," so I was pretty sure the place wasn't about to explode.

"Pssssst. It's me. Where are you?" a soft voice whispered. Then I heard a tapping on the window.

But not *my* window—uh-oh!

I ran to my sister's room and threw open the door—one second too late. From where I was standing, I could see Katie Beth's back, her hands still on the curtains where she had flung them open. Franklin's face was just outside the glass. His expression was sheer terror.

I'm not sure which of them screamed louder, but they woke every dog in a two-mile radius. Someone hit the lights, and it was like our house was the match that

ignited the neighborhood.
The whole block lit up, and
neighbors rushed outside
and all I could do was
watch it happen.

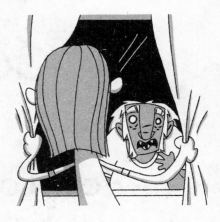

"Bigfoot!" Katie
Beth screamed. "I saw
Bigfoooooot!"

And people say nothing
interesting ever happens
on our street.

By the time Dad rounded the corner, I was already
putting on my sneakers. I knew Franklin would be on
the run, and if he got away, I'd have to go find him. And
if he didn't get away, I'd have to head to Mexico, or South
America, or Antarctica. Having never been a fugitive
before, I wasn't sure how far I'd need to flee.

I was almost out the door when Mom grabbed me by
the back of my collar.

"Just where are you going?" she demanded.

"To look for Bigfoot," I gagged.

"You're not leaving this house. There's some kind of
maniac out there!"

Dad and Stick headed outside with a couple of flash-
lights. Dad checked the bushes and—fortunately, by
my way of thinking—found nothing. Stick looked in the
mailbox. That's right, the mailbox—did he think this was
one of those monsters you see on Scooby Doo? Because in
real life, they don't pop out of mailboxes.

After a couple of minutes, the police showed up. One of the officers took a description from Katie Beth.

"It was Bigfoot," she told him. "Eight feet tall, hairy, with fangs and nice eyes, and he was wearing a pajama-top like the one Nathaniel threw out last year."

I wouldn't want to be the sketch artist who had to work that one up.

The neighbors were a little more helpful. They'd seen a figure, maybe six or six-and-a-half feet tall with long side-burns and a ponytail. He wore red sweatpants and a really, really tight shirt with little cowboys on it. At last sighting, he was headed north and running like a gazelle.

"Don't worry, we'll get him," the officer told us. "He can't have gone far. A guy like that stands out in a crowd."

The police left. One by one, the lights went out in the neighborhood. My mom stayed in my sister's room that night, but at least they both slept. The excitement was over. Things were just as they were yesterday. Well, not everything.

Yesterday, I knew where Franklin was.

When morning came, I headed out early and checked the lab. There was no sign of Franklin. I got ready and headed to school.

He wasn't in homeroom either. Mrs. Ogilvie stopped me in the hall.

"Where is Franklin Stine today?" she asked.

"How should I know?" I snapped, which wasn't a very nice way to respond. I'm kind of a grouch when I don't get any sleep.

Mrs. Ogilvie's forehead wrinkled into a ladder of V-shapes.

"What do you mean? He is your foreign-exchange student."

"Oh," I told her, stumbling to come up with an explanation. "You didn't let me finish. I mean how should I know his schedule? He's still pretty new."

"But you saw him this morning?"

"Yes, of course. Definitely. I saw him this morning, just like always," I said in a blitz of fibs.

Her glare got chillier.

"Do you know why he's not at school? Is he sick?"

"That's it," I said, "he's sick."

"Then why did you say you didn't know his schedule?"

Her line of questioning made me long for a grilling by the cops.

"I meant his *sick* schedule," I backtracked. "He said he might go to the doctor. Or the hospital. He's that sick."

Mrs. Ogilvie stared at me the way I stare at cafeteria meatloaf—curious but untrusting.

"You know, I still haven't received any paperwork about this foreign exchange business," she said, lifting one eyebrow so high I thought it might pop off her head. "Maybe I should just give them a call. What did you say the name of that organization is again?"

That's when I noticed something—a tiny sliver of a smile was on her nearly invisible turtle lips. I couldn't believe it; she was enjoying this! She was enjoying watching me squirm!

Well, we'd just see about that! Howard Boward squirms for bullies, parents, principals, teachers, girls, the dentist, and unusually tough-looking cats. But he draws the line at the lady from the school registration office!

"Oh, I don't want you to go to all that trouble, Mrs. Ogilvie," I said with genuine fakeness. "I'll just tell my parents to pull Franklin out of school until the paperwork gets here. That way, everything will be nice and official. Don't worry about it, Franklin will understand."

She gave me an untrusting look. I smiled considerately.

"It's a real shame, though," I continued. "I guess you'll have to break the news to poor old Coach Fritz. He was really looking forward to having the best player in the history of Dolley Madison play in the city championship. Oh well, rules are rules."

Mrs. Ogilvie's smirk disappeared. Nobody wanted to be known as the person who single-handedly cost the school the city football championship.

Her eyebrows dropped back to human levels. She frowned.

"Your uncle, your parents, the president of Canada—I don't care who it is. I want to hear from an adult!"

That might not have been exactly what she said, but I knew as I watched her shake her head and return to her office, I hadn't won. I'd just outlasted her.

In the meantime, Franklin was still missing. When he didn't show up for football practice, I felt like I'd been run over by a train. As a blocking dummy, that's how I always felt, but somehow doing it without Franklin was even worse.

I ran all the way to the house and dived into the secret tunnel. He wasn't in the lab. The lab was the only place Franklin could call home. If he wasn't there, where else could I look? I thought about filing a missing person report, but he hadn't been missing very long—and he'd never been a person. Besides, after last night, every cop in the city was already looking for him.

I walked the neighborhood until dark then headed home. With the Bigfoot-burglar on the loose, Mom insisted I be indoors by the time the sun went down. I tried to sleep, but Franklin wouldn't leave my thoughts. He was out there somewhere, cold and hungry.

For the record, whenever I can't find something—our dog, my homework, the gray shirt that goes with my blue pants—I always imagine it's cold and hungry. It adds a sense of urgency to my search.

Only this time, it really was urgent. I left my bed and headed outside.

The street felt empty. I don't know if you've noticed, but the dark can be a scary place without a monster. I didn't know where else to look, so I just walked up and down the block waiting for a sign. When I reached the corner, the one where the streetlight is broken, I heard a noise coming from beside the Goldberg's house. I ran toward it. My heart pounded as I left the pavement and cut through Mrs. G's zinnias. Then, just like that, I saw him…

Reynolds Pipkin. He was going through the Goldbergs' garbage.

"Reynolds!" I shouted. "It would have to be you!"

"Who did you think it was?"

"Nobody," I said.

"Then why did you come running?"

This was infuriating! I didn't have to answer questions from a garbage thief.

"Why don't you go home? Bigfoot's out here, you know," I blurted.

Reynolds looked at me a long time, and in the dim light I could see his owlish eyes studying my expression. Finally, he shook his head.

"Wrong climate," he said. "You don't really think Bigfoot is out here."

It wasn't a question. It was a statement.

"Well," I said, "maybe not Bigfoot but somebody. Didn't you see all those cops last night?"

"I saw a lot of things," Reynolds said. "You want to come over to my house?"

"No," I said.

"I'll show you something if you do."

I thought about it. There were few things less appealing than going anywhere with Reynolds Pipkin. But going home and staring at the ceiling for the next few hours might be one of them.

"Fine, let's go," I said.

In the Land
of Pipkins

It was the first time I had ever been inside the gray, pristine house on the corner. I always figured it would be one of those places where the furniture was covered in plastic and dozens of small, porcelain figurines lined the walls, but it wasn't. There were hundreds of figurines!

"Mother calls these her perfect, precious angels," Reynolds said, putting his face so close to the little statues that they could feel his breath. "We're not allowed to touch them."

Then, to my surprise, he picked one up. It was a tiny ceramic boy in a firefighter's hat. Reynolds carried it across the room and put it on a different shelf. Then, from that shelf, he took a porcelain ballerina and moved it to where the firefighter had been. It was an act of diabolical redecoration. When the deed was done, he looked at me and flashed this wicked insect-like smile.

"Sometimes Mother's precious angels are bad," he said.

Without another word, Reynolds walked past several pieces of plastic-covered furniture and disappeared down a hallway. I followed him. We stopped at his room.

The first thing I noticed about Reynolds's room is that it had an ant problem. Covering every inch of it, like wallpaper, were large, close-up pictures of real-life ants. Also, he had at least twenty ant farms that were connected to each other by small, plastic tunnels. I was tempted to give it a clever name like Ant-arctica or Los Ant-geles, but I didn't want Reynolds to think we were bonding.

"Howard," he said. "Do you ever wish you were an ant?"

From anyone else, this would have been a bizarre question, but I could totally see Reynolds as an ant. I mean, he's a hard worker, he's efficient, his brain is too big for his body, and no one wants him in their house. Come on, he's a natural. If you were to miniaturize Reynolds in a lab experiment, he would immediately take his place in the ant line and start bringing crumbs back to the mound.

So I got why Reynolds would want to be a bug. But why did he ask me if I ever wanted to be one? Then I looked at the small, plastic tunnels and the holey-roamin'-empire they connected and that's when it clicked: ants all belong to the group. That's something neither one of us could say.

Reynolds knew me better than I thought.

"Well, thanks, Reynolds. This has been educational," I said. "If I ever run out of stuff to have nightmares about, I'll think of your room."

"Oh, this isn't what I wanted to show you," Reynolds

said, as if he couldn't imagine what gave me that idea. "I wanted to show you my secret hiding place."

"I know what the space under the sink looks like, Reynolds."

He wasn't listening. Or maybe he was; you could never tell with Reynolds. He just turned and walked into the kitchen, expecting I'd follow, and opened the brown cabinet door underneath the sink. There, squeezed around a maze of pipes, was what he'd brought me here to see.

"Franklin!" I gasped.

Franklin's head was down, and the trimmed mane hung across his face. In order to fit under the sink, he'd bent his back into a painful curve, and his knees were pulled up in an impossible scrunch. He was trembling, and his tail was wrapped around one of the pipes.

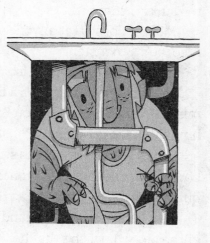

I quickly covered it with my hand.

"That's a scarf," I said to Reynolds, more as a command than an explanation. "Canadians wear scarves."

Reynolds nodded.

I touched Franklin's shoulder just so he'd know I was there. He winced and pulled away. I didn't blame him. It had been a hard day for both of us.

"Where did you find him?" I asked.

"He was in your garbage can."

"Well, why didn't you bring him to me?" I asked.

Reynolds shrugged.

"I thought you threw him away."

My eyes rolled back in frustration. Franklin still hadn't looked at me. I knew he must be furious—someone his size forced to spend hours inside a dark, cramped cabinet. Reynolds was an idiot.

"Reynolds, why in the world would you stuff him under the sink?" I snapped.

"Mother doesn't let anyone stay over on a school night. Also, he's a monster."

I swallowed hard and tried my best to look shocked.

"He's not a monster! He's a foreign-ex ... Oh, never mind!" I yelled and pulled on Franklin's arm. "Help me get him out of there."

At first, I thought he was stuck. I tugged, but the big body didn't move. When I touched him again, his flesh quivered like the business end of an automatic toothbrush. That's when I noticed his hand was gripped around one of the pipes. It wasn't that he couldn't come out; he didn't want to come out.

"It's OK, Franklin," I said. "It's safe. I'm here. You can come out now."

He hesitated but then slowly reached out his hand, and I took it. Reynolds grabbed an arm, and a second later, Franklin emerged from the hiding place.

His eyes searched the room. I could imagine what he was thinking. Was a screaming teenage girl going to bust out from behind the curtains? Were loud sirens and angry lights going to fill the living room? After yesterday, anything was possible.

When Franklin finally spoke, his voice was all fluttery like a wounded bird.

"I didn't know where to go, Howard," he said. "I didn't know if you wanted to be my friend anymore."

You know how when a bully hits you right in the middle of the stomach you feel bruised and sick at the same time? I felt like that. Did this pile of goo not realize how he'd changed my life? Because of him, I now spent my afternoons getting pounded by gigantic linebackers. I had humiliated myself on stage in front of the whole school. On more than one occasion, I had left my warm, safe bed to roam dark, empty streets. Worst of all, I had voluntarily gone into Reynolds Pipkin's room, an action that might very well have scarred me for life. In fact, there was only thing I could think of that would be worse than spending another day with Franklin Stine—and that was spending another minute without him.

"Me not want to be friends with you?" I asked him. "Never!"

If you knew me, you'd know that I am not a hugger. Even long handshakes make me squirm. But I grabbed that giant, and all the worry and fear and insecurity of the last twenty-four hours rushed out through my fingertips. Franklin threw one massive arm around me and, with the other one, he swept up Reynolds.

Now I know for a fact that Reynolds does not like to be

touched. He'll deny it if you ask him, but I saw it with my own eyes: he hugged that monster like an ant hugs a sugar cube.

"Come on, let's go home," I told Franklin.

He followed, but before we made it to the door, he turned around and said, "Thank you for helping me, Reynolds Pipkin. You're a good friend."

I'm not much on sharing, not when it comes to the big things. I mean, I might give you half my egg-salad sandwich, but if it's apple pie or a cream cheese brownie, you're on your own. Franklin was a lot bigger than a pie or a brownie. He was my only friend. Now it looked like he was Reynolds's friend, too. I guess that should have bothered me, but, for some reason, I didn't feel like I'd lost a thing.

☆ ☆ ☆

"I thought it was your window," Franklin told me when we were back safely in the lab.

Franklin had never been inside our house. It was too risky. But when I'd failed to show at the lab that night, he came looking for me. I'm not happy about this, but according to Franklin, I smell like my sister. That's why he ended up at the wrong window.

"So that was Katie Beth," he said, remembering the shrieking girl behind the curtains. "She seemed nice."

I grabbed a bag of Nacho Cheese Doritos from the snack stash I keep in the lab and handed it to Franklin. I didn't know how long it had been since he'd eaten.

Now that the crisis was over, I thought about the reason he'd come looking for me in the first place. The memory made my stomach hurt.

"So I heard you went to PizzaDog with Dino Lincoln," I said. "I guess you had a lot of fun, huh?"

"I had a vanilla shake," he told me. "It's kind of like a Gooshee but with milk instead of ..."

"I've had shakes before," I said.

"You have?"

"Sure," I said. "They're great."

Franklin looked puzzled.

"Then why didn't you come?"

"What?"

"Why didn't you come to PizzaDog? I thought maybe you didn't like milkshakes."

"No, it's not that," I told him. "It's just, well, I wasn't invited."

Franklin looked confused.

"Invited ... what does that mean, Howard?"

"It means that someone has asked you to be some place, so you belong there."

"You belong with me, Howard," he said.

He stuffed his face with a handful of tortilla chips.

It's strange how the simplest things can get twisted around in your mind. Just like that, I knew I'd been worried about nothing. When Wendell told me Franklin went to the PizzaDog, that was my invitation. It was so clear now! Wherever Franklin was, I was welcome and vice versa.

"Well, I didn't want to butt in," I said, trying to sound

like it was no big deal. "You were there with Dino and the gang."

"We waited for you a long time," Franklin said crunchily. "Dino was disappointed when you didn't show."

This is why life needs a rewind button. I really wanted to hear that again.

"Wait a minute," I said. "Dino Lincoln was waiting for me?"

"Yes, I told him all about you. He really wanted to meet you."

"Dino Lincoln wanted to meet me?"

I didn't mention that I had been introduced to Dino at least a dozen times—usually from the other side of a wedgie. Still, it's possible he wouldn't have recognized me from the front.

"They all wanted to meet you, Howard," Franklin said.

Imagine that, a roomful of UPs all talking about me. My head whirled from this sudden rush up the popularity ladder.

"I'm sorry I missed it," I said. "Anyway, it must have been cool riding in a sports car, huh?"

"It was fine. But I prefer walking places," Franklin said.

"Why?" I asked.

"Because I walk places with you, Howard."

I had a big smile on my face, and I couldn't have wiped it off if I wanted to. I'd like to tell you it was there because for the first time in my life I had a best friend who was happy just hanging out with me—but it wasn't. I was smiling because Dino Lincoln knew my name.

CHAPTER 32

A Change in Foreign Policy

I'd been up most of the night, so come breakfast, I had to drag myself to the table. Mom was asking questions, which is the way she stays informed about our lives. I heard her interrogating Katie Beth about her plans for the day. Katie Beth said something about taking an English test or going to England or passing the English muffins—who knew?

Then it was Stick's turn. He said he was going to be stupid and stink all day. Well, that's not really what he said but—trust me—that's what he was going to do.

Orson held up a toy car and pointed to Dad. That meant Dad was going to drive him to kindergarten. See? Orson communicates just fine. I don't know why everybody makes such a big deal about him not talking. Like our house needs more noise!

That's when Mom turned to me.

"Howard," she said. "I had the most interesting talk with your uncle this morning."

"Uncle Ben?" I asked.

I didn't like the look in her eyes.

"Yes," she said. "I called him just before you came down for breakfast. It seems a letter with his name on it came in yesterday's mail. Howard, why do you suppose your school would be writing to my younger brother?"

I don't know what it looked like to everyone else, but the lump in my throat felt like it was as big as a grapefruit.

"Could be a lot of reasons," I gulped.

"And why do you suppose they thought he lived at this address? That just seemed odd to me."

"Well, he is here a lot," I said.

"But not nearly enough to be getting his mail here, don't you agree? That's why I thought it might be nice if we read the letter together over the phone."

"Together?"

"Yes," my mother smiled. "Ben and I used to read together all the time when we were kids. I've missed that."

"Oh," I said.

"Also, I thought the letter might be about you. Call me quirky, but I have this strange need to know what my children are up to."

I took a swig of my apple juice.

"Was it about me?"

"No."

The tension left me, and I let out a great sigh of relief. Crisis averted. I returned to my cereal.

"It was about our foreign-exchange student."

I heard a symphony of spoons and forks clanging

against the floor as my entire family simultaneously dropped their breakfast utensils.

"What?" Katie Beth shrieked.

"Yes, apparently we have one. Your uncle was good enough to tell me all about him."

I knew it was a mistake to bring Uncle Ben in on this! He's a great guy, but one grilling from Mom and he cracks like a fortune cookie—a fortune cookie filled with bad news.

"He told me that there is a homeless boy who needed to use our address so he could go to school. He said you're trying to help him. Is that true, Howard?"

Uncle Ben was faster on his feet than I thought. At least he'd left me with a cover story. I didn't know exactly where this was going, but I nodded.

"Why didn't you come to us, Howard? What were you thinking? You could get into serious trouble, did you know that? Who is this boy? Is he really a foreign-exchange student?"

"Oh, he's foreign all right," I said.

I really didn't know if *foreign* was the right word, but it was true that Franklin wasn't born in this country. He wasn't born anywhere.

Quickly, I made up a story about how he'd come here from Canada but his sponsor-family moved away.

"Why didn't he go back to Canada?"

"He ... he ... he wanted to finish the school year," I stammered. "It was a big honor to be chosen to come here."

"Has he been living on the street?"

"Oh no," I said, not wanting my mom to worry. "He's been staying in the garage."

Stupid, stupid, stupid! I wanted to take the words back even before they left my mouth.

"The garage! You let him sleep in that filthy garage?" my mom exploded.

"Well, just for a little while ..."

She was revving up for a full verbal assault when, all of a sudden, she stopped. Her face told me she'd just had a major revelation.

"Howard," she said. "Am I correct in assuming this explains our prowler?"

I nodded slowly. Then I heard a scream from the other side of the table—Katie Beth's scream.

"Bigfoot is our foreign-exchange student?"

My sister can be a tad dramatic. This wasn't going well. I looked to my Dad for support, but he shook his head. He was getting nowhere near this one.

"It was not Bigfoot!" my mom shouted. "It was a child! A child your brother has had sleeping in a garage! Howard, how could you?"

Then her face flushed pink and her eyes welled up the way mothers' eyes do when they hear awful things about anyone's children.

"Well, Howard, there's only one thing to do," she announced. "When you come home from school today, this boy will be with you. Tell him to bring his things. He's going to stay with us for a few days until we get this all worked out."

Oh no! Oh no, no, no! This couldn't be happening!
Franklin? In the house?

"You don't understand!" I said. "He's ... big."

"We'll find room," Mom said, giving me that cold, deci-
sive stare I've come to know so well.

The only thing that saved me that morning is that my
mom is one of the world's great organizers. Instantly, her
focus shifted away from me and onto a checklist of things
that had to be done before our guest's arrival.

"We can move your desk to the attic and put the roll-
away bed where the desk is sitting now," she told me.
"You'll clear some space in your closet and give him a
drawer in your dresser."

"He doesn't really need a drawer," I said.

"This is a home, not a garage! He'll have a drawer!"
Mom informed me and most of the neighbors. "You will
find out if he is allergic to any foods or medicines and
make me a list. Is that clear? I am extremely unhappy with
you, Howard. As soon as we take care of this situation with
the boy, we'll figure out your punishment—starting with
you quitting that football team!"

Dad, who had been staying out of the line of fire,
suddenly spoke up. "Gee, dear, I don't know. Football is a
good thing for a boy. It builds character—makes him one
of the gang."

Football was the first thing I'd ever done that my dad
found the least bit interesting. He wasn't ready to give that
up. Too bad, though—it would have been a great punishment. I didn't even like football.

"We'll come up with something," Mom said. "In the meantime, are we clear on the plan?"

I nodded. When I looked around the table, all the other heads were nodding too. You didn't challenge Mom when she was in a mood like this one. Slowly, everyone went back to their breakfasts. But not me. My appetite was gone.

A half-hour later, I met Franklin around the corner from the schoolyard. It's where he always waited for me.

"Brace yourself," I said. "We've got a lot to talk about."

☆ ☆ ☆

"I think I've got it," Franklin told me as homeroom came to an end. "I am a foreign-exchange student from Canada. My host family moved away, but I refused to go back to the wild Canadian jungle without an education. So I have been sleeping in a garage and hoping to find another family to sponsor me. I met you while I was standing outside the window of a restaurant watching other people eat. You fed me and told Mrs. Ogilvie that your family was my sponsor so that I could fulfill my dream of attending middle school in America. Is that right, Howard?"

"Yes. Just stick to those points and we'll be OK."

"I don't know. This sounds dishonest."

"No," I said. "It sounded dishonest the first couple of times, but this last time you were very convincing."

"I mean the whole thing sounds dishonest. Should we be lying to your mother?"

I still had a lot to teach him about being a kid.

"We're doing this for my mother," I explained. "This story will make her happy! Particularly the part about me being a hero who had no choice but to help a lonely, starving soul on the street. Don't you see? There's no more noble cause than making a mother happy."

"If you say so, Howard."

"I absolutely say so," I said.

We walked out of class. I was about to assure him for the thousandth time that everything would be all right as long as we stuck to our story, but a girl approached us.

"Hey, Big Frankie," she said in a voice like never-ending bubble gum. "Don't tell me this is the famous Howard Boward?"

Famous? Me? I would have settled for the tolerable Howard Boward ... the so-so Howard Boward ... the not-entirely-repulsive Howard Boward. But here this girl was calling me "famous." And not just any girl, Crystal Arrington! Or, as she was better known, **"Cheerleader— Go! Team! Fight! Win!—Crystal!"**

"Howard, this is Crystal," Franklin said. "We met at PizzaDog."

"We were waiting for you, pokey," Crystal said, her brown hair effortlessly framing her perfect face. "Frankie said you're some kind of genius, like an Einstein or something. He said you'll probably win the Noble Prize someday!"

I was sure Franklin had said

Nobel, and I was equally sure Crystal didn't know what that was. I was also absolutely positive she'd never have to.

"I'm also on the football team," I told her, though I had no idea why.

"Wow! Brains and brute strength—you're the complete package. See ya, How-Cool!"

How-Cool? Did she just call me How-Cool? It had finally happened. I had a nickname I didn't have to erase off the bathroom wall!

Crystal skipped down the hall. Mom could do with me as she wanted now. Whatever the punishment, whatever the torture—it had been totally worth it.

CHAPTER 33

Bowards and the Beast

"Stick," I said.

"What, dork?"

"Howard's a dork!" squawked Precious.

"Shut up, Precious!" I yelled.

Stick gave Precious a cracker.

I didn't like talking to Stick. Or listening to him. Or looking at him. Or living on the same planet with him. Now I was doing all of them at the same time. These were dark days.

"Mom wants me to bring Franklin to live here ... inside the house."

"So?" Stick asked.

"I'm not sure that's a good idea," I said.

"Why? What's wrong with him?"

"Nothing," I told him, taking it a little more personally than I'd expected. "He's just a little ... different."

"Is he different from you? Or is he different from normal people?" Stick asked. "Because if he's going to live here, different from you is mandatory."

"He's different from everybody," I said. "You see, Franklin is a ..."

I struggled to make the proper description come out of my mouth, but the closest I could come was *Canadian*.

Stick shrugged.

"Everybody's from somewhere. You're a troll we found under a bridge, but we got used to you."

I was about to deliver one of my patented snappy comebacks when I heard Mom's car pull into the driveway. My time was up. I walked the path of doom.

"Is he here?" Mom said when she spied me.

"Not yet," I said.

"Grab some groceries. They're in the car."

I checked out the bags in the back of the Dodge. My guess is Mom didn't know what people from Canada eat because she got a selection from around the world. The first bag I picked up had English peas, taco seasoning, bratwurst, baklava, Chef Boyardee, and Swiss cheese.

I scooped up a couple of other bags and carried them into the house.

"So where is he?" Mom asked as she put away a frozen pizza and some Russian dressing.

"He'll be here. Coach kept him after practice so they could go over some new plays," I said. "I'm supposed to go get him when you're prepared."

"Prepared?"

"I mean ready. I'll get him when the house is ready."

"The house is as ready as it's going to get," Mom said. "Go get him."

The walk to the garage was the saddest, slowest shuffle I could manage. Why did this have to happen just when things were starting to look up for me? I was doomed. I mean, it was one thing to fool the people at school—you trim the claws, duct tape the tail, and move on. There are tons of weird-looking kids in middle school. I'm pretty sure the teachers are legally prohibited from even noticing.

But a family? Families notice everything. I could hear it now: "Franklin certainly is hairy for the seventh grade, isn't he? And I think we need to have the orthodontist look at those fangs."

I crawled through the cooler door for what I feared might be the last time, turned left at the cabinet, and came out through the dryer.

Franklin was standing there, stiff and sweating. In one hand he was holding a suitcase and, in the other, a small bouquet of daffodils. He wore a light-blue jogging suit that Reynolds had retrieved from the Goldbergs' garbage (there was nothing wrong with it, Mr. Goldberg just hated jogging) and one of Dad's old ties.

"Lose the tie," I said. "It's time."

☆ ☆ ☆

I thought about trying to sneak past my family, but that would have only delayed the inevitable. My mother was expecting company.

So I decided I'd go in first and break the ice.

When I stepped through the front door, I saw that Mom had assembled a small welcoming committee. She stood in the center of the entry hall with Stick and Katie Beth winged out on each side. Orson stood behind Katie Beth peeking out to see if it was safe.

Dad wasn't home yet, which was too bad. That meant there would be a repeat performance later. If you haven't brought a monster home to meet the family, it's a lot like ripping out one of your eyebrows—nobody wants to do it twice.

"Mom," I began. "I think it was Shakespeare who said, 'Beauty is in the eye of the beholder.' As you know, it takes all kinds to make a world and ..."

"Just bring the kid in!" Mom ordered.

I reached outside the door and found a massive, trembling arm. Gently, I eased Franklin into the house.

It's hard to describe the faces across the room other than to say I could see all of their tonsils. Their skin had turned the color of plain yogurt. Instinctively, Mom threw her arms in front of Stick and Katie Beth as if she were slamming on the brakes of a car.

I was still holding Franklin's arm. It was shaking like a jackhammer. The veins in his neck pulsated, and his teeth were clenched and gritted. As near as I could tell, he was "extreme smiling." That is to say, smiling as hard as anyone can possibly force themselves to smile.

It was a horrifying sight.

No one spoke. No one dared. I'm not sure we breathed.

Mom's eyes were fixed on the creature in her entry hall. In unison, she, Stick, and Katie Beth took a collective step backwards. But Orson, for some reason, did not.

Orson had found his way out from behind Katie Beth's knees, and he wasn't going anywhere.

It's hard to explain, but Franklin's effect on my five-year-old brother was the same as one of those fuzzy muppets on Sesame Street—Orson was drawn to Franklin. Orson moved forward, and when he was directly

173

in front of the sweating, teeth-clenching giant, he held out his small hand.

Franklin took it as one would take the wings of a butterfly.

Orson smiled and, at long last, Frankin un-smiled. The pressure left his cheeks, and his neck muscles relaxed. What was left behind was a very nice grin, the one he got from Winnie McKinney. The improvement was nothing short of plastic surgery.

My little brother led Franklin across the floor to where my mother was standing. Her eyes were still wide, and her hands still trembled, but she stood her ground. As politely as she could muster, she nodded to the visiting creature.

Franklin's arm sprung up stiffly. The daffodils stopped about two inches from my mom's nose, and she winced to avoid being pollinated.

"Th-these are l-l-lovely ... Franklin," she stammered. "As p-p-p-pretty as the ones in Mrs. C-C-Craddock's garden."

I thought it was the wrong time to reveal they were *exactly* as pretty as the ones in Mrs. Craddock's garden.

"Man-oh-man-oh-man-oh-man!" Stick cackled. "Wait until I tell the guys!"

"Nathaniel!" Mom snapped then quickly found her manners. "Do you really think the guys need to be alerted every time Howard has a friend over?"

"I don't know," Stick said. "It never happened before."

"You must be Stick," Franklin said cheerfully.

Stick frowned, and the daggers coming out of his eyes

were aimed straight at me. "Just call me Nate. No matter what anyone else tells you!"

I'd been watching my mom. Something happened when Franklin spoke. Her face changed right in front of my eyes. All of a sudden, she wasn't looking at some enormous, threatening beast that had invaded her family. It was something else. It talked. It talked like a boy, one who was far from home and slept in a garage and had no one to look after it. She softened, I could tell, and she touched his arm lightly with her hand.

"Franklin," she said, "this is Howard's sister, Katie Beth."

"We've met," Katie Beth grunted.

"Oh, at the window," Franklin remembered. "I am so, so, so sorry about that. You see, I was looking for Howard, and it turns out you smell . . ."

"Franklin!" I yelled, stopping him before he could say the word "alike" and complete a sentence the world must never hear.

"I what?" Katie Beth demanded.

"Nothing," Franklin, clearly terrified, said. "You just smell."

There was no fear in my sister's face anymore but what replaced it was much, much worse! Hurriedly, I rolled my finger in a spinning manner, urging Franklin to keep talking.

"Good," he added at last. "You smell good."

Katie Beth looked at him like he was from another planet—which wasn't really all that much of a stretch. She rolled her eyes.

"Thanks," she said and stomped into the other room.

"Franklin," Mom said, "I didn't know what you'd like for dinner on your first night ..."

"I like Gooshees," he said.

"Gooshees?" Mom said, transitioning into full mother mode. "No, no, no, those things are nothing but sugar. You shouldn't drink those because they'll hurt your ..."

She was going to say "teeth," but I could see her looking at Franklin's fangs.

"Oh, never mind. We're having pot roast," she said.

"I'll take Franklin to my room," I told her, and we turned to head up the stairs.

"Just a minute," Mom said. "We're not done here yet."

I knew more was coming. She'd been too stunned by Franklin's appearance to get into the details, but now she'd regained her composure. We were doomed.

"Franklin," she said, "My son is a very imaginative person. So I assume he has already concocted some story explaining why you've been living all alone. One which, no doubt, casts him as a hero."

What can I say? My mom knows me like a book.

"So I will not test how well you've memorized his story by asking how you got here," she said. "We'll get to all that later. What I have to know right now are three things, and I want straight answers. First, are you in any trouble with the police?"

"No," Franklin said.

"Fine. Second, how do I contact your family to let them know where you are?"

"I don't have any family," Franklin told her.

"You mean ... no one at all?"

He shook his head.

At first, Mom seemed like she didn't believe him, but then she looked at me, and I shook my head too. That's when I noticed her eyes starting to well up, and she bit her lower lip the way people do when they're trying to hold something back. It wasn't the answer she'd expected.

"I see," she said at last, and her voice cracked a little. "Well, you boys run along."

Franklin blinked.

"Wasn't there a third question, Mrs. Boward?" he asked.

"What?" Mom said, and it was like her mind was in a faraway place. "Oh right, my third question is ... can I make you a whole bunch of cookies?"

Franklin smiled. I don't think that was the question she'd planned on asking him, but when you just find out a seventh-grade boy is all alone in the world, you figure he's got a lot of catching up to do in the cookie department.

CHAPTER
34

Care and Feeding
of Your Monster

If you're interested, Franklin likes pot roast. He also likes potatoes, carrots, English peas, wheat rolls, and banana cream pie. For the first time in Boward family pot-roast history, there were no leftovers. We were barely able to save the plates.

He had seconds, and thirds, and whatever Orson didn't finish, plus the fat and bones we were saving for the dogs. To be fair, he'd never had anything like it before. He'd also never had a family. More than anything, I think, he just didn't want dinner to end.

"Wow! We've gotta put him in one of those hot dog–eating contests," Stick said. "We'd make a fortune!"

Franklin seemed to have made a good impression on my brothers. Stick had already come up with a dozen ideas for making money off this enormous kid's weirdness. Orson was just fascinated. It was as if some magnificent wild-thing had popped out of a storybook and stayed for dinner.

As for my sister, she hadn't really warmed up to Bigfoot. Her groans grew louder with every plate he consumed, and she kept making comments like "Would you like some salt with your everything?"

At least Franklin had told her she smelled good. Things could have been worse.

But of all the reactions, the most surprising was Dad's. I had prepared myself to repeat the introduction I'd made to the rest of the family since I didn't think it was fair to spring Franklin on him all at once. But Dad walked in just as we were coming down for dinner.

"Who's this?" Dad said as he met us at the bottom of the stairs.

I froze for a second.

"Um ... Franklin," I told him.

Dad looked him square in the eye.

"Welcome aboard, Frankie," he said.

Then he slapped him on the back and sat down for dinner. That was it. I guess when your job means you might have to deal with a bear or a Rottweiler or a gorilla, one giant houseguest is no big deal.

That night, I was so tired I could barely make it up the stairs. Mom had gotten Franklin a brand new, yellow toothbrush because she likes everybody to have their own color. We brushed, we spat, and we headed to bed.

"This was my very best day," Franklin told me. "I really like your family, Howard."

"Yeah, they're pretty nice. If you don't count Stick," I yawned.

Mom had given Franklin a pair of my dad's striped pajamas. They were tight but, as pajamas go, kind of comfy-looking. The headboard of Franklin's brand-new bed was right next to mine so the two of them made a big L-shape against two walls.

His eyes darted around the room, taking in my treasures.

"Is everything in here yours, Howard?" he asked

"Pretty much."

"Wow!" he said. "Are those your coat hangers?"

"Yes."

He gave a long, happy sigh. "Howard, is it wonderful to have things?"

"It's OK," I said. "I never really thought about it."

I didn't see what the big deal was. It's not like I had that much stuff. But I guess if you'd never had anything at all, a coat hanger is pretty fantastic. I thought about that for a second, then crawled out of bed and went to my dresser.

"Here you go, Franklin," I said.

I handed him my autographed baseball I caught at a real Major League Baseball game.

"What's this, Howard?"

"It's a foul ball I caught at a baseball game. Well, I didn't really catch it. I was eating some popcorn, and it landed in my bucket. You can have it."

From the look on his face, you'd think it was Christmas morning. He gently rotated the ball between his fingers.

"Look, it's signed and everything!" I told him.

"Who's Dusty Reynolds?" he asked.

"He's the guy who sold me the popcorn."

"Really?" Franklin said. "Are you sure you don't want this anymore?"

"Oh, I want it," I said. "But I want you to have it more. Everybody ought to have some stuff."

He cradled it like an enormous, autographed diamond.

"Now, let's get some sleep," I said.

"Yes, sleep," Franklin said, "That's a great idea. Let's get some sleep."

"Goodnight, Franklin," I said.

"Goodnight, Howard," he told me.

I was about an inch away from dreamland when he spoke again.

"Howard?"

"What?" I grumped.

"How do you sleep?" he asked.

"What do you mean?"

"I mean you told me to get some sleep, but I'm not sure how you get it."

That's when I realized that Franklin had never slept. Maybe he didn't need to. Or maybe he just didn't know he needed to. I thought about him sitting up all night in the garage, just waiting. And it made me feel bad.

"I don't know if sleep is something you can teach," I told him. "Your body gets tired, you start to yawn, and you lay down. Then you just stop thinking, and before you know it, you're asleep."

Franklin didn't say anything. He sat up and stretched his long arms while making a huge, fake yawn. Then he laid his head back on the pillow. After that, I fell asleep. I can't be sure, but I like to think he did the same.

☆ ☆ ☆

"Good morning, Franklin," Mom said when we came down for breakfast. "Did you sleep well?"

"I don't know," he said. "It was my first try."

"In this house! It was his first try at sleeping in this house," I shouted nonchalantly. "And he slept great!"

"Why, thank you," Franklin said, taking it as a compliment.

I finished my breakfast. Franklin finished two. And we headed to school.

The first face I saw there was Winnie McKinney's. She was grinning like Orson does when you give him a cookie.

"Well, look at you," she said. "First, you win the talent show, and now you're running for class president. I knew we'd get you out of your shell."

No doubt about it, this was an odd morning.

"Class president? I didn't sign up for class president!" I told her.

"I signed you up, Howard," Franklin said, as if ruining a friend's life was a good thing. "You should be president."

"No I shouldn't!" I protested. "To be president, you have to be ... to be ..."

"Smart?" Franklin asked.

"Not particularly," Winnie said.

"Helpful?" he asked.

"Hardly," Winnie said.

"Popular?" he offered.

"Bingo!" she cried.

"Then there's no problem. Howard is very popular," Franklin said.

Now it's possible that Franklin might have gotten the wrong idea about exactly where I sit on the popularity scale. Maybe I let it slip that the reason he hadn't met my

friends is that a lot of them are secret agents and can't reveal their true identities. Or it might have been the emails I showed him that said things like "Wow, Howard! You're the most popular kid in school!" and "Hey, Howard, let's hang out when I finish the world tour with my rock band!"

I don't know who this BenFranklinFan@sciencegeek.com is, but I wish he'd stop sending me these embarrassing messages.

So I can understand why Franklin would think of me as presidential material. The trouble was, the rest of the school tended to think of me as, well, they didn't tend to think of me.

"Don't you think Howard would make an awesome president?" Franklin asked Winnie.

She hesitated longer than was comfortable for any of us.

"I'd vote for him," she said after an eternity and a half.

And so the **"Howard Boward for President"** bandwagon began to roll with everyone on board except for Howard Boward.

CHAPTER 35

A Cool Spell

Our next football game was against the Hilltop Hoot Owls, and I finally saw action. Donnie Ortega, our receiver, had left his helmet on the bus.

"Boward!" Coach yelled for me.

I swallowed hard and rushed to his side.

"Yes, Coach?" I said.

"Give Donnie your helmet!" he told me.

I did. It felt good to contribute.

Franklin had a good game too. He ran back a punt sixty-three yards for a touchdown, caught a twenty-four-yard touchdown pass, and scored a touchdown on defense. I wasn't sure the one on defense should have counted. The Hoot Owls' quarterback saw Franklin chasing him and didn't stop running until he was back across his own goal line. Then, in a state of sheer terror, he threw the ball at Franklin's head.

It stuck in Franklin's facemask. Apparently, that counts as an interception.

Anyway, we won.

"Look at this!" I told Franklin after the game. "I got a mark on my helmet!"

"Wow!" Franklin said. "That's a big one too!"

We both knew that it happened while Donnie Ortega was wearing my helmet, but it was still my first mark—and I got it in a real game!

If you can't brag about something like that to your best friend, what's the point of messing up a perfectly good helmet?

☆ ☆ ☆

I was coming out of my fifth-period chemistry class where everyone hates me—one little explosion, and you're black-listed—when I heard Franklin come up behind me.

"Hello, Howard," he said politely, which was the only way he ever said anything.

That's when I saw he wasn't alone. He was with a tall kid in a white T-shirt and perfectly matched blue jacket and pants.

"This is Dino Lincoln," Franklin said, as if it were possible for me not to know that. "He's been wanting to meet you."

Has your mouth ever been so dry that it didn't have enough juice to form words? Sure, I'd spoken to Dino plenty of times. But those were kind of like speaking to a statue or the TV—you don't figure they hear you, and you'd be stunned if they actually replied. Now he had come all the way down the hall just to meet me!

"Hey, I remember you," Dino said when I turned around. "You're that unitard dude, right?"

My intestines twisted into a knot.

"Oh that," I tried to laugh. "That was an experiment. You see, I was . . ."

"It's cool, it's cool," Dino said in the coolest possible way. "My boy Franklin told me science is your gig. I respect that."

Dino Lincoln respected my right to wear a stretchy unitard to school! Nobody respected that. Vice Principal Hertz said if I ever did it again, he'd make me wear the "Marvin the Manatee" mascot costume for the rest of the day.

But Dino? Dino was "cool" with it. You have to understand, Dino Lincoln is in the upper-echelon of the UPs. He's the captain of the basketball team. He's the homecoming king. He's the guy who single-handedly held Moose Oliver upside down over the toilet and gave him a cosmic swirlee. Moose Oliver weighs 174 pounds!

I felt bad for Moose but, come on, that's a middle-school record.

Popularity just seems to attach itself to guys like Dino. Yes, he'd stuffed me in my locker and thrown me in the girl's restroom and ran my swimsuit up the flagpole, but I could see now that it wasn't personal. We hadn't been formally introduced.

Everything was different now.

"Howard is running for class president," Franklin told Dino.

"Is that so?" Dino said. "Are you going to make the school days shorter and the basketball hoops bigger? I could always use a bigger hoop."

"The last thing we need is to give you a bigger hoop," I said. "Our scoreboard only goes up to a thousand."

Dino laughed. It was a great laugh, the kind that made every other laugh sound like a honking goose.

"You're all right, little dude," he said. "President, huh? Tell you what, I'll put some of the chess-club kids in a headlock until they say they'll vote for you."

"Oh, you don't have to do that," I said.

"Naw, it's all good. I was going to put them in a head-lock anyway. Might as well be for that."

And with those words, he glided down the hallway. But his coolness lingered a while longer.

"See, Howard?" Franklin said. "Dino's going to help with your campaign. He's already getting you votes! You're going to win, I know it."

Poor Franklin. He saw no levels, no social order—a nerd was the same as a jock was the same as an UP. In his mind, we were just different flavors poured from an enormous, educational Gooshee machine. Any flavor could grow up to be class president.

I knew it didn't work that way. Victory was impossible.

Then again, in a very short time, Dino Lincoln would be giving knuckle-noogies to pint-sized chess champions and telling them to vote for Howard Boward.

I'm pretty sure I would have told you that was impossible too.

CHAPTER 36

A Big Hand for Katie Beth

When Franklin and I got home, we saw Katie Beth in the living room wearing a bulky, gray sweatshirt and black tights. That meant she was practicing dancing, a sight that's normally hilarious, but not at that particular moment. That's because instead of pretending she was a swan or a cat, she was just sitting on the floor watching a DVD with her best friend, Hannah.

The DVD was of a dance routine and was even more boring than the usual stuff Katie Beth watches. My sister is on the high school dance team and thinks that gives her the right to hog the TV anytime she wants to watch a bunch of people jumping around in matching costumes.

"We can totally do this," Katie Beth said, grabbing the remote and punching the pause button. "I've been working on that jump. It'll be amazing!"

Hannah nodded. Hannah was taller than my sister, and blonde, and had an overbite that Katie Beth was always telling her no one noticed. She was on the dance team too, which explained why she'd walked over to our house in an oversized t-shirt and purple leg-warmers.

"Oh, you can so do that jump," Hannah said. "But what good will it do you? None of the guys can do the lift. And without the lift, it's nothing."

Katie Beth had an irritated look on her face—the same one that had been there for years.

"Hello, Katie Beth," Franklin said as we walked by.

I hadn't yet taught him the fine art of ignoring my siblings.

Katie Beth didn't answer, she just rolled her eyes the way she did any time one of us spoke. Hannah, on the other hand, was experiencing Franklin for the first time. I saw her eyes widen and you could hear that long gasp that comes just before a scream when—

"Oh, knock it off, Hannah!" Katie Beth shouted. "It's just my goofy little brother and Franklin. I swear, you're such a drama queen. Now, like I was saying, we just need to find some guy who isn't a complete feeb, and then I'll do the jump—something like this."

She took three steps and threw her arms back as she made some kind of leap that looked a lot like a spazmatic dolphin coming out of the water. I was pretty sure she was going to do a belly flop right there in the middle of the living room, which I would have paid money to see, but she didn't. Instead, she went up ... and up ... and up.

Franklin was holding her with one arm above his head. He looked up.

"Is it kind of like this?" he asked.

"No!" Katie Beth screamed, and I thought she was about to let loose a stream of foul-mouthed names like I haven't heard since I used her toothbrush to clean the guinea pigs' cage.

But all she said was, "Your feet are all wrong! Now let's try it again!"

They tried it the rest of the afternoon. After a while, even Hannah tried it and Franklin lifted her too. And I'll tell you something—even though dancing looks pretty dorky when you see it on TV, it's not half bad once you add monsters.

CHAPTER
37

Sunday Surprise

"Is he ready?" Mom said.

"Not yet," I said. "He's trying to get extra clean."

"Well, we've got to go. We can't wait any longer."

"You go ahead, I'll drive them, Mom," Katie Beth said. "We'll be over in a few minutes."

What was that? Katie Beth had just offered to drive me somewhere—something I usually have to beg her to do and she still drops me off twelve blocks away. Being that this was a Sunday, I put it down as a miracle, especially since the place she was offering to drive us was church.

I was kind of nervous about taking Franklin to church. It was one thing to introduce him to my teachers or my family, but I thought the people at church might be a little uncomfortable getting a visit from someone with fangs and a tail.

But Mom said as long as Franklin was under our roof, he was part of the family—and the family was going to church.

The bathroom door opened.

"How do I look, Howard?" Franklin asked.

He was wearing a suit I'd pieced together from the collective wardrobes of Dad, Stick, and me. Don't get me wrong, the clothes were fine, it was just that Franklin was pretty hard to fit. Plus, he was kind of like Uncle Ben in that he just looked weird in a suit. The collar and tie were strangling him, the sleeves of the jacket came down just past his elbows, the pants were too short, and his toes were doubled over inside Stick's shiny, black shoes.

Worse, he had slicked back his hair with what appeared to be several gallons of styling gel. It looked like we had laminated his head. I almost laughed when I saw him, but I stopped myself. This was going to be his first time in a church, and I couldn't blame him for wanting to make a good impression.

"Suave," I told him. "Let's go."

Franklin's face lit up the minute we pulled into the parking lot. His eyes grew bigger, wider, swallowing up every sight in front of them. I couldn't imagine why—I mean, it was just our church. But if you've never seen a steeple rising up to poke the sky or windows made of every color in the crayon box, I guess even a regular, old church can be kind of a big deal.

"You go on in, Katie Beth," I said. "We'll be there in a second."

I wanted to take our time going inside. If we walked slowly enough, there was the possibility we could hover near the back and not draw a lot of attention. But it wasn't just that. You only get one chance to do anything for the first time. I didn't think it was fair to rush Franklin through it.

Katie Beth hurried away.

Me and Franklin took the long way around the building so that he could see the swing set and bicycle rack. There's nothing special about them but he seemed to think so.

Finally, we reached the entrance. The doors of the sanctuary were already closed and I could hear the organ music, which meant the service was about to start. I took a deep breath.

We pushed open the doors.

All I can tell you is I'll bet Reverend Boyd wishes church was as quiet during prayers as it was in that moment. The organist stopped playing. The people stopped shaking hands. No one was laughing or telling stories about what happened to them during the week. It was as if, by opening the doors, we'd let all the noise run out of the room.

Pew by pew, heads turned completely around until everyone was staring in our direction.

I felt a lump in my throat.

"This," I said, sensing the need to make an announcement, "is my friend, Franklin Stine."

For a second, nothing changed. Then a voice from near the front said, "Franklin Stine? Franklin Stine the football player?"

"The kid who scored three touchdowns in one game?" another voice asked.

"Hey, my son goes to school with him!" someone in a choir robe said.

Franklin smiled. It was one of those big, warm Winnie McKinney smiles that had a way of making everything all right.

After that, you'd have thought we just walked into a pep rally. People were rushing up to shake his hand or pat him on the back. I half-expected someone to dump a cooler of Gatorade on his head.

Tugging on his coat sleeve, I dragged Franklin through his new fans to the place where my family was sitting. He sat next to my mom, and I plopped down by Stick.

"I sure didn't think we'd get that kind of welcome," I whispered. "I was afraid someone might scream or faint."

"I know, it's a pretty horrible sight the first time," Stick whispered back. "But then again, most of these people have seen you before."

If we hadn't have been in church, I'd have kicked him in the kneecap.

When the service was over, I wanted to leave before people had the chance to ask Franklin a lot of questions, but Mom insisted on stopping to thank Reverend Boyd.

"Well, I'm certainly glad you brought this fine young man to see us today," Reverend Boyd said. "It's always good to meet a member of the Manatee football team."

"Howard is on the team too," Franklin said.

"Howard? Our Howard? On the team?"

The reverend had stopped smiling. He looked deeply concerned.

Franklin nodded.

"Does Coach Fritz know about this?" the reverend asked.

"I'm only there because of Franklin," I told him. "I don't get into any games."

"Thank heavens!" he said. "I mean, thank heavens our church is so well represented by the two of you. Go Manatees!"

It took forever to get out of the building because everybody wanted to shake Franklin's hand again. A couple of people had their picture taken with him. That's when I realized that I only thought I'd made a friend in my lab.

What I'd really made was a celebrity.

CHAPTER 38

How to Run for President Without Really Trying

"Hey, How-Cool!" Crystal Arrington said when she saw me in the cafeteria. "Dino said I'm supposed to make sure you get the cheerleader vote. So I told the squad you were Frankie's friend and just super-awesome and, well, mission accomplished!"

I started to pinch my arm to wake myself up. This had to be a dream. Crystal Arrington had called me super awesome—in front of witnesses!

I cancelled the pinch. Who'd want to wake up from that?

There was just one thing that bugged me—why did she think I was super-awesome? I suppose there could have been a lot of reasons, like my excellent penmanship or how shiny I kept my braces, but I was pretty sure it was something else: I was "Big Frankie's" best friend. These days, that was something a lot of people wanted to be.

Who could blame them? Franklin had scored three touchdowns in one game. Franklin won the talent show. Franklin was a seventh-grader who, for reasons no one could explain, was the newest member of the high school dance-team.

Franklin, Franklin, Franklin! After a while, it got kind of old. So can you really blame me for pretending, just for a second, that some of my awesomeness was my own doing?

"Thanks a lot, Crystal," I said. "And you tell those cheer-leaders to **Gimme a V! Gimme an O! Gimme a T! Gimme an E! Voooooooote Howard!**"

Winnie McKinney happened to be walking by just as I started my cheer. She laughed so hard I thought she was going to drop her tray. It wasn't a sweet laugh either—it was the kind of laugh Mom makes when Stick asks if he can have a motorcycle.

Crystal, on the other hand, thought it was "cutie-patootie."

"Some of the kids are going to PizzaDog after school," she said. "You should come. I mean, a future president has to get out and meet the people, right?"

"Absolutely!" I said. "I'll be there."

This dream was getting better and better, and then...

"It's Franklin!" someone yelled.

The great one had entered the cafeteria.

"Look! There's Frankie! Hi, Big Frankie!" Crystal squealed, and then she waved her hand like a humming-bird wing. "Oh! I've got to go meet Missi! We're working on a new Franklin cheer! See you around, Harold."

Meanwhile, Franklin made his way across the room.

"Sorry I'm late for lunch, Howard. I was putting up a sign for your campaign."

I gave Franklin a look that said I didn't care about the sign, or the campaign, or lunch. What I cared about was that one minute I was "super-awesome" and the next I was "Harold."

My wrinkled up forehead is surprisingly chatty. But Franklin didn't seem to notice. Instead, he just smiled. He smiled so big it made my eyeballs burn.

"I think you'll like the sign, Howard."

I sighed.

"Franklin," I said. "Do you mind going home alone after school? I've got something I've got to do."

"I can help you with it, Howard."

"No," I said. "It's something I've got to do on my own."

You've probably guessed that what I had to do on my own was go to PizzaDog. Look, I know I said Franklin was welcome wherever I went, but there's something you don't understand. No one ever invited me any place. That was changing. I was changing. OK, maybe I wasn't exactly super awesome, but everybody sure thought Franklin was.

And it seemed to me that maybe, just maybe, a little of the glory ought to go to the guy who made the goo!

I pictured what it would be like hanging out at the PizzaDog—just me and the UPs.

"Another pepperoni dog, How-Cool?" Josh Gutierrez would say.

"Hey, get out of that chair!" Crystal would demand. "It's my turn to sit by How-Cool!"

Oh, it would be sweet all right—a pepperoni dog with a side of UPs. My appetite started growing.

I'm pretty sure my head did too.

After school, I didn't wait to see Franklin. I just hit the heavy exit doors and kept going. I wouldn't have stopped until I got to PizzaDog except that a bunch of kids had gathered in front of the school and were pointing at something. I glanced over my shoulder to see what was so interesting.

Framing the doorway like the entrance to a tunnel was a ten-foot-tall drawing of my face. Next to it were the words "Vote for Howard. A Loyal Friend."

☆ ☆ ☆

The PizzaDog was UP-loaded. It had UPs in there I didn't even know were UPs. At first, I felt out of place but, as luck would have it, Crystal and Missi had brought their homework with them. You know how cheerleaders are—always studying.

201

They figured since I was good at math, I could help them with the confusing parts. Apparently, that was any part that didn't involve running around the restaurant and talking to your friends.

But it wasn't all bad—at least Josh Gutierrez let me buy him a pepperoni dog. OK, he just stole the one I bought for myself, but it amounted to the same thing. We were bonding.

The point is, I spent a whole afternoon hanging with the UPs and not as Franklin's shadow! It was magical.

When I got home, the family was just sitting down to dinner. I had already had two pepperoni dogs and a pineapple shake, but I took a chair anyway to keep up appearances.

"What are we having?" I asked.

"Fish sticks," Mom said.

Franklin looked confused.

"Are we having pizza too?" he said. "I smell pepperoni and pineapple."

That blasted nose! I should have known better than to try to hide anything from the super-snoz. He'd probably smelled me from a block away.

"Just fish," Mom said.

I sneaked a glance at Franklin. Had he figured it out? Did he know I'd gone to PizzaDog without him? How could he not? One whiff of me, and it was like I'd signed a confession!

He knew all right. His odd behavior the rest of the night practically proved it. Franklin was obviously avoiding me—he'd barely said two words in my direction since I got home! And instead of us doing something together after dinner, he sat in the corner with Orson playing around on the computer until bedtime.

Well, that was just fine. If he had nothing to say to me, I had nothing to say to him.

I kept a healthy distance between us until we were in our beds and the lights were off.

"Goodnight, Howard," the voice from the next bed said.

I stared his way trying to make out the expression on his face. Had I hurt him? Were we still friends? It was too dark to tell.

I had a knot in my stomach that might have been guilt. Or it might have been two pepperoni dogs and a half-dozen fish sticks. The feeling is surprisingly similar.

"Night," I said quickly.

Then I rolled over. In a few hours, it would be daylight—and I didn't want to know if his eyes were still on me.

CHAPTER
39

Geekboy
and Maditron

All right, it was guilt. I should've invited Franklin to PizzaDog. I guess I couldn't blame him for snubbing me after dinner. That's what I would have done to him. But as it turned out, he hadn't snubbed me, at all. I don't think Franklin knew how to snub. It was true that he'd been avoiding me, but that was because he had a reason.

The next day at school, that reason became clear.

"Awesome video, Boward!" a skinny kid wearing an orange T-shirt called out to me. I had no idea who the kid was.

"Are you him? Are you Howard Boward?" asked a girl in a plaid skirt across the hall. "That video clinched it. You've got my vote!"

It happened again and again. People I didn't know would hold up their hands in classic high-five fashion and say things like "You rule, How-Bow!" and "Killer video! I hope you win!"

This newfound attention felt good in a nauseating sort of way. I was being congratulated for a great accomplishment I knew nothing about. Still, who's to say I hadn't done something awesome while sleepwalking? Or maybe I had amnesia? There could be a lot of explanations.

"You are full of surprises, slick," Winnie McKinney told me just before lunch. "To be honest, I didn't think you had an iceberg's chance in the Sahara of being president. But that video? Whoa!"

"Oh, thanks," I said, trying to sound humble in a still-deserving kind of way. "Sometimes these ideas just hit you. What I was really trying to get across was, well, I think it's obvious. No use dwelling on it."

"You don't have the slightest idea what I'm talking about, do you?" she said.

"Not a clue."

She grabbed her phone and pulled up something on a FaceSpace page—my FaceSpace page.

On the tiny screen was a video, set to music, that showed our school transforming into a cartoonish Japanese-style robot. The building-bot then walks across town and stomps William Bonney Middle School, our hated rival, under its titanic feet. Bonney, of course, had it coming—they call us the Dolley Madison "Cupcakes" when they know perfectly well we are the "Manatees."

Later, Dolley Madi-tron scored a touchdown, dunked a basketball, skateboarded through an asteroid belt, and made fireworks shoot out of its nose. The video concluded with a close-up of a tiny window in the robot's eye through which you could see who was controlling the mechanical middle-school. It was yours truly. Really, it was just my head pasted onto a superhero-like body, but the point was clear enough.

An instant later, these words appeared:

"Transform Dolley Madison. Vote for Howard Boward."

Apparently, it had spread to every seventh grader in DMMS.

"I wish I was a robot," I said, not meaning for it to be out loud.

"You didn't do this?" Winnie asked.

I shook my head.

"Do you know who did?"

I did. Having seen the video, I knew what Franklin's absence after dinner was all about. He'd spent the evening at the computer with Orson creating this small master-piece for my campaign.

I looked at Winnie and shrugged.

"Well, whoever did it is sure a good friend," she said.

I guess I should have told her it was Franklin. But I didn't want him to get conceited. Besides, he didn't put his name on it or anything. Maybe he wanted everybody to think I made it myself.

I didn't really believe that, but I had a lot of things to consider before I started passing out credit. Things like the UPs. Had they seen the video? Did they think it was awesome? Did they think I was awesome? Because if I didn't know me, I'd think I was awesome.

What the UPs thought had become very important to me. I mean, now they knew I existed. In fact, it was just about the most important thing in my world.

CHAPTER 40

The Dweeb Factor

Franklin met me at my locker before football practice. He was wearing Dad's old hockey jersey and a pair of shorts that hung down to his shin bones.

"Did you hear about the video, Howard?" he asked me.

"Oh, yeah," I told him. "Dino said it was cool!"

"Orson did a lot of it," he said.

"He's a smart kid. He gets that from me."

We walked through the heavy double-doors of the athletic building.

"You know," I said, "at first, this whole president thing seemed crazy. But you should have heard people today. I think I really might win."

Franklin nodded, but his face said he wasn't so sure.

"What? Don't you think I can win?"

He didn't answer, which worried me.

"Howard," he said, "what's a dweeb?"

"It's an insult. One of the worst," I told him.

"I see," he said. "What are its characteristics?"

"The usual. Smart, clumsy, non-athletic. Why?"

Franklin's eyes had that I'm-so-sorry look. It was the same look Mom had when she told me my turtle had run away and gone to live on a farm.

"I've been doing some polling, Howard," he said. "You are a dweeb."

A dweeb? I didn't need a poll to tell me that. And I sure didn't need my best friend to tell me that!

"I don't mean you actually are one! That's just your public image," Franklin continued. "The voters know your name. They like your message, but they're having a hard time accepting that their president could be, well, a dweeb."

The rush of energy I'd been feeling all day was gone. My body slumped ... dweebishly.

"You aren't a dweeb, Howard," Franklin added. "Dweebs are non-athletic. You play football."

"How would anybody know that?" I said. "I've never actually gotten on the field."

Franklin nodded.

"There is that," he said, and then we both got quiet.

I was numb through practice, which, if you're a blocking dummy, is not such a bad thing. But it didn't take away my misery. Here I was thinking I was getting popular when it turned out my freakishness had just found a wider audience.

People at school mentioned the video the next day but not nearly as many. Fame is short-lived. I asked Franklin if there was any change in the polls.

"No change," he said apologetically. "But there's a large group of undecideds out there."

Undecideds? What was there to decide? Whether I was a dweeb or a dork? Did it matter?

Why couldn't they just see me the way I was in the video? I mean, I controlled a giant rampaging robot! What more did they want in a president? What else could I do? It's not like handing them a campaign button that said **"DMMS: Powered by Howard"** was going to change their minds.

This wasn't a good day for politics anyway. We were playing the William Bonney Demons that afternoon, the biggest game of the year. It's the only thing anyone at school was talking about.

I ran into Winnie McKinney as she was leaving her algebra class.

"So," I said, "excited about the big game?"

I asked her because I thought it was mandatory. I'd heard other players saying it all day. They'd add a punch to the shoulder or some kind of primal grunt, but, as I was new at this, I stuck to the basics.

"I could take it or leave it," Winnie said. "I'm not really into football. I like wrestling but only the kind on TV. If you have to wrestle with rules, what's the point?"

That's the way I felt about it. Back in the lab, Franklin and I would play my Wrestling Pro-Extreme video game then have our own live-action match where we re-created the game moves. He was great because he was built pretty much like the wrestlers in the game, and he could do all the things they did. We even invented a move, the Stine Stainer, in which he'd pick me up over his head, fall backwards, and then drop kick me across the room. If performed properly, there would be nothing left of me except a gooey stain on the wall.

In case you're wondering, it was never performed properly. That's because we came up with the Howard Hypnotizer, a move that let me reverse the Stainer at the very last second. So, instead of me getting drop-kicked and becoming a stain, I hypnotized Franklin into unconsciousness. Then I would fall across his chest for the pin.

So far, I was undefeated.

"So, you're not coming to the game?" I asked Winnie.

"I don't know. I haven't thought about it," she said. "Why? Are you asking me to come?"

Asking her? Why would I do that? Like I was really going to say, "Hey Winnie, I'm going to be doing some tough, rugged bench-warming at the game today—and it would mean the world to have you there pulling for me!"

The truth was, I didn't even want to be at the game. Why would I want her there?

"Well, I . . ." I started.

"Hey there, How-Cool!" Crystal yelled as she came down the hall. "Come talk to us at the game today. Maybe we'll do a cheer just for you!"

"That sounds good," I said.

"Super! See ya, cutie!" she said with her electric light-up smile. "Oh, I almost forgot—do you have my English paper? Gross old Mr. Craven's going to ask for it sixth period."

"Yeah, I was going to give it to you at lunch."

"Awesome! And Chandra wants to know if you can help her make a potato clock? It sounds all sciencey, and I just knew you'd be good at it!"

I told her to tell Chandra that if she's got the time, I've got the potato.

"You are just the best. Bye!" Crystal said.

She bounded down the hall.

I turned to leave and bumped into Winnie. I'd forgotten that she was still behind me.

"Oh, hey," I said. "What were we talking about?"

"The game."

"Right, the game," I said.

Winnie rolled her eyes.

"I just hope you play William Bonney as well as she just played you," she said.

Then she gave me what was a pretty darn-good impression of a fake Crystal Arrington smile, and was gone.

CHAPTER
41

Game Changer

Everybody was at the game. And by everybody, I mean the bleachers were jammed with several generations of Dolley Madisonites and an even longer wall of humanity stretched down the sideline. The other side of the field was equally crowded with Demons and their Demon kin.

I saw Mom and Dad on the top row of the bleachers. I started to wave but decided it was too risky. The yearbook photographer had been roaming around, and I didn't want the only picture of me in my uniform to say "Howard Boward, number 27, waving at Mommy."

I had taken my usual place near the equipment manager as far away from the real players as possible. I didn't like to stand too close to my teammates because sometimes, when they were excited, they liked to hug people. This was a problem: most of my teammates were sweaty. I couldn't see any reason why I should have to take my second shower of the day just because someone else made a good play.

I usually didn't pay much attention to anything happening on the field, but this game was kind of interesting. The interesting part was that it involved a lot of numbers. I like numbers.

In the fourth quarter, with twenty-two seconds to go, the score was the Bonney Demons twenty-eight, the Madison Manatees twenty-four. Franklin had scored two touchdowns and kicked the only field goal. We had the ball on their thirty-yard line, and I knew Coach would call Franklin's number again.

Coach Fritz called our last timeout, and the offense gathered at the bench.

"We're going to run a pitch-left to Stine," I heard Coach tell them. "They'll be expecting a pass. Stine, find some daylight and head for the goal line. We're out of timeouts and there are just twenty-two ticks left on the clock, so if there's nothing there, make sure you get out of bounds!"

"OK, Coach," Franklin said and then he grabbed me by my jersey. "Come on, Howard."

The next few seconds were a nightmarish blur. I was actually being pulled out onto the football field! My cleats were barely touching the ground!

"Boward, get off the field!" Coach screamed.

"I can't!" I yelled back.

"Stay with me, Howard," Franklin said calmly.

When we reached the huddle, Franklin tapped Scott Smith, our fullback, on the shoulder.

"Howard is coming in for you, Scott," he said.

Scott Smith turned to run off the field, but Coach

screamed at him to go back to the huddle. I started to leave.

"Stay with me, Howard," Franklin said sternly, pressing down on my shoulder pads.

I didn't move.

We were out of timeouts. There was nothing Coach could do. Finally, he waved Scott off the field.

The huddle broke. Franklin planted me where I was supposed to stand—in a split formation about three yards to his right.

"Whatever happens, stay with me, Howard," Franklin said, and then he repeated the words deliberately. "Stay ... with ... me!"

I nodded. What choice did I have? He was the only reason I was on the field—the only reason I was on the team!

Kyle Stanford, our quarterback, called the signals.

"Hut! Hut! Hut!" he barked and the center snapped the ball.

"Follow me, Howard!" Franklin yelled.

He started running toward the left end and, like a puppy on a leash, I tagged along behind him. Kyle pitched the ball to Franklin and just when it looked like there might be an open hole, a behemoth-sized linebacker filled it. I had a very good view of what was happening—much better than the one I got from the bench.

With the hole plugged, I assumed Franklin would run out of bounds and stop the clock like Coach told him to. He didn't. What he did do was the last thing in the world I would expect anyone in any kind of athletic endeavor ever to do.

He tossed the ball to me.

Against my better judgment, I caught it.

"Stay with me, Howard!" he yelled.

Stay with him? That's how I'd gotten into this mess in the first place! This couldn't be happening!

For a second, everything, including my legs, moved in slow motion. I was half the size of anyone on William Bonney's side of the ball and a mountain of Demons was headed straight for me. Now, whether I actually heard Coach Fritz crying or just imagined it, I cannot say. All I know is, an instant later, the game resumed its normal, hyperactive speed and I heard the single loudest collision of my life.

Franklin had connected with the large linebacker blocking our path and sent him flying. The hole was open and I dutifully followed Franklin through it. Then I spied a cornerback approaching from the left. BAM! Franklin steamrolled him without breaking stride.

I felt like a chariot racer—my one job was to stay behind this horse and let him run! My teammates, who had initially been too stunned to move, were now tearing down the field and blocking anything in a red jersey. Franklin pulverized two more invaders, and I stayed on his hip. When we reached the ten-yard line, only the safety stood between us and the goal.

"It's all yours, Howard," Franklin called and he threw himself into the smaller defender.

It was like using a wrecking ball to open an egg.

The next ten yards were just for me. When I crossed the goal line, I thought hard about not stopping. There were, after all, a lot of large, unhappy Demons behind me. Then I heard the crowd. The eruption came at me like a wave, and I floated on an ocean of joy.

That's when they hit me. Hard. I went down and the ball went flying. It took me a minute to realize this assault was being committed by my own team! A second later, I was hoisted into the air and a parade of Manatees carried me off the field.

I, Howard Boward, had won the game!

The fact that my contribution was entirely involuntary didn't seem to matter. I had slain the Demon horde!

Even Coach smiled. I honestly didn't think his face was capable of that maneuver but darned if it wasn't there. Sure, we'd defied his authority and likely stripped years from his life—but hey, a win is a win.

Back in the locker room, for the first time since our encounter at the Beatdown Palace, I found myself nose to nose with Kyle Stanford.

"Boward!" he yelled and I'm pretty sure my hair turned a half-shade whiter.

I turned to face him, expecting to be eaten alive.

"Nice game," he said, slapping me on the side of my helmet. "There's a victory party at my house tonight. You be there!"

I couldn't believe it. Kyle Stanford and I were having a conversation—and it wasn't about how he was going to send me to the emergency room!

"OK," I said. "We will."

He shook his head.

"I said YOU. Leave that in its cage."

He was looking at Franklin. Apparently, Kyle hadn't forgotten about *everything* that happened at the Palace.

"Oh," I told him. "Well, I'll try."

I suppose "I'll try" could have meant "not without my buddy" or "I hope you choke on the guacamole dip," but it didn't. Kyle was an UP, so it meant "I'll be there."

CHAPTER 42

The Rise of How-Cool

I went to the party without Franklin. I wish I could say it was no fun without him, but that would be a lie. It's not that anything particularly fantastic happened—to be honest, I'd always pictured UP parties with fireworks and elaborate dance routines. There was nothing like that— but it was still amazing. It was amazing because I was there. Me! And everybody in sight wanted to shake the hand of How-Cool, the touchdown machine!

I'd gone from the bottom of the popularity ladder to rising star!

It was pretty late when Kyle's mom dropped me off at my house, but I saw there was a light on in the den. Dad was in there, as usual, but not in his usual way. By that I mean he wasn't wearing dorky pajama bottoms, and he didn't have some dumb monster movie on TV. Instead, he was just sitting there looking through some pictures in a folder.

They were pictures of bears.

"Hi, Dad," I said.

"You're home," he answered.

That was all he said. I kind of expected a "Hey, you're home, Champ!" or "How was the big UP party?" but it didn't look like he was in that kind of mood.

"Did you see me today? I made a touchdown," I said.

"I saw. Congratulations."

This was the least enthusiastic I had ever seen Dad when discussing sports.

"Franklin helped ... a little."

"I saw that too," Dad said. "Why didn't Franklin go with you to the party?"

"He wasn't invited."

"I see. Do you think it was right to go off to a party while you had a guest here at the house?"

I shrugged. "I can't spend every minute with Franklin."

For the first time since I'd entered the room, Dad looked up from his photos. His gaze stuck me like a dart.

"I like Franklin. He's a good kid," he said. "But you're the reason he's here, Howard."

If only Dad had known how true that was. I nodded my head, and he went back to his pictures.

"Are those pictures of Rollo?" I asked.

"Some of them are. The rest are of other bears out on that property."

I realized then that Dad's bad mood wasn't because I'd ditched Franklin. That didn't help, but the main thing was that he was worried about the bears. I picked up one of the

photos. It showed a gigantic, brown, vicious-looking creature with his mouth open in a full roar.

"That's one mean bear, huh, Dad?" I said.

He shook his head.

"It's just a bear," he told me. "Somebody's making him live in a world he doesn't belong in. Things are bound to go wrong."

The man who owned Rollo and the other bears couldn't have been very nice. I'd never met him, but I already knew I wouldn't like him. It didn't seem right for him to keep some big, old, furry creature around just for his own entertainment. The whole thing was unnatural.

"Who does this guy think he is?" I asked. "He's playing God with the animal kingdom!"

Dad gave me an uneasy look.

"Where'd you hear that expression?" he said.

I'd heard it a few times. The first was when I told Mr. Z my idea about switching one of the guinea pig's brains with Precious. Then the guinea pig would be able to talk and, more important, Precious wouldn't.

"I don't know, Howard," Mr. Z had told me. "I don't think a boy your age ought to be playing God."

I didn't ask him how old you had to be before it was OK

to play God, but I was pretty sure there weren't that many birthday candles in the world.

"I just heard it around," I told Dad.

He cocked an eyebrow then looked back at his pictures.

"The owner's not a bad guy," he said. "He's just never looked at things from the bears' point of view."

I said good night and headed upstairs to my bedroom. Franklin was already tucked in, and I kept the light off. But he wasn't asleep.

"Did you have a nice time at the party, Howard?"

If it was anyone else, I'd think he was only asking that to make me feel guilty. But not Franklin—he genuinely wanted to know. So I felt even guiltier.

"I guess so," I said.

"What do you want to do tomorrow, Howard?"

The voice in the darkness was asking a question that had been in the back of my brain since I left the party. Did I want to hang out with Franklin? Because that's what Franklin wanted—it's what he was made for.

Or—and this was purely hypothetical—did I want to hang out with the UPs?

I tried to imagine doing both—hanging out with Franklin and the UPs at the same time. But if I did, would I still be How-Cool? Or would I just be Big Frankie's dippy friend who was always tagging along? I didn't know. What I did know was that Josh and Kyle didn't like Franklin. That hadn't mattered a few hours earlier, but now they were two of my closest friends. Things could get awkward. What if I had to choose?

"I'll figure that out tomorrow, Franklin," I told him.

"Goodnight, Howard."

"Goodnight, Franklin," I said back at him, and then the silence between us got too loud. "Thanks for, you know ... today."

He was a good friend, the best I ever made. I rolled over and tried not to think about the future. Why worry? I was sure everything would work out between me and Franklin and the UPs. At least I hoped so.

How do you tell your monster you're moving on?

If you're going to have large, angry guys chase you around a field while you're carrying a pigskin, I recommend you do it before an election. My touchdown had been just enough to overcome my dweebishness.

I, Howard Boward, was class president.

It was a pretty cool experience, but it turns out the seventh-grade class president doesn't get any real power. He also doesn't get a sash. That was disappointing.

The only thing that really changed was that I had to attend a few meetings that first week and a couple of parties. I spent practically no time with Franklin. Somehow, I managed to spend more time with the UPs.

CHAPTER
43

A Brief Encounter

I was walking with Winnie McKinney to my English class when out of the corner of my eye I saw a set of feet. This naturally caught my attention. Feet normally have a floor under them.

These didn't. Turns out, the floating, blue sneakers belonged to Wendell Mullins, the kid from Franklin's gym class.

Dino and Kyle were holding him in mid-air.

"How-Cool!" Dino summoned me. "Come give us a hand!"

"What are you doing?" I asked.

"Gravity wedgie!" Kyle laughed.

A gravity wedgie, for the uninitiated, occurs when a small, helpless participant is held high in the air by two large, good-natured pranksters. Then a third prankster, equally good-natured if not more so, grabs the waist-band of the suspended figure and holds on for dear life. Ultimately, the hover-nerd is dropped, the underpants remain suspended, and gravity does the rest.

It's physics, beautiful in its way. Last year, Butch Thornton used me as his science fair project.

I'm kind of an expert on wedgies. As I recall, this version is not nearly as painful as the dreaded "puppet wedgie," a technique which requires the victim to be dropped from a high platform, such as the window of Mr. Furley's biology class. The subject—whoever that might be—is then left dangling puppet-like by his underpants until his mother sees him on her way back from taking Stick to the orthodontist.

I wouldn't wish the puppet wedgie on my worst enemy. But this was a gravity wedgie. Compared to the puppet thing, it was wholesome family fun.

I caught a glimpse of Wendell's eyes. He was squinting so they were almost impossible to see, but if there's one thing I can recognize, it's fear.

"Gee, guys," I said, stalling. "I really have to get to class. One more tardy slip, and they'll yank my library privileges."

"That's wimp-talk, Boward!" Kyle yelled. "I thought you were cool!"

Now let's be honest—Kyle never thought I was cool. But the message was clear: if I backed out now, I never would be. The next thing I knew, my hands were tightly gripping elastic and I was watching Wendell plummet. He seemed to fall forever before coming to an awkward, sudden stop.

I've got to admit I felt a momentary rush of power, and, for a single second, I understood the entertainment I'd been unknowingly providing for years. That thrill passed quickly. I couldn't see the familiar, startled expression I was sure was on Wendell's face—I was stationed on Wendell's opposite end—but I could see a face. It was Winnie McKinney's. She looked horrified. Without saying a word, she conveyed dismay, disappointment, and the dismembering of our friendship. My eyes followed her down the hall until they landed on another figure—this one much larger.

Franklin was looking at me. No, not at me—he was looking *through* me. I released the waistband.

"Are you all right, Wendell?" Franklin asked.

"Why wouldn't I be?" Wendell barked. "Just leave me alone!"

He didn't mean it. It's just what you say.

In case you're wondering, Franklin didn't ask me if I was all right. I mean, maybe I wasn't physically hurt, but I had just witnessed a particularly horrible gravity wedgie—the kind that can cause nightmares. And I'd seen it up close! A thing like that can scar you psychologically.

But he didn't say a word. He just turned and started walking away.

If he could've just kept walking, maybe everything would have been all right. But he couldn't because Kyle stepped in front of him.

"You think everything's your business, don't you, Freakshow?" Kyle snapped, grabbing Franklin by his shirt collar.

I knew then that Kyle had never gotten over being humiliated at the Palace. He had a score to settle.

Now, a gentler soul than Franklin Stine has never strolled the DMMS hallways. I believe that. And even then, he didn't actually shove Kyle. It was more of a persuasive redirection—Kyle was one place and Franklin moved him to another. But it was such an easy and peaceful action that I doubt there would have been any fuss at all if someone hadn't yelled, "You get your hands off my friend!"

I recognized the voice. It was mine. For several tense seconds, the words hung there with no one really sure who they were intended for. I mean, Kyle's hands were on Franklin and Franklin's hands were on Kyle. But then I saw Franklin's face and, for the first time, I knew who I'd been speaking to.

I knew because he knew.

The time had come for me to choose, and I'd chosen Kyle.

The minute I said the words, I felt sick and ashamed and empty. It was too late to take them back. People were watching—popular people.

Franklin let go of Kyle, and his eyes started to search me. Maybe he was trying to find something familiar, like whatever remained of the Howard who bought him a Gooshee and gave him a home. But Howard wasn't there. This was How-Cool. And at that moment, in those deep, black pupils where I'd seen that first glimmer of friendly recognition, someone turned out the light.

He walked away like something out of the movies, the

ones where the picture fades to black and the final credits roll. I watched as the heavy double doors that lead out of the building opened. When they closed again, Franklin was gone.

☆ ☆ ☆

"Boward!" Coach Fritz barked.

I jumped. The word sounded angry, but that didn't mean anything—Coach always sounded angry. As far as I could tell, Coach Fritz only had the one volume.

"Where's Stine?"

That was an interesting question—one I was wondering myself all afternoon. And now, thanks to the red-faced man with the whistle, so was everyone on the practice field. I couldn't actually see them staring at us because my helmet is two sizes too large and cuts off my peripheral vision. But the sudden silence let me know I had the squad's complete attention.

"There was sort of an emergency," I said, "and he left."

There's something I should tell you about Coach Fritz. The man's face is made of stone. He has these deep grooves in his forehead and around the sides of his mouth that have become permanently embedded after a lifetime of frowning. Only his eyes tell you what he's really feeling. The madder he gets, the more they bulge.

Currently, there was a real danger his pupils would knock me down and pin me to the grass.

"Where ... is ... he ... NOW?" Coach demanded.

"I don't know."

If you're not familiar with the sport, football is a game filled with penalties. I had just committed one.

"Every player has a job, Boward," Coach informed me. "Yours is simple—you get Stine here! When you fail to do your job, you hurt the team. Now gimme a lap!"

"But Coach ..."

"Two laps!"

I finished my three laps around the practice field. I know he only said to run two laps, but they tack on a third if you don't look like you're enjoying it. I wasn't. I wasn't enjoying anything about this day.

"Boward!" Coach screamed as I came off the field.

Then he moved in real close.

"Is he going to be here tomorrow?"

I could have told him I didn't know, but that would have meant more laps. There was only one answer that would get me back to the locker room.

"Yes, Coach," I said.

CHAPTER 44

Beware the Butt

When I got home, I was sweaty and I was mad and I was in no mood for some monster's nonsense. I'd been forced to do something I hate (run laps) at a place I didn't want to be (outside) while participating in a sport I'm terrible at (just pick one, it really doesn't matter).

I made a quick search of the house, but I didn't find Franklin. That wasn't a good sign because he's almost impossible to miss. Katie Beth was sitting in the kitchen.

"Have you seen Franklin?" I said.

"Why? Did you lose him?" she asked, then she took a bite out of her banana.

"Hey!" I said. "That's the last banana! What am I going to do for a snack?"

She shrugged. "You snooze, you lose."

Just great. First, I'd lost my monster; now I'd lost my favorite after-school snack. Why was losing the only thing I was good at?

"Oh, and Uncle Ben called," she said. "He wants you to call him back."

Uncle Ben? I didn't have time to talk to my uncle, there was a monster on the loose. I thought about the places I might go if I wanted to be alone.

"The lab!" I said to myself.

Of course, Franklin would be in the lab.

I rushed outside, slid open the garage door, and crawled through the tunnel. When I burst out of the dryer, I saw two large, owl-like eyes staring at me. Sitting there on the table with his clunky shoes and his white shirt buttoned all the way up to his chin was Reynolds Pipkin.

"Reynolds!" I yelled. "What are you doing here?"

"I like crawling through the tunnel," he said.

Oh, that's all I needed. My lab was an amusement park for people who wanted to be ants!

"I don't have time to deal with you right now, Reynolds. I'm looking for Franklin."

"He isn't here," Reynolds said.

"I know that! Don't tell me things I already know, Reynolds," I said. "If he comes here, tell him to wait for me. I've got to go inside and call my uncle."

I was turning to leave when Reynolds pulled something out of his pocket. It was a cell phone. Reynolds Pipkin had a cell phone? That was so unfair! Who was going to call Reynolds? I knew more people than Reynolds did! I seethed knowing Mom wouldn't let me have one until I turned sixteen.

"Give me that!" I said and snatched it from his hand.

I dialed Uncle Ben's number.

"Hi, Uncle Ben. It's Howard. You called me?"

"Franklin's here, Howard," Uncle Ben said.

I felt relief, which instantly turned to anger. I'd run laps!

"He's there? What's he doing there?"

"I'm not sure. I saw him just walking back and forth in front of the store so I told him to come inside. He hasn't said much. Did you two have a fight?"

"Sort of. I'm sorry about this, Uncle Ben. I'll come get the big doofus."

"Why don't you let me talk to him for a while, Howard? He's pretty upset. It might do you both good to let this blow over. Besides, it'll be nice to have some company around here for a change."

I wasn't so sure that was a good idea. Uncle Ben had limited experience with children and almost none with monsters. But I didn't really feel like getting into it with Franklin, not after what he'd put me through.

Uncle Ben said he'd call me later. I punched the "end" button on Reynolds's phone. It was a nice phone, thin and light and all sci-fi looking. Man, I wanted a phone of my own. If I had a cell phone, I could call people from anywhere. I wouldn't even need a reason! I'd just say, "Hey, it's Howard. Just wanted to call to say I'm out in my garage but it's totally cool because I have a cell phone." That would be sweet. I tried to think of someone else I could call.

"Oh, Crystal!" I said out loud. I needed to tell her I'd finished her math homework and she could pick it up at lunch tomorrow.

"Reynolds, can I make another call?" I asked.

He nodded.

I dialed Crystal's number, but it went to voicemail. I didn't leave a message. I'd see her at lunch anyway. I just wanted to know what it would be like to call a cheerleader on a cell. It felt right. Everything about having a cell phone felt right! I wondered how people carried them around with them all day. Were they bouncy? I slipped it into my pants pocket. Awesome. I barely even noticed it was there.

"I heard you and Franklin had a fight," Reynolds said.

"It wasn't a fight," I said. "It was Franklin being a baby. Anyway, how do you know about it?"

"I hear things," Reynolds said.

That was true. Reynolds did hear things. For someone who was friendless, he stayed surprisingly well-informed—probably because he had his own cell phone.

My mom was ruining my social life.

"Franklin is the blob you made from Wonder Putty, isn't he?" Reynolds said.

It's not the kind of question you'd expect to just come up out of the blue, yet it didn't shock me. This was Reynolds. Reynolds says weird things. It was obvious he knew. He knew when he stuffed Franklin under his kitchen sink. What was the point of denying it?

I nodded.

"I won't tell anybody," he said.

"I know. If you were going to tell somebody, you'd have done it before now," I said. "What I don't get is how a simple thing like making your own friend in a laboratory could become so complicated. It's like every second of my day has to be about Franklin. He's around when I'm with my family. He wants to be with me when I'm hanging out with the UPs. Today, I had to run three laps because of him. Don't get me wrong, Franklin's great and all, but some-times it's just too much."

It felt good to talk to somebody about it, even if it was Reynolds Pipkin. I reached into my pocket.

"Here's your phone back. Thanks."

I started to hand it to him when I noticed something—something almost too terrible to contemplate. The phone was on—and by on, I mean connected.

I had butt-dialed!

CHAPTER 45

Blackmail in Purple Socks

Now I knew why my parents wouldn't let me have a cell phone. I couldn't handle the responsibility. I had butt-dialed Crystal Arrington!

If, like me, you don't have your own cell phone, you might not be familiar with the devastating act known as the butt-dial. It happens when you stick the phone in your pocket and then bump up against something that causes your butt to redial the last number you called.

In this case, that was Crystal. How much had she heard? If it went to her voicemail, it could have been everything! But there was no way to know until I saw her the next day at school.

This was all Reynolds's fault—him and his stupid cell phone!

I rushed inside and called Uncle Ben on a good, old, reliable land line and told him I needed to talk to Franklin. He put him on the phone.

"Franklin, we need to talk. Urgently!"

I couldn't go into specifics with my family all over the place, but I wanted him to know this was an emergency. But I was getting nowhere—all I heard on the other end was silence. Just when I was about to tell Franklin to stop being a supersized whiner, I heard Uncle Ben say—

"The words come out the other end, Franklin. You have to put it against your ear."

I forgot that Franklin had never talked on a phone before.

"Franklin Stine speaking," he said so loudly I'm not sure we even needed a phone.

"Come home," I told him. "We have things we need to discuss."

"No, Howard."

"But you don't understand," I told him.

"I do understand, Howard. I was there."

"Wait a minute," I said. "Are you talking about what happened at school today? Because I don't care about that."

It was the worst thing I could have said. All I meant was I didn't care about it right at that moment because my butt had just handed us a much bigger problem. Only that's not the way it sounded to Franklin.

To Franklin, it sounded like "I don't care."

"I'll be staying here tonight. Your uncle has invited me. Please tell your family so they don't worry. Goodbye, Howard."

The line went dead.

The night passed like cold syrup from a sticky spout. Drip, drip, drip. I wished Franklin's bed wasn't right across from mine. It's easier to stare at an empty wall than at an empty bed where someone is supposed to be. When the sun came up and people were around, I knew I'd go right back to being mad at Franklin for being mad at me. But here in the quiet, it seemed like maybe he had a right to be mad. Maybe Wendell and Winnie did too.

I remembered how when Franklin first moved into my room, it felt crowded. Now it just felt lonely.

☆ ☆ ☆

I didn't have any classes with Crystal in the morning so all I had to do was dodge her in the halls. She hadn't hunted me down or anything, so that was a good sign. Maybe she never got the message. Maybe the phone dialed after I'd finished talking. I'd know soon enough. It was almost lunch time.

The bell rang.

Franklin hadn't been in homeroom, and I didn't see him in the cafeteria. I didn't see Crystal either, and I was hoping to keep it that way. I wanted to eat and run literally. But the lunch line had never moved slower. It's true we were all dreading the creamed, chipped beef-on-a-bun, but when you've got to go through something unpleasant, it's best to get it over with quickly.

Hadn't these people ever pulled off a Band-aid?

I sat down in my old chair on the back table. It was a

nice, out-of-the-way spot for eating alone. I had just stuffed my mouth with an unnaturally huge wad of mashed potatoes when I heard the voice.

"No ... way!"

Even looking down I could make out the trendy, tan, lace-up shoes that appeared to be wearing little brown saddles. These were Crystal's feet.

She knew.

"Now it all makes sense!" she squealed. "The hair! The fangs! The tail!"

"Crystal, it's not what you ... wait a minute, you know about the tail?"

"Everybody knows about the tail," she said dismissively. "He's in gym class for Pete's sake!"

My worst nightmare was becoming a reality. I struggled for damage control.

"Look, I don't know what you're thinking but ..."

"Of course!" she yelled. "That's why Franklin said you were a scientific genius! Well, obviously! Duh!"

I felt the walls caving in on my secret world. Things were crumbling quickly—and publicly.

"Please, not so loud, Crystal!" I begged. "That call was a huge mistake! This is not something I want people knowing about. Have you seen the movie *Frankenstein*? Villagers! Torches! It gets ugly."

She wasn't listening, but her eyes sparkled like neon

glitter. Even though I knew the words were coming, I could not prepare myself for their impact.

"Make me one!" she screamed.

I looked at her. She was giddy.

"What?" I said, feeling queasy.

"Make me one! Make me a Franklin, a monster, whatever you call it! I want one!"

This could not be happening! I shooshed her and looked around to see if anyone else was listening.

"Crystal," I whispered, "I know that sounds like a great idea but it's not that easy."

"Sure it is! I mean, it is for you, 'cuz you're a genius, right? So you go make me a Crystal companion and this stays our little secret. No villagers, no torches, no angry mobs looking for dear ol' Franklin. You'll do that for me, won't you, How-Cool?"

She chose that moment to reach out and grab my hand, and, I'm almost certain, shoot some kind of mind-control beam out of her corneas. There is simply no other explanation for the unspeakable word that came out of my mouth next.

"Yes," I said.

"Awesome!" she squealed, and she hugged me in what will undoubtedly go down as one of the most wonderful and agonizing moments of my life.

There was no escape. I was in too deep. I sighed and explained that I'd need a little of her hair. Without hesitation, she plucked a couple of brown beauties from her scalp.

"Now you can't tell anybody about this. Nobody," I reminded her.

"I know, stop worrying!" she said and then floated off to class. I could almost see the vision of a bouncing baby-monster dancing in her head.

CHAPTER
46

The Pit

The walk home from school that day was excruciating for two reasons: first, because my secret was in the hands of the biggest gossip ever to have a FaceSpace membership; and second, because I had to run five laps around the practice field.

That was the penalty for not having Franklin there two days in a row.

"You do know the city championship is tomorrow?" Coach Fritz said.

His temples were throbbing.

"Yes, Coach," I answered.

"We're game-planning, son! What do you think is going to happen tomorrow if our best weapon doesn't know the plays?"

It was a ridiculous question. Franklin didn't need to know the plays. When it was time to run, he ran. When it was time to tackle, he grabbed somebody. He was an absolutely instinctive football machine. But that's not what the coach wanted to hear.

"He'll be ready," I said.

When I'd finished my laps, all I wanted to do was go home, crawl in the tub, and pack my aching body in a thousand popsicles. But I had a stop to make first.

☆ ☆ ☆

The Vietnamese donut shop had been closed for hours, but the air still smelled good enough to eat. I walked into Uncle Ben's store. Uncle Ben was standing behind the counter, but the one I really came to see was across the room sweeping the floor.

"Greetings, Uncle Ben," I said in a formal voice. I thought that would make it more punishing when I deliberately shunned Franklin.

"Hail, good nephew!" Uncle Ben replied. He might have been making fun of me.

Then, after glancing at Franklin and then back at me, he said, "Well, I've got some things to do in the back. I'm sure you boys have some catching up to do."

He picked up a black notebook and walked out of the room.

I looked at Franklin. He didn't look at me. This wasn't going to be easy.

"I hope you're happy," I said at last because it seemed as good a conversation starter as any. "I had to run five laps today because you weren't at football practice! I walked three of them, but still, it was terrible!"

"Hello, Howard," Franklin said without looking up from his sweeping.

"Well?" I asked.

"Well what, Howard?"

"If you have something to say to me, this would be the time to do it," I told him.

He moved slowly through the store, a pouting hulk in a faded blue button-down tucked into torn jeans. But his only response was the steady swish of the broom against the white-tiled floor. It was annoying.

"Franklin, would you stop sweeping for a minute?"

"Why did you come here, Howard?"

A dozen reasons tried to rush out of my mouth at once, but the only one that made it was, "I came to take you home!"

"*Your* home?"

"Well, duh!" I said.

"Why, Howard?"

"Because you belong there!"

To me, that seemed like the right thing to say. Who doesn't want to belong some place? But Franklin just kept sweeping.

"Like your bike belongs there? Like your computer belongs there?"

"Right," I said. "Let's go."

I couldn't imagine what was wrong with that answer. Of course like my bike and computer! He belonged there like the TV and the dogs and Precious and Orson and Katie Beth. Heck, he belonged there more than Stick. Stick belonged there like the ugly carpet in the den — it's part of the house, but you're always hoping we'll replace it with something better.

"I thought so," Franklin said.

I rolled my eyes.

"Look, I know I didn't handle things all that great with you and Kyle Stanford," I said.

"And Wendell?"

"Wendell either."

I cringed when I remembered Wendell dangling there in mid-air.

"Look, Franklin, there's still a lot of stuff you don't understand about middle school," I said. "Sometimes things seem like they're mean ... OK, maybe they are mean ... but that's just how kids act."

"Is that how the class president acts?"

That was low. He'd kicked me right in the seat of power.

"What do you want from me, Franklin?" I asked impatiently. "I know I hurt your feelings, and I'm sorry. Do you want me to say I was wrong? OK, I was wrong. Do you want me to say we'll spend more time together? We'll spend more time together. Do you want me to say we're still best friends? Fine, we're still best friends. Are you happy now?"

That's when Franklin gave me the strangest look. It wasn't exactly sadness. It was more like pity.

"Howard, do you think I left because I thought you didn't want to be my friend anymore?" he asked.

"Didn't you?" I said.

"No, Howard. I left because I don't want to be your friend anymore."

There's a reason it's called the pit of your stomach. It's deep and dark, and you put things there that you hope to never feel again. That's where Franklin's words were going. I could tell because my gut burned like the red ashes in a fireplace.

He turned his eyes from me and went back to sweeping.

"You don't want to be my friend anymore?" I asked more quietly than I intended.

He didn't answer. His silence went into the pit too. I'd spent twelve years wondering why it was so hard to make a friend. But the joke was on me. It was a whole lot harder to lose one.

"All right," I told him. "If that's how you feel … I guess we're not friends."

I watched his face to see if maybe he'd changed his mind, but I didn't really think it would happen. I mean, if being my friend was such a great job, how come nobody wanted it before Franklin came along?

I turned to leave, and then I remembered something. Crystal!

"Franklin!" I said, whirling around frantically. "You've got to come home! You've got to come home now!"

"Howard …"

"No, no, no. This isn't about us being friends," I told him. "Crystal knows!"

Franklin looked confused.

"Crystal knows what?" he asked.

"Everything! She knows about you! She knows about me! She knows about the lab!"

"How?"

"Butt-dial!"

"What's a—"

"Never mind!" I yelled. "The important thing is that she knows and she's got a big mouth! That's why you've got to come home where I can protect you."

"Protect me from what, Howard?" he said.

"How should I know? Villagers, torches, pitchforks—that's how they do it in the movies! Or maybe they'd just want to study you, like a fungus under a microscope."

Franklin's eyes widened.

"Would they do that, Howard?"

"They're not going to do anything," I said. "I just have to do Crystal a favor. And if I have to do her a hundred favors, that's what I'll do. But we'll all be a lot safer with you back at the house."

Franklin stopped sweeping.

"All?" he asked.

"Right, all of us," I said. "You, me, Mom, Dad, Uncle Ben. They'd come after all of us. But you're the one I'm worried about. So come on!"

Franklin slowly walked to the corner of the room and propped the broom up against the wall. He looked worried. He waited for a minute then rushed past me without looking in my direction.

"I have to get out of here, Howard."

"What? Where are you going?"

"I have to go!"

In a flash, he was out the door, moving fast and smooth like only he could. I ran outside.

"Franklin! Franklin!" I yelled.

It was too late. He was gone.

Uncle Ben came out of the back room.

"He'll be back," he said. "You're his best friend."

Only I wasn't. Not anymore.

CHAPTER
47

The Trouble with Secrets

Normally my "prey-dar" kicks in the second I step on school grounds, but my troubles must have distracted me. By the time I sensed the predator, a large sleeve-covered arm already had my skull in a bone-crunching headlock.

"Hey, Boward!" Josh Gutierrez said, rubbing his knuckles violently into the place where I keep my brain. "I heard about what you're doing for Crystal. I'm in."

"Ow!" I said. "What are you talking about?"

He stopped mid-noogie and freed me from his underarm.

"I'm in. You know, that thing you're making for her. I want one too."

It wasn't a request. Josh was placing an order.

"No, Josh!" I pleaded. "You don't know what you're asking. I can't! It can't be done."

He reached into the back pocket of his cargo pants and handed me a black, plastic comb.

"She said you'd need hair. Take it out of there but I want that comb back. It was a gift."

He punched me hard in the shoulder the way a friend punches a pal. It hurt just like a regular punch but with less emotional bruising.

"Big game today! Go Manatees!" Josh howled.

He strutted down the hall and disappeared into a crowd of adoring fans.

How had things gone so wrong? I was now being pressured to create two new monsters, and I couldn't find the one I already had. It was a disaster. I had to track down Crystal fast and stop her before she opened her mouth again.

Like that was even possible. To stop Crystal Arrington from blabbing a secret this big, I would've needed a time machine. I knew that the minute Joni Jackson stopped me in the hall.

"Are you Howard?" Joni said. "You're Howard-something, right?"

"I'm Howard Boward," I said, wondering how I'd managed to go to school with someone since kindergarten yet remain completely invisible to them.

"Howard Boward!" she squealed. "I was going to vote for you for president, only I forgot."

My electoral victory was losing prestige by the second.

"Can I help you?" I asked.

"OK, it's like I heard you're making these friend-thingees for Crystal and Josh and Dino and Missi and, well, I want one too."

My stomach ached. Somewhere between the school entrance and homeroom I'd become Monsters 'R Us.

I looked at Joni. She was short with four holes in each ear, not counting the two God gave her, and in each hole was a shiny ring. Her jet-black pony tail was as long as an actual pony's, and her dimples screamed "I'm perky!"

"Who is telling you this?" I gasped.

"Well, Crystal told Missi, Missi told Dino, Dino told Josh, and Josh told me. I'm Josh's girlfriend. OK, not officially, but I told him I will be if you'll make me a monster. So am I Josh's girlfriend or not?"

Oh, great—just what I needed! On top of everything, I now had to worry about wrecking Josh Gutierrez's love life. It was no use arguing. The blank stare told me that whatever I said would go right in one ear and out the various holes in the other.

I rolled my eyes, took a deep breath, and pocketed some of Joni's ponytail.

By lunch, I had orders for six monsters in all. I spent the rest of the day avoiding all human eye contact. But I would have given anything for the non-human kind. I missed Franklin.

It had been a miserable day. The only person at school who could have cheered me up was Winnie McKinney—at least she and Franklin had the same smile—but she wasn't speaking to me. I've made a lot of people mad in my time, but when I wedgied Wendell, Winnie reached a shade of red previously seen only on tomatoes. So I was keeping my distance. But when I caught a glimpse of her coming out of fourth-period science with Kyle Stanford and Dino Lincoln, they were all laughing. I took that as a good sign.

"Hi, Winnie," I said, giving her a nice, friendly wave.

Dino mistook my upraised hand for a sign of coolness and slapped it. It stung, but I finally understood the appeal of the high-five. He trotted off down the hall.

Winnie walked by me like I didn't exist.

"Hey!" I said. "Why are you mad at me and not at Dino and Kyle?"

She stopped, whirled around, and gave me a look as cold as liquid nitrogen.

"You really don't see it, do you, Howard?"

I shrugged. Of the three perpetrators of this wedgie, I had definitely played the smallest part. It seemed to me Dino and Kyle should have been in way more trouble.

"What they did was stupid, but what you did was cruel. It was cruel because you know what it feels like!"

She was right. You can get away with stupid. Stupid means you don't know any better. But I knew. I'd been on the other side of that elastic waistband more times than I wanted to remember.

Winnie turned and stormed away. She was gone—just like Franklin.

At that moment, I wished that undergarment designer Arthur Kneibler had never invented tighty-whiteys. Those things had caused me nothing but trouble.

CHAPTER
48

Field of Screams

My after-school encounter with Coach Fritz did not go well.
His star player, the one who looked like he was born to
stand on top of a championship trophy, was still missing.
Since Franklin had not returned the coach's many tele-
phone calls, I was the last hope for getting him to the
game.

I had, in the coach's words, "let the team down."

From the agony in his voice, I just naturally assumed
we'd forfeit. Well, not so much assumed as hoped. When
it comes to sports, my motto is, "Just give up—there's no
shame in quitting before you embarrass yourself." But
apparently Coach doesn't see it that way.

What I hadn't realized is that, even without Franklin,
the Madison Manatees were a pretty decent football team.
With only fifty-eight seconds left in the fourth quarter, we
led the undefeated Wolverton Cubs twenty-one to twenty.
The city championship was in reach.

We even had the ball for one more play. It was fourth

down, and we were on our own end of the field, which made it a punting situation. Still, the game was ours to lose. All we needed was one, maybe two stops on defense—do that and it's over. From my usual place on the sideline, I could sense "pep" that went way beyond what they're always forcing down our throats at those rallies in the gym. The fans' cheers were louder, the sports drink was sweeter, Coach Fritz's screaming was, well, not happy, but definitely less terrifying.

Sure, I had loads of trouble off the field, but in terms of my athletic life, this was about as good as it could get. I mean, who'd have ever thought I could be on a city championship team? Then, out of the corner of my eye, I saw Carson Beggs coming off the field. He was limping.

"Let me see it, Beggs!" Coach said, bending down and examining the treasonous leg. "It looks like a cramp. Sit down and let the trainer work on it."

He did. Meanwhile, the punt team ran onto the field.

Coach Fritz turned to Assistant Coach Lopez and said, "We need somebody to go in for Beggs."

Coach Lopez was younger than Coach Fritz. Coach Lopez had more hair and more patience and he smiled more. Of course, if he smiled once a season, that was more than Coach Fritz. But even by normal human standards, Coach Lopez flashed a respectable amount of teeth. That's probably why I didn't automatically turn away when he was scanning the sideline in search of a body—any body—that could give him just one play.

I say "any body" because, on this particular substitution, Coach didn't have to be especially picky. Carson's position was in the backfield, and his job was to slow down anyone who got through the line to try to block the punt.

Only Wolverton wasn't trying to block the punt. They were setting up for a punt return. That meant their players would be falling back to block instead of rushing. With no one breaking through the line, Carson's replacement would just need to stand there and take up space.

Not to brag, but that's sort of my specialty.

I looked at Coach Lopez and smiled, but not for the reason you might think. I smiled because I was absolutely certain there wasn't a chance in a million he'd pick me. After all, I'd only been in an actual game for one play all season.

Little did I know that one play would come back to haunt me.

You see, that play had come at a terrible cost: it had made me famous. I don't mean famous with the coaches. They knew I'd only scored because of Franklin. I mean famous with the fans. For completely logic-denying reasons, they were thrilled by my amazing tackle-defying, monster-following, touchdown-making abilities.

So I guess it shouldn't have been a huge surprise when, with less than a minute on the clock and the lead in our pocket, a chant began to drift over from the bleachers. It was quiet at first: "How-ard, How-ard."

But then it gained strength: "HOW-ard! HOW-ard! HOW-ard!"

My initial hope was that they were just trying to get my attention, like to let me know I had something stuck in my teeth or that my shoulder pads were on backwards. But no. The second I realized what was happening, I tried to hide.

A football sideline doesn't offer much cover.

The coaches looked at each other. Perhaps Coach Fritz heard the happy chant of the crowd, and like the Grinch he so much resembled, felt his small heart grow three sizes that day.

I'll never know for sure.

"One play," he said. "Just one and he's out of there."

Coach Lopez laughed. "Boward, you're in!"

In? No! In was the last place I wanted to be. That field was filled with monsters, and I wasn't going anywhere near it without mine! But I had no choice. The coach had spoken. I picked up my helmet, which I'd been using as a portable seat, and put it on.

"We're punting out of bounds," Coach whispered. "They won't get a return so you won't be tackling anybody. Your job is to do nothing and then get off the field. Got it?"

"I'll do nothing," I pledged and ran toward the huddle.

At the sight of me, the crowd went off like a fireworks display.

Our linemen spread out across the thirty-four-yard line. I found a nice secluded spot about five yards behind them. The punter, Jeff Miller, was farther back and to my left.

"Don't do anything, Howard," I motivated myself.

"HUT!" Jeff yelled.

If you're new to this game, *hut* is the word they call out when they want the center to snap the ball. I'm not sure why they say, "Hut." Maybe it's to confuse the defense.

Personally, I've always thought if they really wanted to fool the other team, they'd have the punter point to the sky and yell, "Aliens!"

Now, that's what I'd call razzle-dazzle.

Anyway, when the center heard the meaningless word "Hut," he snapped the ball to the punter. And by "to the punter," I mean nowhere near the punter. For some reason, instead of going to Jeff, the ball rolled across the ground and landed at my feet.

"Pick it up!" Jeff yelled.

Don't do anything! I reminded myself.

"Pick it up!"

In a moment of pressure-packed insanity, I did.

I remember catching a glimpse of the sideline and seeing Coach Fritz's face. It was completely white like he'd just suffered some traumatic, life-changing experience and might faint at any moment. The next thing I remember is hearing someone yell "Run!" This was the most unnecessary piece of advice I had ever received. A Wolverton Cub of considerable size was headed straight for me. From that point on, instinct took over.

When you've encountered as many bullies as I have, you learn to flee at the first sign of attack. I am not fast, but I am slippery. Using the skills that had gotten me through so many recesses, I passed the line of scrimmage weaving and dodging away from anyone who looked like a threat. When I crossed midfield, I noticed my teammates were clearing a path for my escape. I took it, running past Cubs and Manatees and referees and cheerleaders until I had reached the thirty-yard line, the twenty-yard line, the ten—and that's when I saw him.

The punt returner—the last Wolverton player between me and the end zone—was standing on the five yard-line. He was big and kind of fierce-looking, and he eyed me like a rodeo bull eyes a clown. Quickly, I considered the possibilities. On the one hand, I might score. On the other hand, he might pile-drive me into the ground and make me eat yard-line chalk.

I've never tasted yard-line chalk, but if it's anything like regular chalk, no thank you.

So I did what any red-blooded, American nerd would do. I turned around and ran. This was not a conscious decision. I was running on instinct and adrenaline. This was about survival. I snaked my way back through the same giants I had avoided on my initial journey. Only this time, the strangest thing happened—it was the Wolverton players who were blocking a path for me, throwing their massive bodies in front of my own teammates who were desperately trying to tackle me.

Once again, I crossed midfield, only this time in the wrong direction, and reached the thirty, the twenty...

In case you're wondering, no, I did not run into our own end zone. Give me a little credit. Even in my frenzied state, I wouldn't score points for the other team. All I wanted was to find a nice, safe place to fall down without a pile of large, sweaty bodies ending up on top of me.

"Out of bounds!" I heard a voice from the sideline call. "Run out of bounds!"

It sounded like Winnie's voice—the voice of sweet salvation. Of course! Out of bounds—the coward's way out. No one could hit me if I ran out of bounds

I turned at a ninety-degree angle and headed for the sideline. I vaguely remember a loud, panicked "NO!" coming from the general direction of Coach Fritz, but it was too late. My foot stepped out at our own fifteen-yard line.

One play later, with four seconds left on the clock, the Wolverton kicker hit the field goal that gave his team the city championship. It was quite a kick—not only did it clear the goal post, it knocked me all the way off the Dolley Madison Middle School popularity ladder.

☆ ☆ ☆

Looking back, I realized it wasn't Winnie who told me to run out of bounds. I have no idea who it was, but I'm almost positive they were rooting for Wolverton. It might have been helpful to think of that sooner. The only thing that mattered now was that I had lost the game, I had lost the city championship, and I was surrounded by a horde of murderous Manatees. They wanted to return my helmet to the equipment manager with my head still in it. One word from Coach Fritz about my epic flub and they'd be on me. There was no out-of-bounds in the locker room.

I backed away from the team until I felt my legs bump against the heavy wooden bench that ran the length of the wall. I fell back onto it. That's when the crowd divided, and I saw Coach coming straight at me. He reached out his hand and I could almost feel his powerful fingers gripping my throat, but they didn't. Instead, they landed on my shoulder and he gave it a squeeze.

I still don't understand why he saved me. All I know is he stood there with his hand on my shoulder speaking more calmly than I'd ever heard him. He wasn't talking to me. He wasn't even talking about me. He was just addressing his team. But the fact that he chose to stay right there not shunning me, not physically assaulting me, sent the kind of message you just can't say with words.

"I'm proud of you. I'm proud of every one of you," he told us. "I'm proud because we won as a team and we lost as a team. It was a great season. When you lose a tough game, you can look back and wonder what would have happened if so-and-so caught one more pass, or this guy got one more block, or that guy made one more tackle. But that's not what winners do. Winners look in the mirror and say what would have happened if I caught one more pass, or I threw one more block, or I made one more tackle. Winners don't blame other people, they just try to be a little bit better next time. Mark my words, men, there's going to be a next time. This is a great team. This is a team of winners!"

With those words, Coach slapped me on the back—probably not nearly as hard as he wanted to. The whole team started to howl and yelp and slam their helmets together. Forget what the scoreboard said—we were winners, every one of us! Even the scared kid who ran the wrong way!

I savored the moment because I was going to be dead as soon as this speech wore off.

CHAPTER
49

Making New
Friends

When I got home, I called Uncle Ben. He hadn't seen
Franklin, but he said he'd keep looking. We agreed not to
tell Mom he was missing because the first thing she'd do
is call the police. I like the police and all, but if I had to
answer a bunch of questions, things could get ugly. You'd
be surprised how fast "looking for a lost kid" can become
"hunting down a monster."

I'm pretty sure those are handled by completely
different departments.

Of course, if I didn't give Crystal and the UPs what they
wanted, Mom and the police and everyone else would find
out soon enough. I couldn't let that happen. I couldn't let
them turn Franklin into some kind of freak. There was
no use putting it off. When everyone had gone to sleep, I
quietly slipped out to the lab.

I suppose I should have been shocked to find Reynolds there waiting for me, but I wasn't. Pipkins are nocturnal creatures.

"If you're going to stay here, Reynolds, you have to be my lab assistant," I told him.

He looked confused.

"But you fired me," he said, which was true.

"That was a mistake. I see now that the best way to deal with your incompetence is to promote you. Reynolds Pipkin, you are hereby promoted to *chief* lab assistant."

Reynolds's eyes grew wide, and his face broke out in what I can only describe as a smile with training wheels. It was creepy.

Not that I was complaining. If you watch any of the old monster movies, you know that dedication and creepiness are the two most important parts of a good lab assistant. Reynolds had both. Besides I needed him. I had six new friends to make and only one night to make them.

☆ ☆ ☆

A good scientist is always looking for new and better ways to do things. With this in mind, I took steps to streamline the monster-making operation. That's the great thing about having a lab full of stored junk. When you need handy building materials, they're as close as the nearest box.

Using parts from an old bicycle and gears from a broken lawnmower, Reynolds and I set up a primitive-looking conveyor belt to move the goo through its various stages. Meanwhile, I gathered up the bits of fur and claws and animal grossness left over from the lab explosion that created Franklin.

A good scientist never lets anything go to waste.

We were doing pretty well considering I hadn't even made up my mind whether to go through with this scheme until I was walking home from the game. I'd been debating it in my head ever since Crystal decided monsters were collectible. I didn't know what to do—then I saw the sign in the window of the Super Bargain Mart. It said they were having a sale … on Wonder Putty! Right there in the parking lot, I took out a pencil and paper and started a list.

Lists, I've found, are the best way to make any tough decision. My list was divided into two parts. Part one was—

Reasons This Is a Bad Idea:

1. Not sure how I did it the first time.
2. Greatly increases the chance of getting in trouble.
3. If God wanted more monsters, Stick would've been twins.
4. It's not like UPs don't have enough friends already.
5. They'll probably just run away from me — like all my other monsters.

And part two was—

Reasons This Is a Good Idea:

1. If I don't do it, Crystal is going to tell on me.
2. Might make the UPs forget that I lost the big game.
3. Franklin won't be hunted down by angry villagers with torches and pitchforks.
4. Wonder Putty is 25 percent off!
5. If the new batch turns out like Franklin — what's so bad about that?

I thought about Franklin out there roaming the streets all alone. That's when I realized something: Franklin was always alone. He wasn't always by himself, but there wasn't anyone like him in the whole world. That made him special. But did it also make him lonely?

"Franklin won't be alone," I wrote on the list. That was the clincher. I walked inside the store and bought six packages of Wonder Putty.

Back at the lab, I pulled the Wonder Putty out of the brown paper shopping bag, opened the containers, and placed the small pink blobs on the conveyor belt. In each blob, I wrapped a single strand of hair given to me by the UPs. Reynolds sprinkled the animal DNA generously over the wads of goo while I sprayed them with the mysterious O.G.R.E. formula, just as I'd done with Franklin. Finally, I lowered the electrical arc from the rafters and positioned it above the conveyor belt.

"Assistant, assume your station!" I yelled.

Reynolds took his place on the half-bicycle contraption we'd built at the end of the table.

"Initiate substance conveyance!" I said.

"What?" Reynolds asked.

"The conveyance!"

He blinked.

"Just pedal the bike, Reynolds," I sighed.

Good help was so hard to find.

He began slowly rotating the pedals, causing the conveyor belt to push the tiny goo-wads through the electrification process. Smoke erupted, sparks flew, blobs enlarged and contorted.

"Cover your eyes, Reynolds!" I yelled as flashes of unearthly lightning flew through the lab.

But Reynolds didn't cover his eyes. He stood there with his mouth open. The entire incredible process was happening right in front of him like a fantastic TV show being broadcast on the tiny reflections in his glasses.

I rushed forward and inserted logic boards and access ports into the still-forming figures.

"Now, the cable," I demanded, but Reynolds wasn't listening.

I clapped my hands. "The cable!"

"Oh, sorry," he said and brought me the long cable from the laptop.

I connected it to the first port.

"Download information," I ordered, and Reynolds pushed "Enter."

We transferred human anatomy data to each of the blobs—male for those going to the boy UPs, female for the girls. While the shapeless wads took form, Reynolds and I dug through boxes of old clothes so that when they started to look more like people than goo, they'd be, well, dressed for it.

☆ ☆ ☆

Because of the streamlined process, the new creatures developed much faster than Franklin. After an hour, they had faces and were roaming around the room. After two, they were beginning to grow fur. We spent the rest of the night downloading information the creatures would need before they'd be ready to join their new best friends.

It was almost sunrise. Even though it was Saturday, someone would notice if I wasn't in my room. I left the creatures to finish forming on their own and followed Reynolds out the tunnel.

"You can't tell anybody about this, Reynolds," I said. "I mean nobody."

"Can I tell Franklin?" he asked.

The question stung. If there was anybody in the world who needed to know about this, it was Franklin.

"You know Franklin's missing."

"Oh … right," Reynolds said. "I just meant if I ran into him anywhere. You never know about these things."

Since odd was normal for Reynolds, I thought nothing of the look on his face. Besides, I was too tired to dig for the deeper meaning inside his ant-mound of a brain.

"Go home, Reynolds," I said, and I turned and headed into my house.

CHAPTER
50

Creature
Discomforts

I slept for a few hours then went down to the kitchen for brunch. That's what I call it when I eat a bowl of cereal at lunchtime. I scarfed down my heaping bowl of Choco-Socco's and was in the middle of a huge yawn when Stick walked in.

"What are you so tired for?" he asked.

Stick was wearing his black T-shirt with the Batman symbol on the front, which always irritated me. Like Stick could be Batman!

"No reason. I just didn't get much sleep."

"Not much sleep?" he said. "You just got up ten minutes ago!"

"I meant I didn't get much *good* sleep. I had a nightmare about having the world's creepiest brother."

He punched me in the arm muscle with his knuckles. It turned beet red.

"Dad!" I yelled.

"Did you deserve it?" Dad yelled back from the living room.

Stick scrunched up his nose and smirked.

In case you're wondering, leaving six brand-new monsters unattended in a laboratory is not a good idea. The place was a wreck. Beakers and test tubes were broken, the lab table was turned upside down, and one of them was wearing the electrical arc antennas on his head.

The good news was that the monsters were fully formed now, each of them unique and individual in ways I never imagined. The biggest one, for example, had a muzzle mouth and a flat nose, kind of like a gorilla, but his eyes were warm and bright like Dino's. One of the girls—or "creaturettes" as I called them—had a red beehive hairdo, and she held her arms in front of her chest like the forelimbs of a bat.

They were all as different as they could be, and yet every single one of them reminded me of Franklin. I looked around the room and realized it didn't matter if I made six

friends or sixty or six thousand. They weren't the friend I wanted. He was gone.

"You don't know it, but you've got a big brother out there," I told the ghoulish group. "I don't mean like my big brother. This one's awesome. I hope you meet him someday."

I don't think any of them had the slightest idea what I was talking about, but Franklin would. And it felt good just knowing that.

I felt like a cowboy watching over my monster herd. When one got too close to the exit tunnel, I'd corral it and send it lumbering back in the other direction. My goal was just to keep them from breaking things until I could deliver them to their new best buds.

"FaceSpace!" I yelled. I couldn't believe I'd forgotten. I still needed to download the FaceSpace profiles of Crystal, Josh, Missi, Kyle, Dino, and Joni. The profiles helped establish the furry friends' personalities. Without them, they'd just be . . . I didn't know what they'd be.

I took one of the creaturettes by her enormous hand and led her to the computer. A minute later, I was streaming information about Crystal's likes and dislikes

along with photos and videos and personal messages from her FaceSpace account. The change was eerie. Within seconds, the monster moved more like Crystal. She even had some of Crystal's facial expressions.

I repeated the process with each monster.

They were ready.

Looking back, maybe I should have taken the time to get to know the creatures. If I had, things might have turned out differently. But the UPs were waiting, and every minute I was in the lab was a minute I could be looking for Franklin.

Our time together had been special in a monstrous kind of way. But now it was over. I was off to make my deliveries.

CHAPTER 51

Congratulations— It's a Monster!

"Oh, it's so darling!" Crystal said when she saw the large, curly-haired girl-blob before her. "Do you have it in purple?"

I was talking to someone with the IQ of a squirrel—and giving her a monster.

"They're not off the rack," I said.

"That's OK, I'll have it wear something purple."

I don't know what it is about girls that makes them want to play dress-up, but I felt the need to remind Crystal this wasn't some doll left under the Christmas tree. Dolls don't have shoulders like a professional wrestler. Dolls don't have furry arms that reach to their knees—farther if you count the retractable fingernails.

Crystal thought it was adorable.

"What … is … your … name?" she annunciated slowly, in case the thing did not speak cheerleader.

"You know it can't talk, right?" I said.

"Yours talked!" she yelled. "I want one that talks!"

I rubbed my temples.

"We discussed this. It knows how to talk; it just can't form words yet. You have to work with it."

"Well ... I guess that's all right," Crystal said.

"And you'll have to name it."

I'd learned that lesson the hard way.

"Yea!" she cheered. "I think.... Pookie! Don't you think it looks like a Pookie?"

I had never seen a Pookie. But if it is six-feet tall with pink hair and porcupine quills then, yes, this was a Pookie.

"Good luck, Pookie," I said and walked quickly away.

My other deliveries only confirmed my fears—the UPs were not monster-ready. They all seemed surprised their model wasn't as complete as Franklin. But at least they gave them names right away. I almost wished they hadn't. The creatures seemed more real to me now that I had something to call them.

I wasn't saying goodbye to blobs of putty, I was saying goodbye to...

Big Ape. I could see why Dino called him that. At first glance, he sort of reminded you of King Kong. Most of that was because he was supersized and always had this goofy, monkey-type expression on his face. But the gigantic arms and spiky brown hair didn't help either.

Tarzana. Tarzana had this broad, goonish face and her long, black ponytail looked a lot like Joni's. Well, not exactly like Joni's. Joni's didn't come out of the very top of a completely bald  head. I don't mean Tarzana was completely bald. She was really hairy everywhere but her head.

  *Mutt.* Kyle's new best friend looked more like man's best friend. It was as if someone took the head of a pit bull and stuck it on the body of a furry California-surfer.

Buffy. Missi yelled out "Buffy" the second we arrived. It was as if she'd been saving that name and finally had a chance to stick it on some- thing. In this case, that something was a short, wide gargoyle with a red, beehive hairdo and arms that stuck out in front like a kangaroo's.

My last delivery was to Josh. It's name? *Steve Evil.* Personally, I'd have thought of something a whole lot nicer, but nothing could have fit any better. There was a fiendish look about this one. Steve Evil was not a hulk like the others. He was sleek and lean like a leopard or a Doberman Pinscher. His hair was dark and short, and it came together to form a little peak at the top of his forehead. He had what I can only describe as the face of a rat—  except for his eyes. Steve Evil had the eyes of a snake.

Since these monsters were only one day old, they didn't know I was leaving them with people I wouldn't trust with a house plant. But what choice did I have? I told myself that it would be all right, that the UPs must be good with friends—why else would they have so many of them?

I still felt sick inside. It was like giving away six giant puppies.

CHAPTER
52

Another Side
of Franklin

My mind was racing. On the walk home, all I could think of was what Dad had said when he had to go capture Rollo the bear.

"Things are bound to go wrong."

He wasn't just talking about bears. Things were bound to go wrong when people tried to play God. Especially if they played as badly as I was.

My stomach hurt like the time I had three Super-Slime Ghastly Green Gooshees in a row. But at least that felt good before it felt awful. There's nothing like a Gooshee when you need a quick burst of happy—and I needed one now.

I stopped at the Grab 'N Git three blocks from my house.

The Grab 'N Git was like most convenience stores in that they had a little bit of everything: car deodorizers, tiny boxes of detergent, week-old donuts, motor oil, good candy, crummy candy, newspapers, the great-wall-of-soda, and something I didn't expect—Reynolds Pipkin.

I saw him filling a super-sized cup at the Gooshee machine.

"What are you doing here, Reynolds?" I asked.

He jumped back, leaving a multi-colored trail on the floor.

"Nothing," he said.

I eyed him suspiciously. He was wearing black canvas sneakers—Reynolds never wears sneakers—and the sides were covered in dirt. Curious since Pipkins are ultra-clean. The top button of his shirt was unfastened, which made him look normal, and normal was odd for Reynolds. Maybe I'd seen too many detective shows, but something didn't add up.

It wasn't just the way he looked. It was the way he was acting. First of all, he was using the Gooshee machine all wrong. He'd only pulled the handle halfway down, which means you get mostly juice. Only a first-timer makes that mistake. Also, he was holding the cup perfectly still when everyone knows you need to rotate it so the Gooshee comes out in little swirls.

I raised one eyebrow and leaned in toward him.

"Nice Gooshee," I said. "Who's it for?"

"It's mine," he answered, a little too quickly for my taste.

Let me explain something about Gooshees. They have their own social order. I couldn't picture Reynolds drinking a Gooshee at all, but if he did, it would be a Peach Passion or a Choo-Choo Cherry. They're milder with less of a kick.

Oh, one day, years in the future, he might boldly sample a Lucky Lemonburst, but that's as far as it would go.

Reynolds was a lightweight. But here he was holding a Rainbow Extreme, the grand-poobah of Gooshees. Reynolds couldn't handle the Extreme! It was out of his league. I circled him slowly.

"Really?" I said, the way the cool TV cops do. "Then why don't you drink it?"

Reynolds hesitated. I saw a thin layer of sweat forming on his enormous forehead.

"It's pretty cold," he said.

"And?" I inquired.

"And I like my Gooshees room temperature."

"You're going to be room temperature if you don't tell me where he is!" I exploded, grabbing the lapels of his jacket.

It was all so clear now. That's why he'd asked me if he could tell Franklin about the new creatures. Reynolds knew where Franklin was!

I gave him my most intimidating glare, the one I reserve exclusively for people I'm sure won't hit me. He blinked twice, which I took to mean he was terrified. Reynolds doesn't exactly have a wealth of facial expressions.

"He's at the dump," he said at last. "But he told me not to tell you. He doesn't want you there."

☆ ☆ ☆

I jumped on a bus headed for the west edge of town. I'd been to the dump tons of times on my bike, but it's a pretty long ride and I was carrying a Gooshee—a *Rainbow Extreme* Gooshee. When did Franklin move up to Rainbow Extremes? It had only been two days since I last saw him at Uncle Ben's store, but it seemed like years.

I had to walk the last few blocks because the bus didn't go all the way to the dump. Somebody at city hall would be getting an angry letter about that. I arrived at my destination and crawled through one of the many holes in the chain-link fence.

To me, the dump always looked like an archaeological dig that had uncovered a lost civilization of litterbugs. I'd found lots of neat stuff here, but today there was only one find I wanted to take home.

"Fraaaaaaaank-linnnnnnnn!" I called.

The sound echoed through the endless piles of cereal boxes and truck tires. I walked slowly past the brown, trash-filled mountains hoping nothing leaped out at me except a monster. I couldn't believe Franklin would stay here with the garbage when he had a nice, warm bed at home. Then again, if I ever needed a place to disappear, this might be where I'd come. The junk was stacked up in high, unsightly mounds—glass bottles over there, scrap metal over here—so you'd never run out of hiding places. Also, you could count on it being more or less deserted. Unless you were a monster or a twelve-year-old inventor, you probably didn't spend your weekends hanging around the dump.

"Franklin, I know you're here!" I yelled. "Just talk to me! I brought you a Gooshee!"

I heard the wind whistling past the hill of disposable diapers. Smelled it too. But there was no reply.

The dump was laid out like a maze, and with all the twists and turns, he could have been standing ten feet away and I'd never have known it. It was clear that Franklin didn't want to be found. I was about to give up the search and head for home when I came across a spot that looked strangely familiar. It had two makeshift beds created out of cardboard boxes and old, discarded mattresses. Their frames came together at the ends so that the beds formed a giant L-shape.

I knew what I was looking at—I was looking at Franklin's version of my room. He'd re-created it from things he'd found in the junk piles.

A short walk from the bedroom took me to the kitchen. A three-legged table, a busted refrigerator, a stove—they were all arranged like their duplicates at our house. And that wasn't all. There were figures—five of them. One was clearly my dad, tall and lean, made from a chest, a radiator, and an old baseball cap. Next to him was my mom—not a bad likeness considering it had a bucket for a head topped with an old, brown wig.

Katie Beth, outfitted in mop hair and headphones, came next, and Stick, appropriately, was a stick. As for Orson, Franklin had used two baby-food jars to make his glasses. I knew it was Orson because it was smaller than the others and sat at the keys of a useless, old computer.

I got the picture. Franklin had surrounded himself with a new family—and I wasn't in it.

Everything seemed different now, like I was intruding on someplace personal and private. I took a last look at the little world he'd built.

"I'm sorry, Franklin!" I yelled and put the Gooshee on the table.

Then I walked away.

☆ ☆ ☆

I took a different route leaving the dump than I'd taken coming in. This one was closer to the side fence, meaning it was the fastest way off the property. I felt like I'd already overstayed my welcome.

I was walking along a path filled with everything you

could ever hope to throw away when I came across an old friend.

It was Rollo.

I knew the dump wasn't far from the place I'd met the bear the first time, but it was still a shock to see his big, hairy rump sticking out of a stinking heap of plastic garbage bags. Now the smart move would have been to call my dad but—as I think I've mentioned—*my parents won't let me have a cell phone.* That meant I'd have to wait until I got home. I started to turn around and go out a different way, but then I remembered something Dad said: Rollo thinks he's a person.

I couldn't leave a person standing there eating rotten, putrid garbage. It was disgusting.

"Rollo!" I said, clapping my hands like I'd seen Dad do. "Get out of there. Get!"

Rollo jumped back quickly and looked up at me. That's when I noticed something kind of important. This wasn't Rollo.

It was shaggier than Rollo. It looked meaner than Rollo, and, unlike Rollo, it seemed fully aware that it was a bear.

I'd made a terrible mistake. This had to be one of the big, fierce, brown bears Rollo's owner kept in a cage!

I stood perfectly still while the animal studied me—kind of like how the neighbor's cat studies Precious through the window. The enormous animal growled, and sticky sweat burst from every pore in my body. I held my breath waiting for the next move and, an instant later, the bear rushed me!

The collision was quick, violent, and devastating. Franklin was little more than a blur when he hit the charging bear and took the beast to the ground. I didn't know where he'd come from, and I didn't care. He'd arrived just in time. The bear scrambled to its feet and shook its massive head. After that, it had no more interest in me—it wanted Franklin. With as angry a roar as I have ever heard—and keep in mind I once used Katie Beth's bra as a guinea-pig hammock—the bear lunged. His jaws sprung open like a great steel-trap. And as terrifying as this snarling, salivating creature was, I found my eyes fixed on something much scarier.

It was Franklin—or what used to be Franklin. Somehow during the battle he had transformed into a hulking, hunched-over, other-worldly version of himself. I saw the arched back and dripping fangs and hands that pawed the ground, and it was clear this was not the Franklin I knew.

And then I heard the roar—Franklin's roar! The ear-splitting explosion made me jump out of my sneakers.

The bear jumped too. Eyeing the situation one last time, he seemed to think better of the match-up, turned, and ran away. That's when Franklin's face snapped sharply toward me. I looked into his wild, black eyes. This wasn't Franklin—this was a monster.

He snarled and growled and whipped his head about angrily. At first, he seemed confused by his surroundings but then his piercing stare locked on me. I could see the razor-sharp fangs when he opened his mouth and he made a horrible, savage-sound like the cry of a cougar. He did it again and this time, I realized it was a word.

"How-ard!" he grunted. "How-ard!"

I was too scared to answer, too scared to move. Had this creature actually lived in my house? Had it slept two feet from my bed? What would have happened if ... the thought was too awful to finish.

"Howard," I heard again, but this time in Franklin's voice. He fell to his knees and buried his face in his hands. "I'm sorry ..."

When he looked up, tears were running down his cheeks.

I turned around and ran as fast as my feet would carry me. I was running away from a friend and a monster, and the realization that I'd made them both. My heart was pounding—and breaking.

Monster Alert

When I got home, Dad was in the living room reading the newspaper. My head was still spinning, but I knew there was something I was supposed to ... the bear!

I'd been so shook up about Franklin that I'd forgotten about the bear. What was I going to tell him? If Dad went after the bear, he might come across Franklin—and what if Franklin changed again? What if Dad saw it happen?

Or worse—what if he brought him back home?

"Oh, there you are, Howard," Dad said, looking over the top of his sports section. "Where you been, Champ?"

"Around," I said, my voice squeaking like I'd swallowed a mouse. "I went to the dump."

Dad put down the paper.

"The dump? Howard, you shouldn't go over there by yourself. Slater just called and said they picked up a bear not far from there. One of the big ones this time."

"Oh," I said. "Are they sure it was a bear?"

"What else would it be?" Dad said. He gave me a curious look. "You OK, son?"

"I'm fine."

☆ ☆ ☆

Later that afternoon, the phone rang. A second later, Stick stuck his head around the corner.

"It's for you, doofus. Hurry it up, I'm expecting a call."

I walked into the kitchen and picked up the phone. "Hello?"

"I'm breaking up with Josh," Joni Jackson said immediately.

"Congratulations" seemed rude, so I didn't say anything at all.

"Did you hear me? I'm breaking up with Josh, so you need to come get your monster."

I wondered if her brain had fallen through one of those holes in her head.

"First of all, it's not my monster. It's your monster!" I said. "And second of all, what's that got to do with you breaking up with Josh?"

"I told Josh I'd be his girlfriend if I could have a monster! But now I don't like him, so I need to give the monster back. It's like a ring or an iPod—those are the rules!"

My hands were sweating so much I almost dropped the phone. I had just gotten rid of these things. For the first time in weeks, my house was monster-free.

"Look," I said. "Josh didn't give you the monster, I did."

"Really?" Joni said, and she was silent for ten seconds,

which I'm guessing was a personal record. "I didn't even know you liked me that way."

"It's not that kind of monster!" I yelled.

I explained to Joni that the creature wasn't so much like a ring as a tattoo. Josh wouldn't expect her to give a tattoo back, would he?

"He might. He's kind of a jerk!"

She was missing my point, but by this time I'd come to expect that. I was about to get off the phone when a terrible thought entered my head—what if these monsters did what Franklin did? What if they changed?

"Joni," I said nervously, "have you noticed anything strange about your new friend?"

"Only everything," she said, answering what may have been the stupidest question ever asked.

"I mean has she changed in any way? Does she seem different than when you got her?"

"Not really. But most of the time she's been in my closet so I haven't paid that much attention."

I could barely control the fear building inside me. How could I have been such an idiot?

"Look, everything is probably fine," I said calmly, "but there's a possibility she could change. And if she does, she might be dangerous."

"Stop worrying," Joni said. "She's a big sweetie, just like Franklin."

The idea that she might be just like Franklin was exactly what I was worried about. Before I could explain what I meant, Stick walked in the room. He crossed his arms and tapped his foot.

"Look, Joni, I have to go," I said. "But will you call the others and tell them what we talked about?"

"That I broke up with Josh? I already told them," she said.

"Not that. Tell them about the dangerous thing. Tell them to be careful."

I looked at Stick to see if he was paying any attention to my conversation. The only thing he was paying attention to was the ham inside the refrigerator.

"All right, if I talk to anybody," she said.

"This is really, really important!" I snapped.

"OK, don't freak out. I'll call them."

I was already dreading going back to school on Monday.

CHAPTER
54

The Invasion

I had just walked through the door into the school building when one of the walls suddenly turned purple. Only it wasn't a wall.

Directly in front of me was the single largest purple pantsuit in the western hemisphere.

"Hey, How-Cool!" Crystal squealed. "Doesn't Pookie look adorable?"

She looked like a giant blueberry with a poodle on top.

"You look nice, Pookie," I winced.

Pookie giggled. Or growled. It was hard to tell.

"Crystal," I whispered, foolishly believing a quieter tone would keep people from looking in our direction. "Can she even talk yet?"

"Sure!" Crystal chimed. "I taught her last night, watch! Pookie, do you like living in our garden shed?"

"Awww-sommme," Pookie grunted.

"What do you think of my outfit today?" she asked.

"Awww-sommme."

"See?" Crystal said. "She talks awesome!"

I was going to ask if she'd taught her to say anything else—like "Howard had nothing to do with this"—but I was distracted by something down the hall.

The monsters were on parade.

Leading the way was Josh Gutierrez. He was shadowed by his monster who was not much larger than Josh, but with snake-like skin and cold, black eyes. The face was sort of human, I guess, but you could probably say the same thing about a rat if you shaved it. It wore a white T-shirt, low-top boots, and a dark, leather jacket.

"Tell 'em your name," Josh ordered, grinning at the crowd that had gathered.

The voice leaked out like steam.

"Steevil," it hissed.

Josh laughed. "Steevil! That's classic! Close enough!"

Steve Evil smiled, showing his razor-sharp needle teeth.

As it turned out, all the UPs had brought their new toys. This was the creepiest show-and-tell ever.

I thought back to the first day I'd brought Franklin to school—polite, sweet, articulate Franklin. No one came within twenty feet of us. One kid actually tried to stuff himself in his own backpack. But here were the UPs walking in with Godzilla's first cousins, and the crowd rushed them like they were movie stars with free candy.

All of a sudden monsters were cool. That's the thing about middle school—it only matters if the right kids do it. By the time the bell rang for homeroom, everyone had seen the fancy, new furballs from UP-town and, like magic, the new status symbol at Dolley Madison was having your very own Canadian.

I've decided I could never be an UP. I'm too nervous. Like I couldn't just show up at school with an undisguised, drooling, monster-sized sidekick and no explanation for what it was doing there. But an UP can. They can because they don't worry about things like getting past Mrs. Ogilvie, or being called into Principal Dillard's office, or staring into the angry, flaring nostrils of "Cannonball" Hertz.

When you're an UP, life's little problems just take care of themselves.

I realized that the day the monsters came to school. Any other time and the UPs would have run smack-dab into Vice Principal Hertz, who I'm almost positive has a hall-monitor alarm installed in his brain. But on this particular day, the school was extra crowded. There had been a fire at Theodor S. Geisel High School, a large, prison-looking building that happens to be right across the street from the middle school. It was a small fire that only damaged a few rooms, but they were still using our gym, auditorium, and cafeteria for some of their classes. My guess is that the teachers thought the monsters were just big, ugly high schoolers—of which there are many—and let them wander in with the rest of the herd.

So the UPs got away with it. They didn't even have to answer any questions.

CHAPTER
55

Moment of Truth

"Where is Franklin?"

These were the first words Winnie McKinney had spoken to me in days. OK, they weren't the friendliest words, but it was a start.

"He's not here," I told her, scrambling to come up with some believable-sounding reason. "He, uh ... he moved away."

"Did you make him?"

"No!" I said. "I asked him to stay!" That seemed like an honest enough answer. I mean, I did go after him.

But there was something strange about the way Winnie was looking at me. Her eyes were way too serious for a girl in a pink headband. Finally, she shook her head.

This time, the words were slow and perfectly clear.

"Did ... you ... make ... him?"

There it was. The unimaginable question, the one I hoped I'd never hear. I felt sick.

"Because it's all over school that you made those new kids. Did you?"

This was the point when my brain shut down. It's a defense mechanism I have, kind of like that species of goat that faints when startled. This meant there was no way that I was going to answer that question. I couldn't. My brain wouldn't let me.

Unfortunately, I had forgotten I had other body parts. Without my knowledge and completely against my will, my head began making a nodding motion. I didn't even know it was happening—until I saw Winnie's face. She went pale like she'd just seen a monster. A skinny one with glasses.

"All that genius," she said, backing away from me, "all that brain power and you use it to make people to give to other people. You're unbelievable!"

"Thank you," I said.

"It wasn't a compliment!" she screamed.

I knew it didn't sound right. But in the thousands of times I'd been insulted, never once had anyone called me a genius.

"I thought I knew you, Howard, but I was wrong. You're not special. You're not misunderstood. You're just ... just ... creepy!"

She turned and ran down the hall. Part of me wanted to run after her, but another part of me was afraid I might catch her. The last thing I needed was to get yelled at again, especially when everything she was saying was true.

I turned around and walked slowly toward my next class. That's when I noticed people were watching me. Their eyes felt like invisible spiders crawling on my skin. Winnie was right—everyone knew what I'd done.

And if this was how they were looking at me—how were they going to look at Franklin?

CHAPTER
56

Monsters Gone
Mad-ison

Dolley Madison Middle School had been invaded by
monsters—real monsters.

My first clue came the next morning when I was
walking past the soccer field on my way to school. The sun
was just beginning to rise and everything had this gray,
unreal quality like something in a dream. I remember
hearing a sound—a dull, low, painful moan coming from
the shadows underneath the bleachers. I walked toward it.

What I saw then was something that will stay with me
for the rest of my days—nine swinging figures dangling
by their underpants. They were all hanging from the
bleachers like some eerie, swaying monument to the
puppet wedgie! Brutal.

I caught my breath then helped them down.

Once he touched ground, Lyle Covington got busy
trying to stuff about eight feet of Fruit-of-the-Looms

back inside his corduroys. It was a dance I knew only too well.

"What happened, Lyle?" I asked.

He didn't say anything, but it didn't matter. I knew it was the creatures.

"Things are bound to go wrong." That's what Dad had said.

I had no idea how right he'd turn out to be.

☆ ☆ ☆

In the annals of Dolley Madison, the rest of that Tuesday will forever be known as the day nobody went to the bathroom.

You'd have been crazy to go. Not alone. Not willingly. The bathrooms were for monsters only. If you dared enter, you were in for the swirlee of your life.

It didn't take long for me to figure out that's where the monsters were keeping themselves while classes were going on. They ventured out only at lunchtime or when there were tons of people in the halls. Then they'd storm through the crowd leaving a path of wedgies, power-noogies, and mutilated textbooks behind them. And everywhere that there was a senseless act of destruction, you'd find an UP watching like a proud parent.

"You have to get them out of here," I told Crystal.

She looked at me like I was out of my mind. Maybe that was because she'd just taught Pookie to shake a vending machine until a soda fell out.

"Why? They're just having fun." she said. "Franklin was here every day until you ran him off. I don't see why you think you can bring a friend to school, but nobody else can. Lighten up, How-Lame!"

Crystal and Pookie were wearing matching purple outfits. But that wasn't the reason it was hard to tell which one was the monster.

I saw Wendell coming toward me in the nearly deserted hall. His head was down, and his walk was fast and nervous. I hadn't spoken to him since the wedgie incident because I didn't know what to say. When he reached me, he didn't look at me. But he stopped.

"Where is Franklin?" he asked.

"I don't know."

"Is he coming back?"

"I don't know that either."

Short conversation, but it told me something—I wasn't the only kid who missed Franklin.

Now that I'd met his replacements, I missed him more than ever.

☆ ☆ ☆

Their ears go up. Their fur bristles. They hide or burrow or run. Middle schoolers are like that when they sense danger.

I could feel the tension in the air. No one was joking around or hanging out in the halls. They were rushing off to their classrooms. They were seeking shelter.

Not that it would do them much good. The monsters were on the prowl.

By the time the morning classes were over, we'd gone way beyond wedgies, way beyond watching Big Ape eat someone's geometry homework. The monsters no longer felt the need to hide in the bathrooms. In fact, they weren't hiding at all.

The school belonged to them now, and no one was safe.

I heard a rumor that Mutt walked into Mrs. Florence's Latin class and threw Doug Bronsky out a second-story window. OK, it was Doug Bronsky—Doug had jumped out that very same window on at least six different occasions just to get out of pop quizzes.

So my guess was that Mutt hadn't actually tossed Doug;

Doug had jumped on his own to escape. But he was escaping from Mutt, so it amounted to the same thing. The point was, the monsters were getting bolder and meaner and more dangerous, and the next person to fly out of a window might not be as springy as Doug Bronsky.

It wasn't just Mutt. All the monsters were on the prowl. Buffy had smashed the trophy case because she wanted something shiny. It turned out to be a trophy with a green, marble base topped by a golden lady with wings that the debate team had won.

She gazed at it like this was the most beautiful thing she'd ever seen. Then she tied it to a ribbon and wore it like a necklace.

"Awwww-sommme," Pookie told her.

Meanwhile, Tarzana was in the cafeteria kitchen happily helping herself to a big bucket of frozen Sloppy Joe

mix. (For some reason, monsters love the Joes.) The cafeteria workers didn't notice this intrusion because they were all outside at the time watching Big Ape who'd climbed to the top of the flagpole and started flinging ... well, I don't know what he was flinging, but we had to get a new flag.

What I didn't understand was why no one from the administration had tried to stop them. Surely, they'd noticed what was happening. I mean, any one of those things was enough to get you expelled or at least sent to detention for a couple of decades.

As far as I knew, no one from the principal's office had said a word. It didn't make sense.

Then I saw the most chilling thing at my own locker. When I opened the door, I found all the usual stuff—a jacket, some books, my portable first-aid kit—and something else.

It was Vice Principal Hertz!

Cannonball Hertz is the enforcement arm of the school

administration. Nobody messes with him. He is five-and-a-half-feet-tall and almost as wide, and I believe with all my heart that he is a single, solid muscle that somehow developed the ability to scream at children. As a scientist, I know that it is physically impossible for the shape of Vice Principal Hertz to fit inside my locker. Yet there he was.

I helped him climb out.

He didn't say anything to me. He just walked away as quickly as he could.

☆ ☆ ☆

I was trying to make it to history class as fast as possible when a hand reached out and covered my mouth. Kyle Stanford yanked me into the janitor's closet.

"You gotta take Mutt back!" he said. His voice was bed-wetter scared.

"I can't," I said.

"What about your dad? He catches animals and stuff, right? Let's call your dad!"

"I can't!" I yelled.

And I couldn't. What would Dad do, take them to the pound? They were monsters. You couldn't take them to the pound. You couldn't take them to a zoo. You couldn't take them anywhere.

Kyle is the kind of person who talks when he's nervous, and today he was spilling buckets. He told me he couldn't handle Mutt so he tried to release him in the alley behind the Super Bargain Mart. But Mutt found his way back— and he didn't come home happy.

"You just left him there in the alley?" I asked.

"Hey, it's not just me!" Kyle snapped. "These monsters are defective or something. None of us wants them anymore. Well, except Josh."

It was clear that Josh had formed an unbreakable bond with his new buddy. To him, Steve Evil (also known as "Steevil") was like an evil twin brother. I say "twin" not because they looked alike, but because I'm pretty sure they were identically evil.

CHAPTER 57

The Lunch Rush

I'd barely made it through the lunch line when Crystal grabbed me by the shirttail and pulled me over to the UPs table. Even on a day like this one, the UPs table was just nicer than the other tables. The food even tasted better. Not good, but better.

I sat down in the nearest empty seat, and she took the one next to it. On my other side was Dino. He had turned his chair around backwards so he appeared to be riding a folding, metal horse. He even sat cooler than I did! I glanced across the long, beige table and saw Missi. She was staring at me. Actually, staring isn't the right word—what do you call it when someone is strangling you with their eyes? Kyle and Joni sat down. This wasn't going to be a friendly, little lunch-gathering. This was a very unfriendly little mob scene.

I was surrounded by unhappy UPs.

"Here's the plan," Crystal said. "If you take back the monsters, you can have Dino's cell phone, and Joni will be your girlfriend."

"Wait a minute," Dino stopped her. "I said he could *borrow* my cell phone."

"And I meant like a secret admirer kind of deal," Joni said. "Like he can leave gifts by my locker."

"It doesn't matter!" I blurted out. "There's nothing I can do!"

UPs aren't used to getting resistance from the little people. It makes them cranky. The next thing I knew, the five of them had closed in on me like a Venus flytrap devouring its prey.

"I go to a lot of stores and every one of them has a return policy!" Missi said. "You're taking back Buffy. My Daddy is a lawyer! We'll sue you!"

Did they really believe we could tell the monsters where to go? They'd go wherever they wanted! I tried to explain, but my words were drowned in a sea of random yelling. The UPs were all talking at the same time, and nobody was listening to anybody. Just when I couldn't stand it anymore, it stopped. An eerie chill came over me.

I don't know if it's animal instinct, or just a sense I've developed after being around Stick my whole life, but I knew something bad was about to happen. Six monsters had walked into the room—well, seven if you count Josh. They moved like a pack of teenage lions entering the grazing grounds of the slow-footed dorkalope.

Then the monsters all opened their mouths and tilted back their heads, even Josh, and howled in some kind of joyful, beast-like cry to chaos.

I'll probably never know who threw the first taco. What

I do know is that once it reached its destination, it set off the kind of chain reaction that janitors probably have nightmares about. This was not a food fight. This was the food version of nuclear war.

It was worse than the legendary Dolley Madison "Swedish Meat-brawl," the clash that got meatballs permanently banned from the menu. Potatoes, beans, and broccoli rained down like little, green veggie-bombs (vegetable hail). Everyone was tossing throwables (food bombs) from their plate or the floor or the walls, or anywhere they could get their hands on something damp, gooey, and disgusting. The air smelled like leftovers and panic. Kids rushed for the exits or climbed through windows, turning

over tables on their way to foodless freedom. As for the fallen, they were left where they went down—their cries lost in the roar, their clothing covered in footprints and condiments. Principal Dillard, Vice Principal Hertz, Mr. Z, and a few other teachers stormed into the room, but they were consumed by the flying food frenzy. Principal Dillard called for order, but the room would have none of it.

But there was no stopping this fight. It would continue until the last slice of custard pie was occupying someone's face.

I did not personally throw any food. If dodge ball has taught me anything, it is that I am not a thrower. I am, however, a natural-born target. When I looked down, I saw that I was covered in a thick, slimy coat of the five basic food groups. I was positive this was the kind of ultra-grossness that must have caused Arthur Scott to invent the paper towel.

When there was a momentary lapse in the food cloud, I spotted a way out through the dirty-dishes window that led to the kitchen. But when I tried to make a break for it, something held me back.

That something was Big Ape. He had me by the underwear.

With one mighty hand, he'd yanked me from the ground by my waistband so that I hung there like a bowling ball waiting to be hurled down an alley. You know how you can pick up a box turtle and he'll keep paddling his legs in mid-air? That was me. I suppose I've had more painful wedgies but few that were as humiliating.

But if anyone was laughing, I never saw it. About that time, boiled chickpeas splatted against my glasses and everything turned mushy and green. Then we started moving. I could hear the blast of the alarm as we rushed out the fire exit and, wiping my lenses, I saw we were headed for one of the portables.

You've seen portables, right? They're those individual,

wooden houses that surround the school like tiny, educational islands. When we reached the nearest one, a door opened and we went through it.

I recognized the room right away. This was the place where the band practiced. The windows were covered with a foam material—soundproofing, most likely—and the wall on the other side held a row of large, wooden cabinets. There were no desks, just chairs arranged in a giant half-a-donut formation. Most of what I saw seemed pretty normal, things like tubas and a bass drum and music stands, but a few things seemed out of place—the monsters, for example.

Buffy, Mutt, Pookie, Tarzana and Steve Evil were all inside the room. Since the band didn't practice until sixth period, they had the place pretty much to themselves. Sitting in a chair in the back was Josh Gutierrez, his feet propped up in front of him and his fingers locked snugly behind his head. He looked as comfortable as my dad does when he's watching monsters on TV—only Josh was seeing them live and in-person. From the look of him, he'd managed to slip out of the cafeteria before the trouble started. I say that because he was the only one of us who wasn't wearing a thick coat of leftovers.

Well, that's not exactly true. There was one other person there who looked as spotless as she had on class-picture day.

"Winnie!" I gasped.

Winnie McKinney was sitting on a short, tan stool in the corner while Pookie and Mutt hovered over her like jailers. She looked at me and rolled her eyes.

"I'm first-chair clarinet," she said, sounding more annoyed than scared. "Mr. Talbert lets me practice in here on my lunch break."

What she didn't say was, "This is all your fault, Howard." But we both knew she could have.

Because it was my fault. And if anything happened to Winnie, that would be my fault too. I wanted to do something, to burst into action the way the heroes did in my comic books. Unfortunately, my only superpower at the moment was the amazing ability to spring up and down like some kind of underpants yo-yo—which was sort of fun but virtually useless.

So I went to my back-up plan: talking. I opened my mouth without having the slightest idea what would come out.

"I was disgusted by what I saw in the cafeteria today," I said sternly, the way my mom would if she was kidnapped by monsters. Big Ape growled.

I took a deep, nervous gulp and continued. "Of course, I'm disgusted by what I see there every day. Which is why I wanted to say thank you for rescuing me before any of it actually entered my body. Your methods were messy, but the important thing is that your hearts were in the right place."

My mouth was still open but it had run out of words. I closed it. Then we played the waiting game.

Steve Evil walked slowly across the room, bent down, and put his face so close to mine that my glasses fogged over.

"I don't have a heart," he sneered. "You never gave me one. Remember?"

This was the first time I'd ever stared directly into those icy, yellow snake-eyes, and I didn't like what I saw. Whatever was behind them was dark and cruel.

He really didn't have a heart.

Then again, neither did Franklin. At least, not a heart like mine. And yet Franklin was nothing like Steve Evil. He wasn't like any of the new creatures. Scientifically speaking, this didn't make sense. Why were they different?

My brain instantly switched from "escape planning" to "monster chemistry." It switched because it couldn't help it.

There's something you should know about me—once you get past my pale, scrawny exterior, you'll find a gooey core of pure nerd. I am constantly thinking about science. And science wanted to know why these mutant goo-balls weren't nicer. After all, Franklin was nice. And considering they were made from the same stuff—DNA, Wonder Putty, somebody's FaceSpace page...

FaceSpace?

FaceSpace! That was it! They were all made from somebody's FaceSpace page! Why hadn't I thought of that before?

See, a FaceSpace profile is like a mirror—it reflects who you are. So if you're nice or caring or helpful, that's what comes across on your page. Only I didn't use people who were nice or caring or helpful—not on the new batch. I used UPs. UPs were spiteful and selfish and conceited. They walked on people. And when they didn't get their way, they behaved—well, like monsters.

It was so simple! Of course these creatures weren't acting like Franklin—they were acting like UPs!

I looked around at my abductors and, for just a second, I felt sorry for them.

What had I done? I knew the kind of stuff UPs had on their FaceSpace pages. Crystal had hateful messages about people she didn't like. Kyle had pictures of himself happily giving wedgies and noogies to smaller, weaker kids. Josh had loud, angry music filled with cursing and screaming.

And I had taken all of that meanness and inflicted it onto some poor, unsuspecting monsters.

"This is my fault," I said. "Please, let Winnie go. Your problem is with me."

Steve Evil drew close, and I could smell the hatred on his breath.

"My problem," he seethed, "is with everybody."

Then I saw that wicked, serpent-smile again—only this time, it was on a different face. I'd never noticed before, but Josh Gutierrez had Steve Evil's grin. He stepped alongside his terror-twin and grabbed a fistful of my hair.

"We start with thisssss one," Josh hissed.

He'd even started to talk like Steevil.

A thousand horrible possibilities raced through my mind—but the one that actually occurred surprised me.

It was a pie in the face—Josh's face.

The banana-cream bomb soared across the room and exploded inside his right ear. Covered in meringue and rage, Josh searched frantically for the hurler. By the time he found her, Winnie had reloaded—this time with a dangerous-looking lemon meringue she'd peeled from the smorgasbord on Pookie's pantsuit.

"You ready for seconds?" she asked.

I heard Josh breathing—hard and quick—and a low, dull snarl rattled in his throat. His look, his sounds, his movements were so much like Steve Evil's it was scary.

"My mistake," he said coldly. "We'll start with her."

I felt sick. The pack was moving in on Winnie, and all the baked goods in the world wouldn't help her now. With each step, the monsters looked bigger and beastlier and angrier and then—they stopped.

They stopped all at once, as if someone had pushed an invisible off-button. Each creature froze mid-stride and cocked its head. They were listening to something...

Sirens!

The creatures' ears were a lot better than mine, but even I could hear them now. The cavalry was coming! Big Ape had made a monster-sized mistake when he tripped

the alarm on the fire exit door—help was on its way.
As the trucks got closer and the sirens got louder, the
monsters seemed more and more nervous. Finally, Big Ape
released his grip on my underwear, and I kissed the floor
with my whole face.

"This isn't over," Josh warned me on his way out the
door, because that's what bullies say instead of "Goodbye."

A second later, the invaders had vanished.

As for Winnie, she didn't go anywhere. She just picked
up her clarinet and started to practice without so much as
a look in my direction. I wanted to thank her for saving me
with the pie but decided I better not. I didn't want to give
her a reason to regret it.

There was no use denying it any longer—I was really
bad at making friends. The only thing left to find out was
whether I was any better at unmaking them.

I walked out into the crowd of assembled seventh-
graders, held out my arms, and let the janitor spray me
with a hose.

CHAPTER 58

When Friends Become Enemies

"I need a virus that makes bad people disappear."

These were words I thought I'd never be saying to my five-year-old brother, but the situation was desperate. I needed two things—a computer wizard and someone who knew how to keep his mouth shut. Orson was both.

"Will you help me?" I asked.

Orson has always been tough to read. He just looked at me with those big, round, processing eyes and waited for more input.

"You see, there are some people at my school, some very bad people," I explained. "And these people have a computer program inside them. I need a virus that makes those people go away."

This time, Orson shook his head.

I was afraid that would happen. Orson would never do anything he thought would hurt someone. For the first

314

time in my life, I wished I was more like Stick. When Stick wanted Orson's help doing something that was mean or evil—usually against me—he'd make Orson think it was a game. I was no good at that.

Lately, I wasn't very good at telling the truth, either, but I decided to give it a try. I told him in terms a kinder-gartner could understand how I had built these things using little bits of bullies, and how no one could control these things, and how they might hurt someone if I didn't do something quickly.

"They're not people like me and you, they're not real," I told him. "They're like ... like Franklin."

I knew my mistake before the words even left my mouth.

Orson never cries. Not even when he was a baby, at least not that I remember. But when I looked at him, I could tell that somewhere on that unreachable inside he was crying now. His eyes got a faint, little glisten. Then he did something else he never does—he spoke.

"Fwanklin is weel," he said.

Then he ran out of the room.

Stupid! Stupid! Stupid! Of course, Franklin was real. Why did I say that? I'd just guaranteed that there would be no virus from Orson ever! It was a dumb idea anyway. I mean, even if he'd made one, how would I have delivered it? I'd have to get close enough to them to connect to their ports. The monsters would never let that happen.

About an hour later, when I was coming out of the kitchen, I saw Orson sneaking into my bedroom. That

meant all was forgiven. It was his ritual. I couldn't tell
what toy he was carrying, but it didn't really matter.
Whatever it was, he'd hide it in my room, and at some
point I'd find it. And in some small, quiet way, that would
make Orson happy.

☆ ☆ ☆

Orson was right. Franklin was real—he was a real friend.
The one good thing to come from all of this was that I
had a whole new appreciation for that. Maybe he looked
like the other creatures on the outside, but he was a lot
different on the inside. For one thing, he had feelings.

I knew because I'd hurt them.

It wasn't my proudest moment. I still didn't know
exactly what happened to him that day at the dump, but
I knew he couldn't help it. Looking back,
those wild changes scared him more
than they did me. But I was the one
who ran away and left him there
alone—again. That's why I had to
find him.

"Have you seen him?" I
asked.

I was standing on the
front porch of the Pipkins'
house.

"I think he's gone,"
Reynolds said.

316

"What do you mean gone?"

"Just gone," he said. His eyes did their owl-blink, and I had an almost uncontrollable urge to strangle him. "I went to the dump after school, and he wasn't there."

"Maybe he was hiding," I said. "It's a big place. Maybe you just couldn't find him."

"I find everything," Reynolds said, and he closed the door.

☆ ☆ ☆

I told my parents I was going to see Uncle Ben.

"Tell him we miss him," Mom said.

She wasn't talking about my uncle. My family still thought Franklin was staying over there for a few days while we got past our fight. They'd have been going nuts if they knew he was missing.

That was just one more reason I had to find him.

I ran up to my room and grabbed my backpack, which is where I kept a flashlight, a granola bar, and a rolled-up windbreaker. You never know what you'll need when you're hunting for a monster.

A second later, I was out the door.

Uncle Ben drove me around for over an hour. Reynolds was right; Franklin wasn't at the dump. He wasn't at the PizzaDog either. I was starting to think he wasn't anywhere. It was after dark when we pulled back onto my street.

"Look Howard, I know you don't want to hear this, but

maybe it's time we told your mom and dad," Uncle Ben said. "Maybe even the police."

I shook my head.

"I have to find him myself," I said.

"Why?" Uncle Ben said. I could tell he was getting worried.

"Because he'd find me."

He let me off at the curb, and I took a long, slow look up and down the street. No monsters. Not on my block. A sinking feeling took over my gut as I made my way toward the house.

That's when I noticed the garage door was raised a little. Someone had gone inside.

As quietly as I could, I lifted the door. The lab was dark except for the light that came from a neon clock I'd hung above my work table.

"Reynolds?" I whispered.

There was no answer. I couldn't see anything but shapes and shadows in the red glow. I knew I wasn't alone.

I put my backpack on the table and started to go for my flashlight, but I never got the chance. Something moved. Even in the dark, I recognized the form—those enormous shoulders, that gargantuan head. Franklin! He was here! I rushed over to the switch and hit the overhead lights.

"I take you. I take you now," Tarzana said.

Terrified, I ducked behind the table. Where did she want to take me? The thought of going anywhere with her made my skin clammy. She was about Franklin's size only with more fur. For school, Joni had covered her head in a red bandana, but the bandana was gone now and I could see the tiny, black horns springing from her scalp. I couldn't believe it—I was about to be dragged away by an enormous, hairy she-devil!

This was number seventeen on the list of my one hundred greatest fears!

"Stand back!" I yelled, grabbing a bottle of liquid I kept on my lab shelf. "I'm not going anywhere with you. One more step and I drop it—then this whole place will be blown sky high!"

Tarzana looked at me. Then she looked at the bottle in my hand. It said *Windex*. If Joni had taught her anything about glass cleaners, I was in big trouble.

"Put down pretty blue drink," she said. "We go."

"I'm not going!" I screamed.

"Come!" she yelled, showing what I thought was an unladylike amount of fang. "We have pie ..."

"Pie?" I shouted. "I don't want any pie!"

Tarzana shook her head wildly.

"No! We have pie girl!"

Pie girl?

"Winnie!" I gasped, and for the first time, Tarzana smiled.

"Wee-nee," she said. "Pie girl!"

Did they really have Winnie McKinney? I put down the Windex.

A few seconds later, I found myself nestled snugly in the hairiest armpit this side of baboon country. Instinctively, I reached for the table—it's my nature to try to delay the inevitable. But I was a fraction too late, and my reach fell short. I grabbed only the hanging strap of my backpack.

320

CHAPTER
59

Return to the Palace

Even toting me under one arm, Tarzana was remarkably fast. We moved through dark alleys—it's not like we were going to meet anything scarier than she was—and ended up at the school grounds. From there, it was a short sprint past the buildings and over the football field to our final destination: Beatdown Palace.

The Palace was a bully's paradise for a reason. It was isolated, sitting in the far corner of a weed-covered field. This was the last place anyone would look for anything, especially at night.

The metal door creaked open, and Tarzana flung me inside. Two hairless hands picked me up off the ground, and I found myself staring into Josh Gutierrez's danger-ously flared nostrils. A grunt, a lift, and he had returned me to the hook I'd occupied on my last visit.

Didn't bullies believe in chairs?

"I told you this wasn't over," Josh said. "I told you all."

Tarzana hadn't lied—this was a group event. Hanging

like meat along the dimly lit wall were Crystal, Kyle, Missi, Dino, and Joni. The floor was reserved for Winnie "Pie Girl" McKinney who sat hugging her knees and directing her eyes anywhere but on the monstrous crowd that surrounded her.

It looked like some horrible initiation ritual for the worst club in the world.

"Winnie! Are you all right?" I said.

I got silence, which I never handle very well.

"Are you not answering because you're hurt, or because you're not talking to me?" I tried again. "Nod your head if it's because you're not talking to me."

"None of us are talking to you, idiot!" Crystal blasted me from her spot down the wall. "This is all your fault!"

"Shut up, Crystal! You're breaking the pact of silence!" Missi whined. "We're supposed to be making him an outcast!"

"Well, how would he know we're not talking to him unless someone tells him?" Crystal snapped back.

"Maybe someone could write him mean note?" Tarzana offered.

"I'm all right! I just don't feel like talking, OK?" Winnie yelled.

Her voice echoed through the building and carried a wave of relief—for me, anyway. She wasn't happy, but at least she wasn't hurt. For whatever reason, the monsters had wanted everyone present before taking their revenge.

But now, all the hooks were filled. Steve Evil held his thin, clawed finger about an inch from my face.

"You," he sneered. "How-Coooool."

"More like, 'How-Lame!'" Missi said.

"How-Gross!" Joni said.

"How-Pathetic!" Dino said.

The nicknames flew like confetti from my neighboring hooks.

"It's Howard," I told the beast. "Just Howard."

Steve Evil showed me his rat teeth.

"You're the reason we exist, Howard," he said calmly. "And now, we will be the reason you don't."

I looked into his eyes and saw there was nothing in them. Not scorn. Not rage. Not even the twisted joy I'd seen in the faces of so many middle-school bullies.

"Why are you doing this?" I asked.

Steevil looked genuinely confused.

"I'm a monster, Howard," he said. The answer was so obvious.

Then he shrugged and turned his back to me.

"We'll start with our favorite pie thrower," he laughed. It was an ugly laugh, and I was sure that I had put hyena somewhere in his lineage.

Meanwhile, Josh circled Winnie like a buzzard.

"You know, you wasted some perfectly good pie today," he sneered at her. "But don't you worry, we've got another dessert for you."

He reached into a large bucket.

"These!"

When Josh pulled out his hand, it was filled with night crawlers, the vilest of the wormy stink-baits. They squirmed between his fingers like living spaghetti, and he waved the disgusting glob under each of our noses. When he'd finished his display, he picked up the bucket and carried it to his victim.

Buffy held Winnie by the hair. Slowly, she pushed her head toward the putrid feast, and I nearly spewed a sympathy puke. If I didn't come up with something in the next few seconds, I was sure I'd never see that warm, Winnie McKinney smile again.

Well, at least not without picturing worms in her teeth.

I glanced around looking for anything I could use—a distraction, a weapon, a projectile. Wait—a projectile!

My backpack! I'd been gripping it since Tarzana hauled me out of the lab. Now, if I could just fling it the ten feet to where the bucket was sitting, I might be able to knock over the worm salad. Still, my aim—never a strong suit—would have to be absolutely perfect.

I swung the strap backwards and forwards a couple of times to build up momentum then flung the pack like a horseshoe. The missile soared through the air and then: CLANG!

Bullseye! A direct hit!

I don't know if you've ever tried to knock over a bucket of night crawlers, but it weighs a lot more than you'd think. The backpack whacked against the side and then, uselessly, fell to the ground.

But then it did something interesting. It spoke.

"Moooooo."

Buffy let go of Winnie's hair. The room got quiet as

everyone looked around for what
had just made the mysterious
cow noise.

I knew exactly what had made
it. It was Orson's See 'n Say.

That must have been the gift
he'd taken to my room after
our argument. He'd hidden it
in my backpack for me to find
later. Orson must have really felt bad if he was willing
to part with his See 'n Say. He loved that toy. He'd spend
hours just watching the spinning farmer point to various
animals that would answer with a "Moo" or "Quack" or
"Oink."

"Grrrrrrrrrrrrr," Pookie growled loudly, and she
kicked at the talking backpack.

"Moooooooo," it responded.

That's when something fascinating happened.

Steve Evil jumped. It wasn't a startled little skip either,
it was a full-fledged "Eek! A mouse!" type leap.

Steve Evil didn't like the See 'n Say—just like Josh.

Josh Gutierrez was terrified of the "The Farmer Says."
It occurred to me that maybe, just maybe he'd passed
that fear along to his DNA-double Steve Evil. I didn't know
exactly how DNA worked, but Josh and Steevil did practically everything else the same—why not that?

I tried to think of a way that a talking toy could save
us from certain doom. I couldn't come up with a thing.
Still, I didn't want to lose the only weapon I had. So when

Pookie lifted her foot to stomp on the chatty backpack, I distracted her.

"Moooooo!" I mooed from my hook. "Don't mind me— just practicing my ventriloquism by making backpacks talk. **Mooooo!** Try it, it's easy!"

Wherever the noise was coming from, Pookie didn't like it. And right now, it was coming from me. She pulled my carcass from its hook and raised me above her head in a prelude to the body slam that would surely crack me like a walnut.

This wasn't necessarily a bad thing. As long as I was being positioned for an eight-foot piledriver, nobody was eating any worms. Plus it supercharged my brain. See, when the body is in danger, it releases adrenaline, which allows the muscles to perform extraordinary feats.

Since I have no muscles, my adrenaline goes straight to brainpower. In that second, every cell in my cerebral cortex was screaming, "Listen to what The Farmer Says!"

The farmer was saying that Steve Evil had Josh's weakness for the See 'n Say. And if Josh had passed that handy little trait along—what about the other UPs?

All this time, I'd been hanging on that hook looking for these creatures' weaknesses. But what I should have been looking for were the weaknesses of Kyle, Missi, Dino, Joni, Josh, and Crystal.

Because Kyle, Missi, Dino, Joni, Josh, and Crystal were the stuff monsters are made of.

I had to think fast because, in a few seconds, I was going to be a skinny splatter on the concrete. I could feel

Pookie's hairy grip tighten beneath me. Nervously, I looked down. There it was! The answer was right in front of me, big and purple as life!

"Pookie!" I screamed. "Those pants make you look fat!"

When you call a monster fat, there's always a chance they'll respond badly by, say, ripping you in half. But I knew that Pookie had Crystal Arrington's DNA—and nobody cared about clothes more than Crystal.

After a few scary seconds, I felt the death grip loosen and Pookie dropped me to the ground.

Let me tell you, if it's a choice between being dropped or splattered, I'll take dropped every time. When I looked up from the floor, I saw Pookie staring over her shoulder and trying to smooth out the bulky wrinkles in the back of her pantsuit.

The purple diva turned around and looked question-ingly at me.

"Still fat?" she asked.

"A little. It's kind of a poofy material," I said.

She resumed smoothing.

My classmates on the hooks were stunned. Especially Crystal.

"What is he talking about?" she cried. "Those pants look great on her!"

Clearly, my genetic scheme was lost on that particular hostage. Winnie, however, who is more scientifically minded, got it right away.

The next thing I saw in her quick, clever fingers was a half-eaten candy bar. Buffy was on the ground beside her,

her face swollen to the size of a Thanksgiving Day parade float.

"Missi's allergic to chocolate," Winnie smiled.

Allergies! Buffy had Missi's allergies! My hypothesis was right! For a second, I felt like laughing out loud, but it didn't last. Funny how quickly your mood can change when someone steps on your skull.

Mutt had my head under his boot.

"Owwwww!" I screamed.

I was in trouble. Mutt had Kyle's DNA, but the only thing I really knew about Kyle was that he was dumber than Wonder Putty. The foot pressed down harder. If this thing had a weakness, I needed to find it fast!

"Kyle!" I yelled. "Do you have any allergies?"

He shook his head.

"What about fears? Is there anything you're afraid of?" I shouted.

"Him!" he screamed and pointed at Mutt.

That particular piece of information was not going to help us.

The creature felt like he weighed a ton, and the pain was unbearable. There had to be something—was he ticklish? Shy? Lactose-intolerant? Anything!

"Kyle! What will it take to get him off me?" I screamed.

"An army!" Mutt growled.

At that very moment, the door to the Beatdown Palace burst open. Big Ape, who had been standing in front of it, flew at least fifteen feet.

"Excuse me," Franklin said. "You're standing on my friend."

I was never so happy to see his face in all my life. And it wasn't because we were being mauled by the knights of King Kong. There in the doorway was Franklin. He was all right! If this mutated hippopotamus wanted to squash my head like a grape, he could go ahead and do it. I honestly didn't care. All that mattered was Franklin was back!

CHAPTER
60

Between Good
and Steevil

"Stine!" Josh screamed. "I thought we were rid of you!"

When he heard the name, Steve Evil hissed. He was finally meeting his older brother.

"So this is the great Franklin Sssssstine," he rasped. "Well, you don't look so great to me. How's he look to you, Pookie?"

"Awwww-sommme," Pookie said.

She sucked in her stomach and smoothed the back of her pants again.

Franklin ignored them.

"Howard, would you like to stand up?" he said.

"Yes, please."

Mutt didn't seem to care much what either of us wanted. He leaned even harder into my skull. I'm pretty sure my ears touched.

That's when Franklin reached into his pocket and

pulled something out. It was the Dusty Reynolds baseball! He still carried it! He flipped it in his hand and, a second later, his arm was a blur as he rifled a fastball across the length of the building. And that's when I found out Kyle and Mutt had something in common after all—neither one knew when to duck.

POP!

The ball caught Mutt squarely in the forehead, planting the autograph of my favorite popcorn seller deep in his memory.

I peeled my face from the floor, and the pressure rushed out my ears. A few seconds later, I was on my feet.

"Franklin! It's you!" I yelled, trying to regain my balance. "Look out!"

Big Ape and Tarzana were storming toward Franklin. They were on him like a pack of wolves.

I started to run to him, and that's when everything went black. Steve Evil backhanded me with a slap that knocked me against the rear wall.

When I reopened my eyes, I could barely make out the struggle at the other end of the room. The monsters were big and vicious, but I knew it would take more than a couple of giant juvenile delinquents to keep Franklin down. I had, after all, personally taught him to wrestle.

Of course, now that I thought about it, Franklin had never actually won any of our matches. Not a single one. I'd pinned him every time—and I was a terrible wrestler! I'd always suspected he'd let me win, but how did I know that for sure? I just hoped neither of those creatures

knew the Howard
Hypnotizer.

It wasn't looking
good. They were all
over him, punching
and clawing.

Then, just like that, I heard it. The
roar, the one I'd heard the morning he
chased away the bear. Only this time, it
didn't frighten me. This time, it
was a beautiful war cry, and I
wanted it louder and angrier. I
wanted Franklin as mean and terrifying as inhumanly
possible. I wanted him to be a monster!

Tarzana left the pile first. It was a sweet toss. Her feet
continued rising until she was upside down and then, she
plunged—headfirst—into the nightcrawler bucket.

Now it was Franklin against Big Ape, monster on
monster. They fought to their feet, and Big Ape swung
wildly. He missed, and Franklin hit him with a straight jab
to the chin then rammed his mammoth hand against the
broad gorilla jaw.

From their hooks, Crystal, Missi, and Joni began
chanting: "Go! Franklin, Go! Go! Franklin, Go!"

I'm pretty sure it's a cheerleader thing.

Another strike, then another, and Big Ape went down—
and stayed down. It was over.

Franklin whirled around, and that's when I saw his
face. We all saw it. His eyes were wild and hungry like

the time he'd fought the bear. He leaned over the fallen monster and roared, and the wall of the room rattled. Then, he rushed in our direction.

I wanted the old Franklin back as much as I'd ever wanted anything—but not yet. This wasn't over.

Pookie, ninja-like, was crouched down waiting to leap on the big fellow's back. But there were two big differences between Pookie and an actual ninja: ninjas don't wear glitter, and they generally know when someone is behind them.

Winnie had removed the winged trophy from around Buffy's bloated neck. Then she crept quietly across the room until she was just behind Pookie and, with a quick, downward motion, put a deep, golden crease in the poodle-haired skull.

Pookie was down for the count.

Mutt, however, had shaken off the strike from the baseball and climbed back to his feet. He charged Franklin and grabbed him around the waist. From the other side, Steve Evil sprung at Franklin like a snake. Steevil was the smallest of all the monsters, but he was amazingly quick. In a flash, he was on Franklin's shoulders, pounding his head as Mutt administered a crushing bear-hug. Franklin cocked back his neck and brought his massive forehead down hard against Mutt's skull. It rang out like a hammer striking a hideous nail.

Mutt fell like a bag of hairy cement. Instantly, Franklin reached for Steve Evil but the rat-boy was everywhere, biting him on the shoulder one second and on the leg the next. The good news was that Franklin appeared to be facing his last monster.

The bad news was I'd miscounted.

Josh Gutierrez was coming up behind them. In his grip, I saw something bulky and stringy—a volleyball net! What was Josh doing?

I realized this was no game. Josh was going to throw the net over Franklin like he was trapping an animal. Once they had him wrapped up, they could do anything they wanted—kick him, beat him, put a tag in his ear, and release him into the wild.

I watch a lot of Animal Planet.

Whatever Josh had in mind, you could bet it wouldn't be good. Every step of his felt like a knife twisting in my stomach.

I don't even remember moving. But a second later, I was on Josh's back, my elbow locked around his chin and my puny, pasty fist banging against the side of his head. He grabbed me, but I wouldn't let go and we both fell to the floor. The fall broke my grip, and Josh scrambled on top of me. He hit me once, hard in the face, and I tasted the blood as it poured from my nose. He punched me again, and again, and my eyes swelled until the form above me was only a shadow. I reached back blindly to find a shield and when my hand connected with something solid, I pulled the object in front of me.

"The cow says 'Moooooo!'" the object said.

It was the See 'n Say from my backpack. Orson's toy had blocked Josh's punch! But that's not all it had done. Josh's face was pale, and his breath grew quick and heavy. I could feel him trembling, and, when he tried to scream, the only sound he could manage was a series of sad squeaks. Quickly, I pulled the string.

"The horse says, 'Nay-ayyyyyy!'"

Josh scrambled to his feet and leaped like a frog in reverse.

"Stay away from me!" he yelled. "Stay away!"

Phobias are odd things. Here was Josh willing to do battle with a gigantic monster, but not with "The Farmer Says." I put my hand back on the string.

"One more move …" I warned.

"OK, OK!" he pleaded. "Just don't make it talk!"

I looked across the room. Steve Evil was on Franklin's shoulders gripping his neck. Franklin's face was somewhere between magenta and blue, and I had the awful feeling he was about to pass out. Yet something about the scene looked familiar.

"Franklin," I screamed. "The Stine Stainer!"

It was the wrestling move Franklin had never gotten to use because I'd always countered it with the Hypnotizer. But Steevil wasn't me. With one great burst, Franklin lifted the rat-thing straight over his head, then fell backwards as the beast floated in air. Before Steevil hit the ground, Franklin raised both legs and drop-kicked the little monster against the Palace wall—where it left a nasty stain.

After that, Franklin laid on the ground, his chest heaving. His eyes were wild, and his fangs were clenched.

An unearthly growl came out of his throat. I didn't care. I went to him and threw my arms around him and put my head on his giant heart.

"You're my best friend," I told him. "You'll always be my best friend."

He was panting too hard to answer.

"How did you find us?" Winnie McKinney asked him.

Franklin just smiled and pointed to the door where a short, stout, blinking figure stood in the shadows.

It was the first time I was glad to see Reynolds Pipkin.

"That's Reynolds," I told Winnie, and I gave him a wave. "He can find anything."

CHAPTER 61

Unfriending

We wrapped the battered creatures in volleyball nets and jump ropes, but it didn't much matter—they had no fight left in them.

"What happens now?" Steve Evil asked me in that dark, steam-powered voice.

"I don't know," I said truthfully.

I had absolutely no idea what I was supposed to do with a gang of outlaw monsters.

"We can't stay here," he growled.

At first, I thought he meant in the Palace. It was already a pretty scary place, but no, they couldn't stay there. Then it hit me—he wasn't talking about staying in this building.

He was talking about staying in this world.

"What do you mean?" I said.

"We never asked to be here," he said. "We didn't ask for any of this."

His words found their target: me.

"The problem with having a friend who's a monster,"

Big Ape said, which surprised me because I didn't know he could speak, "is that someone has to be the monster."

There it was—the truth. The only reason they were monsters is that I had made them that way. They hadn't asked to come here. They were like Rollo, out of place in a world made for humans.

And they didn't want to be here anymore.

I looked at the creatures' faces and claws and fangs, and I didn't feel scared anymore. I just felt sorry.

"This isn't your fault," I told them, though I don't know if they cared. "I just wanted to make a friend. But somehow I ended up messing with the laws of creation. I guess the problem is that I'm not a very good creator."

"Maybe," Steve Evil sneered. "Or maybe it's just that we're very good monsters. Monsters and humans are a bad combination."

"Did you at least like your outfits?" Crystal asked as she rubbed Pookie's bruised skull.

"They were awe-some," she said.

Crystal smiled. Perhaps she'd found her soul mate, after all.

We all knew what had to happen. I pulled the laptop from my backpack and ran a cable to the small port in the back of Steve Evil's neck. I looked at him and said nothing, but the question was in my eyes. He nodded.

I hit "Delete."

The monster in the net instantly turned back into a blob of harmless goo.

One by one, I repeated the process. Large, gelatinous piles filled the floor. It was done.

Almost done.

"Me too, Howard."

"No," I said.

I knew what Franklin was going to say even before he'd said it. And I knew I couldn't do it.

"That's the way it has to be," he said.

"No it doesn't. You're not like them."

"That's the problem," he said. "I'm not like anybody."

I shook my head.

We didn't say anything for a while. No one did. Then Franklin looked into my eyes.

"You made me because you needed a friend. And we're great friends. Best friends," he said. Then he looked at Reynolds and Winnie and smiled. "But you don't need me anymore."

"Yes I do," I said forcefully.

"Howard. I don't want to be here anymore."

Everyone started to speak at once and they were saying things like, "Shut down your monster too!" and, "This isn't fair!" I covered my ears because if I had to hear anything else I was going to lose it. And the last thing I wanted was to lose anything else.

"Not here," I said at last.

There was no more conversation. Crystal, Missi, and Joni left arm in arm. Joni mentioned she might still let me be her secret admirer—as long as I never told her who I was. Winnie just rolled her eyes and walked away with

Reynolds. Dino and Kyle limped off, still feeling the pain of being hung up like slabs of beef. As for Josh, he was still growling a bit as he left. But they all went back to their monsterless lives. Not me. Not yet.

Franklin and I walked together down to the convenience store, and I bought him the largest Extreme Rainbow Gooshee. Then we walked around the neighborhood and remembered the things we'd done, and we laughed about everything. Finally, we ended up back at the lab.

"It was a wonderful adventure, Howard."

I nodded.

"You understand, right?"

I nodded again.

"You're a bear kept in a cage because it makes someone else happy," I said.

He smiled his finest Winnie McKinney.

"If there were another way . . ." he told me.

I connected the cable to the port in his back.

CHAPTER
62

And Now ...

I kept the goo. It's in a barrel in the lab. It kind of makes it feel like Franklin is still here with me. Does that make sense?

As for the rest of my life, well, let's just say my climb up the popularity ladder didn't last. When Mrs. Ogilvie finally checked out my foreign-exchange student story, I was quietly impeached from the class presidency. OK, they just took my name out of the yearbook, but impeachment sounds more official.

I had to do a lot of explaining to the police. There must have been twenty squad cars out looking for us that night. They were particularly curious about some mysterious blob-like substances they'd found in an old storage barn at the edge of the middle school athletic field. I told them the truth—it was Wonder Putty. As for how it got there, well, I left that part kind of vague. I don't think they would have believed me anyway.

We'd decided as a group not to tell *everything* that

happened. Our story was that we'd been taken in a prank—we weren't really sure who'd done it or why—but whoever they were, they were long-gone. I figure that saved us about a combined forty years' worth of groundings and school suspensions.

Without Franklin, the football team had no reason to keep an eighty-pound blocking dummy on the roster during the off-season. Coach cut me, but he said I could try out again if I grew—or made another friend from Canada.

I was definitely out with the UPs. Not only had I made creatures which took them hostage, I stopped doing their homework. So I'm back to being non-existent in the eyes of Dino and Crystal, and I'm pretty OK with it. They don't bully me anymore, and I think I may be wedgie free for the rest of middle school. No one wants to risk a monster rematch.

I realize everybody thinks the UPs are great people to know and maybe they are. But when it comes to friends, I've known better.

Wendell sits with me sometimes at lunch. We're not exactly friends, but he's not mad at me anymore. He was mad for a while, but then I gave him Orson's See 'n Say and some useful information. Half the school was watching the day he cornered Josh Gutierrez and gave him a twister wedgie.

Then he gave me one too. Fair is fair.

Winnie's still mad, but our conversations about why she isn't talking to me are getting longer. One day we might even talk about something else. Anyway, that's what I'm hoping for.

I hang with Reynolds once in a while at home. If he'd stay out of our garbage and stop acting like an ant, he really wouldn't be such a bad guy. I don't know how he found Franklin that night—and I don't think I'm going to ask him. The way I look at it, I have my secret lab so Reynolds is entitled to a few secrets of his own.

It's kind of cool about the way he can find things. But if you tell him I said that, I'll deny it.

Of all the changes in my seventh grade life, the weirdest one happened just a couple of days ago. I was coming out of Cranium Comics, the place where I buy my comic books, and I ran into Josh. He hadn't really gotten over the whole thing with Steve Evil. Wendell's twister wedgie didn't help a lot either.

"Boward!" he said and he put his arm around me like we were old friends.

The truth is, it was more of a headlock, but I'm sure it looked nice and friendly to anyone passing by. He dragged me into the alley next to the shop.

"We've got business to finish, Boward," Josh said, then he pushed me to the ground. "Not so tough when it's just you and me, are you?"

"I'm not so tough when it's just me and anybody," I told him honestly.

Josh ignored me.

"You know, people are always asking me, 'When are you going to get even with that Boward?' They come up to me and say, 'Boward's talking bad about you, Josh—Boward says he can kick your butt!' Is that true, Boward? Can you kick my butt?"

Now, I couldn't kick Josh Gutierrez's butt if someone placed it on a tee. I've never even hinted that I wanted to, which is what I intended to explain to him. That's why I was so surprised when the reply was—

"Yes, I can."

Only the person replying wasn't me. It was Stick.

Stick had been standing around the corner listening to the entire conversation.

"Oh, hey, Nate. I didn't see you there," Josh said nervously.

"You must have," Stick told him. "I just heard you say that people are telling you Boward thinks he can kick your butt. And you know something? Those people are right."

"But I didn't mean you, I meant the other Boward!" Josh explained.

"Really?" Stick told him. "Then there's something you need to know. When you mess with that Boward, you're messing with this Boward."

I looked at Stick. I didn't know what to say. Was he being . . . brotherly?

"Because if anybody's going to beat the snot out of that Boward, it's going to be me," Stick said.

That was more like it.

So I went home. I don't know what happened to Josh after I left. Stick hasn't mentioned it. Maybe being my rescuer was as weird for him as it was for me.

Franklin freaked when I told him about it. He says Stick and I have a classic case of sibling rivalry.

Did I mention I still talk to Franklin? Yeah, we're still best friends. But I've got a lot more competition for that position now. At last count, Franklin had 2,782 friends, and that number seems to grow every day.

Franklin is on FaceSpace. Well, not just on it—he's in it. See, Franklin wasn't happy being a monster in a human world. So when I connected the cable, instead of hitting "Delete," I decided to put him in a different world—FaceSpace. Now he is what he was made to be: a friend.

"Howard," he told me last week, "you wouldn't believe it. I have friends from all over. People I can talk to. People I can play games with. And I'm making new friends all the time! I'd never have believed it ... still, I do miss the Gooshees."

Franklin and I play Wrestling Pro Extreme online almost every day. Only in the FaceSpace version, he can actually do the Stine Stainer because the Howard Hypnotizer doesn't work there. I'm beginning to think he was faking it the whole time in the lab.

"I wasn't faking it. I've just improved," he told me. "Tell Orson I'll play chess with him later tonight."

The whole family talks to Franklin now that he's on FaceSpace. Of course, they think he's back in Canada. But it doesn't seem to have hurt their friendship. Dad wanted nothing to do with the computer before, but now that he can chat with Franklin, he hogs my laptop like he owns it or something. I wonder what they talk about.

And get this—Franklin likes Stick! I'm thinking it must be some kind of computer virus. I mean, I know Stick did something nice for me, but I'm pretty sure that was just because he wanted to do something terrible to Josh. Come on—it's Stick!

"Nathaniel has some good qualities. And he cares about you," Franklin said.

"You lie!" I said.

"It's true," Franklin answered. "Now, I didn't say he likes you ..."

Franklin's body may not be made out of goo anymore, but he's still kind of mushy.

I did something for Franklin the other day, something I'll tell him about later. I went to the dump and found the family he created out of parts and metal—the robot Bowards, I call them. I walked into the junkyard kitchen, and I saw the scrap versions of Dad and Mom and Katie Beth and Stick and Orson. Then I turned the corner, where I hadn't gone before, and I saw that Franklin had made another room—a lab. And in it, made of springs and wires, is a boy about my height with cotton-white hair and braces.

So, next to that boy, I built another figure—a big, hairy one with metal arms and Winnie McKinney's smile. Because, if you ask me, that metal boy in the lab looked kind of lonely.

And if there's one thing I've learned I'm really good at, it's making friends.

The End